# THE HOOSAC TUNNEL

# MURDERS

## A

## GINGER O'LEARY MYSTERY

## BY

## CHRIS H. WONDOLOSKI

THE HOOSAC TUNNEL MURDERS is a work of historical fiction. Any names, characters places and incidents are either a product of the author's imagination or are used fictitiously. Any resemblance to actual persons, living or dead, business establishments, events or locales is entirely coincidental.

Thank you to all friends and family members who so graciously and honestly supported me in in the writing of this story. I promise the next email you receive from me will not have yet another rewrite attached!

For Sharon,

My supporter, my critic, my editor

My soulmate and love of my life

# Chapter 1

## March 20, 1865

I'm sitting in the corner where the fieldstone hearth and the wall of the great room meet, my knees held up to my jaw by my right arm while I gnaw on the knuckle of my left thumb. Rocking back and forth, I stare across the room as the shadows change shape in dancing light of the wood burning in the fireplace.

My name is Virginia and I'm strange. Everyone says so. I'm seventeen, nearly as tall as me Da, and I can look all but the tallest men in town right in the eye. I'm left handed, have flaming Celtic curls and milk white skin sprinkled with cinnamon dust across my nose and cheeks. My emerald green eyes remind everyone of my Irish heritage.

And… I just know things. Things I shouldn't … things no one should. The elders call me the dark one. I'm not sure what that means. But, of this I *am* sure. It's no compliment.

When I walk down the street people avoid looking me in the eye. As they exchange pleasantries with Ma and

Da they check me out with quick sideways glances. Because sometimes events tend to trigger my "sight" they seem to think I can always see right through them. They don't want me to notice them. A smile from me erases theirs.

I've tried explaining. When I do, people use my awareness of their uneasy feelings as evidence that I, indeed, do know what they are thinking.

I don't actually see everything; thoughts just come into my head and stick. I can't shake them; thoughts about people, thoughts about events. And when I do see things, the outcome is almost always bad, really bad. That's why I'm sitting in this corner listening to the grandfather clock pendulum go tock, tock, tock while Ma and Da sleep. I know something and it's clear to me that life would be a whole lot easier if I didn't.

"Ginger... Ginger, me darlin' what's the matter? What's wrong?"

I opened my eyes and there was Ma kneeling in front of me, her hand reaching out to caress my hair. As she swept the locks from in front of my face I started to cry; not soft tears, but gut wrenching sobs.

"Oh, Ma, it's happened again. I just know. This time people are dead. I saw the flashes, heard the screams.

Blood, blood all over, Ma. Sharp and cutting, crushing rocks buried them. A cruel, horrible death it was. This was no accident, Ma. Someone killed them. And that someone was a friend."

As Ma continued to gently stroke the side of my head she said,
"Come on now, up wit' ya'. Sun's just about up and it's time for Da ta' get up. I'll start the stove and put on the kettle."

We both stood up and deeply embraced. My body had stopped shaking, but Ma's trembling hands gave her away. She felt the anguish only a mother can feel for her child in pain. Her nerves were tight as a bodhran because she feared that her child was right.

The first light of dawn streamed through the windows and the aroma of morning coffee wafted through the house. Jolted back to reality, I unsteadily tottered toward the kitchen. I wondered... hoped that this was all some horrible mistake, just a dream. This was, after all, just another day, wasn't it? No, no it wasn't. This was real. Somehow, it seems, I'm privy to a surreal netherworld I don't understand. And, I'm terrified of it. I just want it to go away. I want to be... normal.

Just then, the melodious voice of Constable Captain Charles O'Leary himself preceded his glorious presence as he clomp, clomped down the stairs.

"Woman is that breakfast I whack? A man needs sustenance ta' serve the needs o' this village of North Adams, ya' know."

To which Ma retorted,

"Ya' know it'is, my love. And a fine figure of a man y' are. This village of North Adams is lucky ta' have a man such as yerself keepin' them safe."

At this, Da presented himself to Ma for morning inspection. Six feet tall, fourteen stone with shoulders wide as a doorway, Da always cut an impressive figure in his policeman's uniform. Ma primped, adjusted and finally declared that Da was fit for duty. She stood on tip toes so she could gently kiss him on the cheek. To which Da engulfed her with his massive arms, held her in swoon and kissed her firmly on the lips. Ah, if the town could only see this side of Captain Charles James O'Leary. They would never believe that this was the man who commanded all others, and only the most foolhardy challenged.

The daily revue completed, we all sat down at the table to break our fast and share our plans for the day. Da immediately noticed my red and swollen eyes and could see Ma's shaking hands as she passed the rashers and toast around the table.

"OK, you two. I'm a trained investigator and I get just a hint that all is not well. Did you two have a row already?"

"So Charles, a joke is it now? If you're so bleedin' perceptive, can't ya' see that Ginger and I both have had the shite scared out of us? You amadan."

Cups, plates and silverware skittered around when Ma bumped the table while rising to her feet. She slapped down her napkin, placed both palms on the table, leaned forward on two stiffly held arms and intensely glared at Da.

"Virginia's visions are not goin' away, Charles. And, as she gets older they're no longer about some kid skinnin' a knee in the schoolyard. Last night she was 'wakened by a most disturbin' vision. This time, she says people have died... or will die. She's not sure when, Charles. But the rest is so clear that I believe her."

Tension released, Ma slowly sat down, neatly folded her napkin and placed it on her lap. When she next spoke, her voice was so calm and soft that the words demanded the attention of all.

"Now listen, and listen well. Saorla isn't here ta' explain things and guide Ginger. *We* need ta' try. You've seen what happened ta' those poor souls in the old country who had the second sight and not the brains ta' deal with it. It doesn't matter whether we fully understand An Dara Sealladh ourselves. We need ta' do our best ta' keep our precious daughter whole. Right now, she's reached the edge. We need ta' help her. And we need ta' do it now."

Da's shoulders slouched. His gaze dropped from us and he stared into his coffee cup which was held with both of his enormous hands. At first I thought he was hurt that Ma talked to him in such a way. After a few moments, I could sense that he was just lost in thought and using his coffee cup as some sort of crystal ball.

Suddenly, his shoulders squared back up. His deep blue eyes locked on mine and he said to Ma,

"Maeve love, more coffee. And you, Virginia, stay right here."

Only the lilt at the end of Da's commands saved me from hiding under the table.

His bulk caused the chair to scrape the floor as he pushed from the table. He stood up and walked directly to the mantle over the great room fireplace. He lifted the wooden box that had been there ever since I could remember, brought it back to the table and reverently placed it in front of me.

"Virginia, this box is one of the few things that came with us from Ireland. It was your Seanmháthair O'Leary's. She treasured it and had it as long as I can remember. When it was decided that Ma and I were movin' to America, she put a few family keepsakes in it and gave it to us. She also put an envelope in it for you. She made it clear that its contents were for you and you alone. At that time you weren't even a glimmer in me eye, but Grandma knew. Much like you, she always knew things. Ginger, dearest, this was twenty years ago."

"But, now it's time. Ma and I believed your visions were those of an innocent child. We thought they would go away as you grew up, as they usually did in children back home. America is so different from Erin, though. Everything is new and constantly changing. There just didn't seem ta' be a place for this... this power. But, here y' are; beautiful, brilliant and nearly a grown woman. It's as though Grandma has reached down from heaven and shaped ya' inta' her image. She was revered throughout the county Cork for her wisdom and ability ta' sort out solutions ta' people's problems. She was loved by most and feared by those who should. It was the An Dara Sealladh that gave her this special wisdom, me darlin'. And you have it too. You have the gift."

*There's that word again, damn it. Gift. Gift?*

The box Da placed in front of me had always held a place of honor in our home. It was about a foot long by half that and the same tall. The lid was gently arched and carvings covered the entire surface except for a small oval in the center of the lid. On it was painted a scene foreign to me. Ma once told me that it was of the family home in Ireland.

I was allowed, no required, to dust it weekly. Ma lovingly applied bee's wax and polished it at the change of each season. Other than that, no one touched it. Sometimes, though, late at night when Da got into one of his moods, he would stand in front of the great room hearth, hands in his pockets and stare into the fire. After a few minutes he'd seem to come around, give the box two or three pats on the top, turn to us with a tear in his eye and smile. Next, he'd give Ma and me a peck on the cheek and silently be off to bed.

"Virginia…Virginia, darlin'. Ya' with us? Open the box."

Nudged back to the here and now by the gentleness of his voice, I looked up into Da's imploring smile. My stomach suddenly queasy, I asked,

"Something in this box is mine?"

"Yes, dear. More than something. Answers. Answers ta' things only your grandma understood, and things you need ta'."

I opened the box and peered inside. One by one I removed and placed on the table: first the envelope Da had mentioned; next a small daguerreotype about three inches in width by four long; and finally a fairly long, tapered, round piece of wood which had only fit in the box one diagonal corner to the other.

I picked the envelope back up and examined it. It was yellowed and appeared stuffed full of sheets of paper. On the front was... my name, Virginia. The back was sealed with a rounded button of wax. Indented in the wax was what appeared to be a coat of arms.

What first looked like just a stick turned out to be much more. It was about one inch across on one end and half that at the other. When rubbed with my napkin, it turned into a shiny, though well-worn object of obvious import. It had the patina of something ancient, and had strange letters carved into it.

The glass cover of the daguerreotype was covered with a thin film preventing me from seeing what it depicted. I again used my napkin. Removing the film caused my jaw to slack.

"Da? Is this Seanmháthair?"

Arms crossed, Da nodded, smiled and said,

"Yes, Ginger. And a beauty she was, wasn't she?"

The image was of an older woman sitting in a chair, back ramrod straight. She wore a dark colored dress which had an elegantly embroidered white lace collar and cuffs. Her hair was middle parted and tied back. Even so, it was clear that her hair was light in color, maybe gray, and quite curly. She wasn't smiling, but she wasn't frowning either. One corner of her mouth turned up just a hint and her eyes seemed to twinkle giving me the impression that Grandma had a most mischievous personality. Her right elbow was supported by one arm of the chair while the left was carefully draped across her lap. In her left hand was, saints preserve us, the stick.

"What is this?" I said to my parents.

I displayed the entire length to them by pinching it lightly on each end. To which Ma answered,

"I think it's time you opened Seanmháthair's letter, Ginger."

I put down the stick and picked up the letter. Using my butter knife as a pry I popped the wax enclosure loose and the envelope was opened for the first time since it was sealed nearly twenty years ago. I slid out the pages and

could see that this was a quite lengthy missive.  When I
unfolded it I was greeted by a neat script gracefully flowing
across the pages, seemingly without correction.  It read,

28 April 1845

My Dearest Virginia,

By the time you read this letter I will have
certainly passed on to be reunited with my beloved
Padraig and basking in the love of God. While my
painful challenge is over, yours is just beginning. Rest
assured, confusing and frightening as your life has
been, it is a gift from God to help others. Tis an
ancient gift originating in the time of the Druids.
As you mature, you will learn that with this

power comes constant temptation to use it for selfish advantage. Through the centuries a few keepers of the gift have succumbed. And these people, Lord help them, came to no good end.

My story begins with the clan O'Leary. O'Leary is an ancient and proud Irish name. In times gone by, the family was both powerful and educated. We were landowners, chieftains and included Laoghaire who was King of Ireland at the time of St. Patrick. During his reign the two collaborated with the most learned Brehons or judges to develop the Senchus Mor. The Senchus Mor was a melding of pagan, civil and Christian law and became the Irish law of the land. It was based on fairness and impartiality to all parties involved. Even the Brehons themselves were subject to severe civil penalties if a decision was later deemed unfair or an inappropriate interpretation of law.

For a thousand years before the time of Laoghaire and St. Patrick the Irish were not Christian. We were pagans worshipping the elements of the sun, air, fire and water. Executors of this religion were called Druids. They were also the exclusive possessors of all knowledge. They were the judges, physicians, historians and poets of the time and were the most respected members of Irish society. They were confidants and advisors to chieftains and sometimes even to kings. They often resided with these powerful families and became teachers of the royal children.

During those times women were also a favored

lot, having the same benefits of education and position as men. They were not afflicted with the burden of needing to marry for advantage and often chose directions in life denied most girls today. Some studied architecture or history, while others the Brehon law. They became lawyers who were then called dalaighs, anruths or arbiters of truth. A few chose to become Druids and were called Bandruis.

Tuiren of Tara followed this path. She also studied the Brehon law and became a dalaigh. However, Tuiren was more deeply intellectual and mystical than most Druids. She was said to be one of the truly dark ones; one who possessed the An Dara Sealladh. She was said to have the ability to see the future and predict the death of others. Her visions were manifested as dreams in which the wraith of the soon to die visited her. Sometimes objects triggered certain knowledge that an event would occur. Other times she simply found objects that others could not find.

As a dalaigh, Tuiren had the reputation of being able to resolve cases deemed unsolvable. People believed that she could read their thoughts and hence, know lies from truth. Many of the accused simply babbled out the truth rather than face her questioning.

Although this power wasn't that unusual among the Druid community, her second sight terrified the general public. She was treated as an outcast and lived quite alone until needed to right some wrong.

King Laoghaire hearing of this strange and brilliant woman, summoned Tuiren to his presence. Taken also by her beauty, he took her into his household as his advisor. Within a year of moving into the castle she was taken to his bed. Soon after, they wed and Tuiren presented Laoghaire with three children, two sons and one daughter. All three showed enhanced intuition, but no real signs of the gift. In time, they married and had children of their own.

It was their children, male and female alike, who again expressed the An Dara Sealladh. Since their parents were not blessed with the second sight, it fell upon Tuerin to help nurture their gift, educating them about the responsibility that came with such power.

When each of the gifted children reached

adulthood she presented them with her final gift, a divination rod. Tuerin had three yew rods cut of such a size as to match hers. She painstakingly polished and then carved the sacred symbols of divination into them. She instructed that this rod had the special power of focusing a gifted one's energy. The rod facilitated the user going to the future, rather than waiting for it to visit them in an unnerving dream or vision. It gave the user a feeling of power and control.

When Laoghaire and Tuerin's grandchildren wed, the power of An Dara Sealladh again
lay dormant for a generation in their children only to express itself fully again in the next. So was the manner that the power was spread throughout the descendants of Laoghaire and Tuerin, some named

O'Leary and others not. Regardless, the divination rod was given to the first born of each gifted generation.

This is how I inherited the divination rod I now present to you. It is a matter of fate that you not only have the power of An Dara Sealladh but also the honored Irish name O'Leary. You need to know that you are among the most directly descended from Laoghaire and Tuerin of all Ireland.

Use this power of divination with care, my granddaughter. Divination is fraught with peril and should be employed only when all other means have been exhausted. Those in the past who have ignored this warning and used it for personal gain have ultimately been destroyed by the unintended consequences of their actions.

So, my child, you possess the power to affect tremendous good in this world. You are the chosen one of your generation. Do not fear the An Dara Sealladh. The personal toll you suffer will be small compared to the good that is possible.

Your Seanmh'athair,

*Saorla*

I put the letter on the table and looked up meeting Ma and Da's imploring eyes. All I could muster was,

"Grandma was brilliant. I so wish I had known her."

I gave them the letter to read, rose with the daguerreotype, crossed from the kitchen to the fireplace mantle in the great room and carefully propped it there. I felt such an affinity, such a connection to this grand lady that I wanted to see her image every day for the rest of my life. In gazing upon her countenance I saw myself. And for the first time in my life I liked what I saw. I was *not* alone...this was supposed to be. This was my destiny.

Still gazing upon her countenance I quietly said,

"Da, why did we leave Ireland?  I know most of the poor Irish folk in town came here because of the starvation. But, we're not poor.  We have this fine farm, our house is grand and we want for nothing.  People in town respect you.  Surely, we weren't poor in Ireland either."

As I finished these words, my voice rose and trembled as tears began streaming down my face.

"And, if we had stayed, I would have known Seanmháthair."

At that, Ma came to me, took my hand and led me back to my seat at the kitchen table.

"Ginger, my dearest, I guess this is a day for stories. But, this one is no legend.  This one is fact."

"Many generations ago the English took control of our homeland and imposed their laws upon us.  Instead of Brehon laws, we were subjected ta' their Penal Law system.  No longer was it asked what was fair ta' one and all.  These laws sought ta' affix blame while ignoring circumstances."

"Everyone knows that a starving man will steal. We Irish would ask why he was starving. The English didn't care. They simply punished the man for his theft. Men were taken from their families and thrown into gaols simply for not paying taxes. Deprived of liberty, these men were robbed of the opportunity to ever make things right. Their wives and children often starved as a result."

"And the English called *us* barbarians. Understandably, we saw things as quite the opposite. So, there was constant friction and turmoil between us. However, as time went on a few English governors came ta' understand our culture. They realized that while the crown governed the land, it could never control the Irish people."

"So, in matters civil, a blind eye was turned allowin' us ta' take care of our own problems. Workin' behind the scenes, Irish mediators reinstituted our own Brehon based laws. Your Seanmháthair was such a mediator. The second sight gave her the ability and her reputation for fairness the respect needed ta' hold such an important position."

"Your grandda's name was Padraig. Ach, but a grand and massive man he was. Handsome as they came and blessed with the gift of blarney, not one woman in town's virtue would've been safe if he intended it. But, completely devoted ta' your Grandma he was. And she was woman enough ta' hold him."

"He had the ability ta' put men at ease and immediately gain their trust. English businessmen were neither immune ta' his charm. In this way his humble store in Cork City grew into an import-export business which made him and his family wealthy."

"He loved being the center of attention at the pubs around town, often buying drinks for the house while he held court. Grandda's big problem was that after havin' taken a bit too much of the creature, his true feelings for the English were broadcast for all ta' hear. While he seduced the English and profited greatly from his business dealings, he in fact hated them ta' his core."

"Your Seanmháthair would always hear of these outbursts from her contacts around town. She tried ta' warn him that if she knew, then the English knew. I'm sorry ta' say that Grandda would have none of it. In fact, he started ta' hold meetings at the house with like-minded men from all over southern Erin. The creature flowed freely at these gatherings which were long on talk and short on either means or conviction. The English were just too powerful."

"However, one night the local constables felt threatened enough to act. They showed up at our house in force and demanded Grandda come out for a talk. Well, he greeted them at the door, but being a bit tipsy he made the dangerous mistake of bringing a pistol with him. Two o' the constables immediately grabbed your Grandda and a struggle ensued. A loud roar filled the night air and Grandda slumped ta' the ground, his lifeblood spilling all over the door step. In the confusion, his so called compatriots abandoned the scene leavin' Grandma and me screamin' and your Da vowin' revenge."

"The next day news of Grandda's murder spread around Cork like wildfire. The story became more and more distorted with each telling and soon it was said that the constables had ambushed Grandda on the doorstep of his own home as he arrived for supper. Cork was ready ta' blow."

"Grandma terribly feared that they would come for your Da too. She said that the English would clearly see him as the head o' the snake of a local insurrection. Ta' make matters worse, your Da was stompin' back and forth furious and out of control. He was ready ta' die avengin' your Grandda. Grandma and I had ta' physically block the door and beg him ta' listen ta' reason. She said that *we* knew the truth of the situation, and that Grandda's death was a tragic accident. If it wasn't for the blindin' pistol, he'd at least still be alive. And even one death avenging a lie would be too many. She told Da that the best revenge would be for your Da and me ta' live long and well. We needed ta' leave Erin, and we needed ta' do it straight away."

"Fortunately, Grandda had friends everywhere. We were able ta' book passage on a merchant ship leaving the very next day. Grandma gave us money and a few keepsakes. She promised ta' follow when things quieted down. Other than that we only had the clothes on our backs. This is how we arrived in Boston. We were young, only married a short time with not a clue where ta' go or what ta' do."

"We found Boston ta' be very crowded and extremely dangerous. We heard that Chicago had a large Irish population and was growing by leaps and bounds. So, we started on our way there. But, when we passed through the Berkshires, we stopped cold. Such a piece of home it was. Stone wall lined farms climbed the hills kissing the bases of rolling mountains. There were swift moving rivers and everything around us as green as Erin herself. We were so homesick we grabbed for any piece of Erin that we could. From that day on we called North Adams home."

"So, my dearest child, this is why we left Ireland. Grandma promised that she would follow as soon as things quieted down. But she never did. Letters and money continued ta' come for several years, but she always had some problem or other ta' resolve that she couldn't walk away from. She felt she owed her people and served them until she finally died. The letter we received said she died peacefully in her sleep. Da and I both figure the real cause was exhaustion."

When Ma finished all of our eyes met. Tears quietly rolled down the cheeks of everyone. Theirs were from the sadness of reliving a most terrible time, mine from self-directed anger.

"Oh, Da… What a selfish, selfish eejit I am."

# Chapter 2

## Dirty Scene, Dirty Deed

Just then a loud pounding came at the front door. "Captain... Captain O'Leary, sir." When Da opened the door, two grime and dust covered workmen presented themselves hats in hand. They were haloed by the early morning March sun behind them which was peaking over the Hoosac Mountains just to the east. Their frantic looks revealed that something serious had occurred.

"It's the Bloody Pit, sir. There's been a terrible accident. We think three men are dead. Sergeant Mulcahy has sent us to fetch you. He needs you now, sir."

A man with stern, determined eyes turned to me. Da was gone. In an instant the Captain O'Leary villagers both respected and feared appeared.

"Ginger, go find Stanley. Have him saddle Rusty... and Hessie as well."

When I looked at him with a quizzical vacant stare, he growled,

"Do...It...Now."

As I ran to find Stanley I could hear Ma offering the workmen coffee while Da began interrogating them. It was about fifty yards to the stable. As I ran I wondered why Da wanted Hessie saddled. Hessie, a gentle and beautiful gray Appaloosa, was my horse. She was my baby.

Stanley was in the barn feeding the cows when I found him. Together we went to the stable and saddled the horses. Stanley, knowing better than to second guess Da warned,

"Let it-a be, Lass. Let it-a be. Just do as he says."

As I led Rusty and Hessie toward the house I saw the workmen departing in their wagon. Da was pacing the porch impatiently back and forth.

"Mount up, Ginger. You're comin' with me."

I felt stunned as though I had been hit between the eyes. In our house women did women's work, certainly not police work. Da, now sitting atop his chestnut stallion glared down and whispered,

"Get a grip, young woman. Right now you seem ta' know more about what's happenin' than anyone actually there. I need ya', now mount up."

We didn't follow the mile and a half long west shaft road to the valley floor as the workmen had. Instead, we pursued the more direct overland route across our ten acre dairy farm. The first hundred yards or so from the house followed a gentle down slope. After that the rest of the property, just as gently, rose until a crown was reached. Upon reaching it the entire village of North Adams spread out before and below us to the west and north.

In front of us and toward the south was the massive eruption named Mount Greylock and its attached smaller sisters Williams, Fitch and Saddle Ball. Backlit by the morning sun and still covered with snow from the winter just passed they glistened gloriously. Along with the north-south running Hoosac range just to our rear the gray violet Taconics, some five miles to the west, completed the cradle of the Northern Berkshire valley and also defined the border between Massachusetts and New York.

Splitting the village and running north through the valley was the placid meandering south branch of the Hoosic River. The Hoosic's north branch, having collected its water from mountain streams of Vermont, cascaded and riffled south into town along Union Street, the two joining in the village center.

All along the river the giant smoke stacks of textile mills billowed the refuse of progress. The grid of streets lined with hotels, churches, businesses and houses filled the downtown and spilled up the sides of hills at the bases of surrounding mountains.

Locomotives running from State Street Depot south to Pittsfield and west to Troy, New York rumbled in the distance. This settlement north of Adams was clearly a village in name only. In actuality it had outgrown the mother town of Adams and was a blossoming center of commerce sure to become a city with its own identity very soon.

Once over the crown, we headed down the hill through what was left of winter snow that had been stained by brown dust. Soon we came to two new wooden buildings still under construction on our left. Da reigned in Rusty, pointed to them and said,

"The fools building the tunnel are desperate. They haven't been able ta' keep up with the work on the east side so they plan ta' make this new stuff called "nitro" here. Last few months they've been tryin' it out. Supposed to be a lot more powerful than the black powder they bin' usin'. Terrible dangerous it is, Ginger. Just a spark'll set it off. I'll bet the amadons blew themselves up."

At that, the visions of last night invaded my thoughts.

"Da, it wasn't an accident. Only two are dead. The third is a murderer."

Pondering what I had said for only a moment, Da prodded Rusty with his boots and called,

"Shite…Lets go, Ginger."

It was all Hessie and I could do to catch up with Da and his chestnut stallion.

We soon came to a large gathering of workmen milling about and muttering angrily to one another. All of them swiveled their heads so as to stare intently, hopefully into the huge black hole in the side of the hill. Puffs of soot and dust still regurgitated from the opening they disdainfully called the "Bloody Pit."

The Bloody Pit is, in actuality, an excavation begun in 1852 called the Hoosac Tunnel Project. Its ambitious goal was to bore a tunnel some four and a half miles through the Hoosac Mountains to complete a rail route from Troy, New York to Boston. So far all it had done was devour money invested in it, ruin careers of engineers who designed it and kill many of the men working on it.

Only tattered and stained remnants of the banner proclaiming, "ON TO HOOSAC, ON TO THE WEST" remained above the tunnel mouth as testimony to the boastfulness swallowed up over these past thirteen years by its gaping maw. A small child at that time, I could only flash back to bits and pieces of the exhilaration which had permeated our village.

Today, thirteen years later, more lives had been tragically lost. But this time, for the first time, unknown to all but Da and me the murderer was not the mountain.

In time I calmed down and details emerged before me. I noticed a trio of men standing near the tunnel opening. In the middle was a tall, almost emaciated man I did not know. Head down, shoulders hunched, he hugged himself. On his left, a consoling hand gently reached up and patted his back. This hand was attached to a much shorter, but powerfully built man who sported a shock of thick coal black hair. The cassock he wore had a Roman collar and told me that Father Charles Lynch had somehow already arrived. The purple sash around his neck and book of rites he carried in his left hand mutely proclaimed that his presence was more than to offer consolation. He was here to perform Extreme Unction, the Catholic sacrament of the dying.

Father Charles Lynch is the newest pastor of St. Francis church. Still in his twenties, his boyish good looks, startling blue eyes and effervescent charm have endeared him to the women and girls of the parish. His physical strength, endless energy and willingness to roll up his sleeves to lend a hand have made him a respected friend of every man. Since his arrival, St. Francis has quickly grown from the tiny "church" located on the second floor of Rice's Dry Goods to the impressive construction project soon to open on the hill at the corner of Eagle and Union Streets. When finished, the new St. Francis of Assisi will be the largest edifice of worship with the tallest steeple in all of North Adams.

The third man of the group was the most easily identifiable. Fortyish, balding and so rotund that his girth challenged the integrity of every seam of his clothing, Samuel N. Briggs M.D. "calmly" awaited the casualties. Only the smoke signals puff- puffing from the cigar clenched between his teeth betrayed the feelings of trepidation he so carefully attempted to hide.

Our beloved Dr. Sam clearly never met a vice he didn't like. However, this walking paradox was afflicted with not a single bone of pretention. Though he could afford to own one of the most prestigious homes on Church Street's mansion row, he chose instead to live in a single room on the second floor of the Wilson House Hotel on Main Street. He was often known to chortle, "Why should I have all of those headaches? Living at the Wilson House offers me the best food cooked by the best chef in the county. I have "personal" maid service anytime I desire it. And every evening I hoist a glass or two in the saloon while being entertained by the most interesting and influential men for miles around."

Whether it was a cold March breeze off of the still snowcapped mountains or shades of the victims proclaiming their outrage, sudden body wracking shivers brought me back from my musings.

Sweat soaked rescue workers whose clothing and faces appeared painted with gray mud began emerging from the bowels of the mountain. Squinting against the glare of the morning sun they came one at a time, and then in pairs. Somewhere near twenty men stood either bent at the waist tugging their pants or using the nearby banking to recline. To a man they coughed, wretched and spat attempting to clear their lungs of the poisons they had inhaled.

The sound of squeaking wheels alerted everyone to the mule drawn cart next to come out. It carried two horribly mangled bodies and a third man injured, but clearly alive. Seeing this, Father Lynch and Doctor Sam left the tall man behind and alone; Father Lynch to administer the sacrament assisting the dead to meet their maker and Doctor Sam to assist the injured man so that he would not meet his.

Behind it all limped a short, gaunt figure. In his blue policeman's uniform, painted with the same gray dust and employing a cane to support his weakened left leg the last man to safety was Sergeant Conal J. Mulcahy. That he was the last man to leave the bloody pit after such carnage and danger was no surprise to Da, me or any man who really knew him. Da and I strode quickly to meet him.

"Hi, Cap. Been quite a mornin'."

"Bullshite, Sergeant Mulcahy. What the hell're ya doin' goin' in there."

"Thanks, Cap. I'm fine, thank you very much. Good morning, Miss Virginia,"

"Damn it, CJ…Ya' know how I feel about that hell hole. This whole enterprise has been one huge boondoggle from the start. If I lost any of the men, let alone *you* ta' that awful place…"

"Now, Cap, I had to see what happened for myself, didn't I? Would you want me to take the say so of those gobshites over there? Most of them are so spooked they'll never even enter the tunnel alone. I'm told the flickering light; sounds of falling rocks and whistling of breezes down the shafts play tricks on them so bad most believe Indian spirits of the Forbidden Mountain have appeared to warn them off."

Sergeant Mulcahy then shuddered, hugged himself and gave out a chuckle as he continued,

"Let me tell you, while I was in there I heard the wind go hoo-oo and then a cold breeze hit me in the back of the neck and went right down my shirt. Damn, but it had *me* believing in ghosts for a minute there too."

CJ shook his head not believing what he had just said and refocused:

"But let me tell you, there *is* something real queer about this whole thing."

"Two guys buried by a ton of rocks and the third had barely a scratch? When I found him, he was on the tunnel floor right at the edge of the blast zone. He kept moaning, "A mistake… too soon… no, no." But when I looked him over all he had were a few cuts and scratches, but absolutely no shrapnel injuries. Now how can that be, Cap? I've seen enough men blown to pieces to know that circumstances here are just plain wrong."

Da turned to me with a knowing look, his consternation with Sergeant Mulcahy transforming into curiosity.

"If this guy doesn't have any reason ta' think you don't buy his story, let's keep it that way, CJ. Right now we need ta' know a lot more about nitro and how they go about setting it off."

"See that walkin' cadaver over there standing by himself? That's Franklin Northkutt. He's the head engineer brought in by the state two years ago to replace Hermann Haupt. They drove that poor bastard out and now they're doin' their best ta' do the same to Northkutt. He's also the genius who decided to replace black powder with nitro. Let's go have a chin-wag with him.

# Chapter 3

## Conal J. Mulcahy's Story

When the great rebellion began I was twelve years old and saw the war through the eyes of a child. The Union would certainly win. The actions of all and the exploits of some were reported faithfully in our local weekly, *The Transcript*. In school, teachers and students buzzed with the latest news. At recess the boys played soldier and marched about in ranks back and forth across the school yard. In mock battles some fell down dead. However, when the bell rang putting an end to hostilities the dead magically rose up and went back to class. Every soldier was a hero and death an abstract unreality.

Today my school days are in the past and I find myself at the doorstep of womanhood. While I understand that there are ideals worth fighting for, the toll this conflict has taken on the North and the South has become all too evident. Clearly the Union would survive, but I can't help being left with the question, "Does anyone ever really win a war?"

No story illustrates this point better than that of our dearest local son Conal J. Mulcahy. Newspaper reports and the tales of returning soldiers who served with him along with the telling and retelling of his exploits combined to turn him into a veritable living legend. But again, knowing the details of his story as I do and imagining what it was like to have lived them have left me with a second question, "What price glory?"

Soon after Fort Sumter was fired upon, the 27th Massachusetts Regiment of Volunteer Infantry was formed. All the men in this regiment lived in rural areas of western Massachusetts and were quite adept at operating in the bush independently and with minimum support. They were assigned to General Burnside and given the duty of employing guerilla tactics against rebel forces in North Carolina.

In the early fall of 1861 Conal J. Mulcahy of North Adams, a twenty-one year old law clerk in the offices of Andrew Richmond, Esq. of the North Adams Police Court, joined the twenty-seventh as a first lieutenant. He had graduated from Williams College in 1858 at the age of eighteen, and only recently from Albany Law College.

C.J. quickly gained a reputation as a natural leader. His men worshiped him because his tactics of surprise and ambush resulted in inflicting maximum damage on the enemy while incurring minimum casualties.

In late July, 1862, he left Camp Warner for Bachelor's Creek to establish an outpost. Anxious to get into the fray, he decided to use the cover of night and set out with two companies and a detachment of cavalry to ambush a Confederate cavalry outpost reported to be encamped at Gum Swamp.

Near daylight, his troops encountered a rebel scout who immediately turned tail and ran to warn his mates. Not wanting to give the rebel scout even one breath to think of what he was actually doing, Captain Mulcahy ordered his men to drive him, using the man's panic. He deferred capturing the terrified man until they had reached the edge of the enemy camp.

A very short fire fight ensued. Two Confederates were killed and two wounded; while nine others found themselves surrounded and quickly surrendered. Several horses and all of their implements of war were also confiscated.

This was the hallmark of Lieutenant Mulcahy's tactics. He began with a solid plan, quickly adapted to the circumstances at hand and seized the initiative by boldly challenging the enemy. To him, this was as natural as hunting white tailed deer in the remote forests of the Berkshire Hills back home.

General Burnside was so impressed with the decisive results at Gum Swamp that he rewarded CJ with a battlefield promotion to captain.

Not even a month later Conal and his men again distinguished themselves. They were scouting through the North Carolina woods when they encountered a small body of the enemy approaching. As they set up an ambush, one of Captain Mulcahy's scouts reported women among the group.

Not wishing to risk a firefight under these conditions, he and five volunteers confronted the opposing force while the rest of his men silently moved to positions of advantage. The surprised Confederate colonel smiled, "Young Captain, this is very unfortunate for you. I have you completely outnumbered. For the sakes of the women I have with me, lay down your arms."

Conal merely smiled and said, "Would you, now? Let's see." Just then, the rest of C.J.'s men emerged from their hiding places with rifles cocked and bayonets fixed completely surrounding the rebels. To which the colonel removed his hat and in a mock bow said, "Ah beg your pardon, sir. This does alter the circumstances." "Yes," a smiling Captain Mulcahy retorted. "And circumstances alter cases."

As it turned out, the rebel forces were transporting four women from New York state and Massachusetts as prisoners. The colonel hoped to use them to affect their exchange for confederate prisoners. Unfortunately for the colonel, he instead found himself on the short end of such an exchange. He and his men were used to secure the release of Union troops held captive by the South.

Captain Mulcahy then saw to the protection of these women and personally secured their safe passage back to their homes.

That fall, Conal, Captain John Crowley and their men were left as a detachment to protect the Union stronghold at Bachelor's Creek while remaining Northern forces departed for action at Tarsboro Creek.

Confederate General Martin, learning of this, sent the 31st North Carolina regiment to capture this highly valued prize. Fortunately, Conal had deployed scouts who saw this large force advancing. Terrified, they reported what they saw crying, "We won't stand a chance if we stand and fight."

Always calmest in difficult times, CJ and Crowley had different plans. Crowley split his small force to flank the advancing rebels on two sides. His men opened up, catching them by surprise in a cross fire. In the meantime, Captain Mulcahy's men set up a skirmish line to the front of the advancing forces, hidden behind the Bachelor's Creek battlements.

CJ and Corporal Cooley found some old wagon wheels that were still attached to their axles. When moved, they squeaked with an awful racket. So, Conal and Crowley moved them back and forth behind the battlements hoping to make the Confederates believe that his forces were setting up artillery pieces.

Expecting only the light resistance of a small force, the only slightly bloodied but thoroughly confused enemy retreated buying time for the Union cavalry to literally arrive.

And so the celebrity of Captain Conal J. Mulcahy, late of the small village of North Adams, Massachusetts, grew as the war continued to grind on.

However, these small strategic victories achieved by low level officers through combat tactics most personal only resulted in a seemingly eternal war of attrition. So they were abandoned in favor of tactics employing huge confronting forces. Each side hoped to inflict massive damage to the other in a very short time and hence force a quicker end to the nightmare of this civil war. The day of the General had arrived.

In this sort of war, the Conal Mulcahy's of this world held no more value than a pawn on a chess board. It was in a battle thus waged, that Captain Conal John Mulcahy's war came to an abrupt end.

Late in a May afternoon of 1864, regiments from the 27th Massachusetts were attached to the Army of the James, XVIII Corps under the command of Brigadier General Charles A. Cousins. They were part of a large skirmish line moving toward the Mary Dunn farm located at the junction of the Richmond-Petersburg railroads at Port Walthall. Their mission was to drive out the Confederate brigade led by Brigadier General Johnson Hagood and destroy the rail lines.

Captain Mulcahy, used to operating under his own initiative, advanced toward the rebel stronghold much quicker than the other tentatively moving Union forces. At the time it was quipped that, "the 27th must be trying to catch the Richmond Express." As they emerged from the forest and into a clearing, Conal and his men caught the enemy by surprise and quite unprepared to defend themselves. The confederates were routed and a breakthrough of the enemy lines seemed imminent.

However, as the sun was now setting, General Cousins recalled all troops rather than pressing his advantage. Since the battle was still raging on, the recall appeared to the Southern forces to be a Union retreat and their cheers resonated all over the theater of battle.

General Cousins' weak explanation was that his forces could, "take the damned rebs any time he wanted." Many fine men on both sides would die the next day because of Cousins' arrogant vanity.

The next morning the confederates, reinforced by an additional brigade led by Brigadier General Bushrod Johnson, were confident and chomping at the bit for a new go at the Yanks as they set up behind battlements built overnight. Union forces, on the other hand, were demoralized, exhausted and still tending wounded of the previous day.

Nevertheless, shortly after sunrise an all-day infantry, artillery and cavalry battle commenced in the 100 degree humidity of the Virginia spring. Sulfurous smoke hung over the battlefield stinging eyes and depriving anyone a clear view of what was occurring more than ten yards away. The fog of war was literal as well as conditional.

Each side fired continually in the general direction of their opponent hoping to hit something… anything. Shortly after noon on this day, a cannon shell fired from somewhere in the confederate lines burst in the general vicinity of the 27th Massachusetts. The resulting shrapnel killed five; one piece of the hot steel tearing a gaping hole in the left thigh of Captain Conal J.Mulcahy.

At days end our CJ lay near death in a Union hospital and Brigadier General C.A. Cousins was proclaimed a hero.  After all, his troops had inflicted enough carnage on the rebels to force them to abandon the Mary Dunn farm allowing Northern troops to seize the railroad crossing there and destroy it.  Politically, it didn't matter that more than 300 hundred Union soldiers and 200 Confederates died this day needlessly.

This battle could have been decisively won on the previous day if the initiative of junior officers like Conal were followed.  General Cousins simply could not, or would not, adapt to the unexpected advantage these officers provided him.

Days became weeks, which stretched into months and the well-being of the young captain remained unknown to us in North Adams.  The last report received was a casualty list in the *North Adams Transcript* of those killed and wounded at the battle of Walthall Junction. "Gravely wounded," had always meant, "Soon to die." So, it was assumed that his body lay among the thousands buried far away from their homes. Captain Mulcahy's exploits had made him larger than life. But, in the minds of everyone in North Adams, this damned war had buried even him.

Then, one October afternoon in 1864 amid the brilliant orange, yellow and red foliage of the Berkshires, a smallish, emaciated young man clad in the everyday dress of a workman, limped down from the common car of a Troy and Greenfield train. No one expected him. The few there barely recognized him. But Captain Conal John Mulcahy was not only alive... he was back.

Soon, however, Main Street buzzed with the news. People began funneling into State Street depot to shake hands, slap him on the back or offer him a drink. Captain Mulcahy, head down, ignored them all and assisted by a cane, limped gingerly through the growing crowd.

Just then, two shiny black boots entered his vision blocking his way. A pair of massive hands gently placed on his shoulders massaged him. He looked up, and up, the eyes of his five foot eight inch frame meeting those of the bear, my Da who whispered, "Son, welcome home."

This is how Conal John Mulcahy came into our lives. This is the day he became part of our family and Da's most trusted friend.

Never again to be called Captain, never again to speak of the war or his part in it, Conal J. Mulcahy became, forevermore, just CJ. Haunted by the demons of those terrible days, CJ cringed at the prospect of returning to an office and the practice of law. He instead sought out the next best thing and became a sergeant of the North Adams Constabulary. This twenty-five year old former warrior became a peace officer.

# Chapter 4

## It Seemed Like a Good Idea at the Time

As we approached Franklin Northkutt for the first time I could see how tortured this man was. He was taller than Da and so gaunt he appeared to be a bag of bones. His clothing spoke of a previously opulent life gone inexplicably wrong.

He wore what was supposed to be a calf length top coat. It was camel colored and featured a fur collar, but also had a frayed hem, mud covered from dragging along the ground. Opened the entire length, it revealed a deep blue pin striped suit expensively tailored and made of fine wool. His white dress shirt had a grimy collar and his tie hung loosely exposing the top button. The waistcoat almost billowed from empty space that should have been filled by an ample belly. Mr. Northkutt's black shoes shone with a deep patina, but the heels were rounded at the edges. The toes were scuffed exposing raw leather much like the boots of a common workman.

But it was his countenance that was most shocking. His coal black watery eyes were ringed with dark circles.

His hair was so dark that his attempt at being clean shaven only rewarded him with what looked like a dirty face. A long pointed nose sprouting profuse nose hair and an almost nonexistent jaw made Mr. Northkutt look like a well-dressed, but starving raccoon.

Da stepped forward and introduced first himself, then Sergeant Mulcahy and finally me. I guess I was part of the team, at least for now.

"Mr. Northkutt, sir, a diabolical business this has been…Just diabolical."

Northkutt's vacant eyes came into focus and he said,

"It's my fault, Captain…All my fault. Those men would…This should not have happened. Why did I listen to Mowbray? I really wish it had been me, Captain. Arrogance made me believe I could pull off this bore and vanity won't let me quit. This damned project is slowly killing me anyway. So I might just as well be done with it."

Oh, oh. At this CJ and I exchanged glances and cringed because we both knew what was coming. Da was a staunch believer that whining was the way of the weak. Moments of self-doubt were allowed; but only just…and privately. In the end, leaders had to be the last to cave. It simply wasn't allowed. Da needed to find out what this Mr. Northkutt was made of, whether he could be of any use. So…

He turned red in the face and roared,

"Mr. Northkutt, I think you've mistaken me for the good Father Lynch."

He then added disdainfully,

"You can wallow in self-pity later. Right now I need to know who the victims were and how and why this happened. And I need to know fast. There may be more going on here than meets the eye."

Northkutt's reaction was one of quiet resignation; his response a shoulder shrug. Then he abruptly turned and seemingly without concern we'd accompany him began walking down a tree lined path which led to a shack approximately twenty feet on a side.

Inside was a surprisingly comfortable space. Against the wall to our right was a gigantic desk covered with a disheveled clutter of documents. On top of the desk was a deep cabinet. Its open doors exposed cubbyholes too many to count at a glance. Each space contained a neatly rolled up but dog eared set of blueprints. On the back wall of the shack was a well stoked wood stove which was more than up to the task of defeating the chill of this early spring

Berkshire day. To our left was a conference table with chairs and space enough to easily accommodate eight people.

It was here that Northkutt invited us to sit by silently pointing to a chair, only then joining us. Suddenly and without preamble he began replying to Da's questions as though they had been asked a few seconds ago, rather than several minutes.

"The two men killed were Ned Brinkman and Billy Nash. The injured man is Ringo Kelley. I hired the three of them shortly after the first of the year on the recommendation of George Mowbray."

"If you've been following stories on the bore in the newspaper you know that things have not been going well on our side. The Charlemont side to the east was nearly a mile in and our side only a little over 600 feet when I took over. The main reason for the shortfall is the composition of the rock on this side. It's called porridge stone and has absolutely no structural integrity. As soon as we dig it, the walls and ceiling fall right in filling up what we just dug out. Right now we're temporarily shoring up with jacks and timber. Later on we'll need to replace these supports with a brick lining or the whole tunnel on this side will collapse again."

"I've started a central shaft at the half-way point up on top of Hoosac Mountain in Florida. The composition of the rock there is very stable, just like the Charlemont side. But it won't be ready for another year, maybe two. When it's done we'll be able to dig in two directions from it."

"The west shaft was one of the few good things Haupt did. It was started just before he was driven off the project. It was completed easily and quickly. And it surely has helped. We've been digging in two directions from it and making decent progress because there's no porridge stone that far in, but the damned black powder we've been using just doesn't have the power to blast enough rock fast enough to give us any chance of catching up."

"In the meantime, the damn politicians in Boston and Worcester are beginning to tar me with the same brush they used to vilify Haupt. Sometimes I wonder if they really want this tunnel to be completed. But that's another story for another time."

"Anyhow, this is why I decided to hire George Mowbray and began experimenting with the nitro. He had recently discovered how to make a purified trinitroglycerin. The engineering journal I read promised a blast ratio of 13 to 1 over black powder. I believed it to be an answer to a prayer until I read on to learn it is so unstable that unless it's kept cold to almost freezing almost anything will set it off."

"But I was desperate. So, Mowbray and I exchanged telegrams. In them he assured me that with proper storage and employed by trained men, nitroglycerin was perfectly safe to use. I agreed to allow him to send us enough samples to begin experimentation, as well as three men personally trained by him in the procedures for proper storage and use of this devil's explosive."

"Up until today things had been going so well that I began having the acid house and factory built in anticipation of his arrival."

Northkutt suddenly stood up and angrily slammed his fists down on the conference table.

"And then Brinkman, Nash and Kelly got complacent...Idiots. They've ruined everything.

Having vented, Northkutt just as suddenly deflated and collapsed back into his chair and continued so softly as to almost whisper,

"This is probably what happened. They took the bottle of nitro out of the ice chest, walked all the way to the blast site and poured it into the bored holes. By the time they started to walk out laying the powder trail after them, the nitro was warmed enough that even a friction spark could set the charges off. They simply took too much time. The only reason Kelley survived was because he was the one who poured the nitro and was already on his way out as the other two laid the black powder trail. These three men were trained by Mowbray and should have known better. They got lazy by not keeping the nitro in the ice chest and bringing it with them. And, God help them, they paid the price."

Northkutt had obviously used the time it took to walk to his office well. His oration left little else to say, nothing to ask and him in complete control. Da thanked him and we walked back up the path three across. I know we weren't supposed to let on what we were thinking until we were well clear of the area of probing ears. But to me Northkutt's entire interview had instead been an arrogant and carefully crafted statement. He had built a case absolving him and dismissively blaming the trio for carelessness and incompetence. Listening to him had gotten me so frustrated that I had chewed the inside of my left cheek raw.

And it also now occurred to me that even outside the tunnel Northkutt's proclamations of, "all my fault" carefully ended with an indictment of Mowbray for talking him into using nitroglycerin. Ya, sure… The divil made me do it. Poor me… all is woe.

Finally, risking the chance that I'd be told to shut it, I spoke up.

"Nice story, that. Trouble is it doesn't fit with what I know to be true or what Sergeant Mulcahy suspects to be true. You never really came out and said it, CJ. But you think Kelley set off those charges on purpose, don't you?"

"Sure and I do, Miss Ginger. Now that I know what to look for, I want to go back into that hole and have another look see. What say, Captain. Shall we give it a go?"

"God an' ya' all know how I feel about that place. But I'm convinced as well that weasel Kelley murdered those men. And it's our duty ta' nail him, so it's worth the risk. You two go back in. But...you...will take the most experienced tunnel rat ya' can find with ya'."

"I know you examined Kelley, CJ. But you're not qualified in the eyes of the court ta' testify about his wounds. So, I want ta' talk ta' Doc Briggs. He tended Kelley as soon as he got out o' the tunnel. I'll get him ta' speak on the record about exactly what wounds the bastard has and where."

*So… It's MY duty too? This is exciting. I don't think I'll remind Da just now that I'm just his daughter and only along for the ride.*

On second thought no, that's not like Da. He knows who I am and he still wants me here… And definitely not just for the ride. Da would never tell me what he wanted me to do; he would expect me to simply know... and to do it.

*Seanmháthair Saorla, is this the beginning? Am I really going to do the kind of good in this world you told me about in your letter?*

Well then, it's settled. It's up to me to carve my niche and I'd better not foul up. There's no way I want Da saying later on that this was all a huge mistake, but seemed like a good idea at the time.

# Chapter 5

## An Adventure Ruined, Innocence Lost

The "tunnel rat" assigned to us by the shift supervisor was a sinuously built man of medium height named Napoleon Blais. His bent posture and deeply lined face made him look about fifty years old. The hand which reached out to shake ours was badly scarred from injuries long past and had skin cracked from the wear and tear of the regular work day. Blackened nails were at the end of each gnarled finger. But Napoleon Blais' grip was incredibly gentle. A smile lit up his face that made his eyes sparkle. His soft, slightly accented voice exposed French-Canadian roots when he said,

"Allo, my friends. Please call me Napy."

As we exchanged pleasantries on our way to the tunnel opening Napy told us that word of mouth had carried news of the great bore all the way to Montreal. Having few prospects at home, he decided to come south to seek his fortune. Napoleon Blaise arrived in North Adams in early 1853 and started working on the bore on his twenty-first birthday that same year. Which made him what…thirty-three? My God. I had never before thought about the toll such work takes on the men performing it. I also began to understand why Da was so down on the project.

Clearly, Napoleon Blais was one very special man. The pernicious physical effects of surviving twelve years in the tunnel had not eroded his spirit. Even today, he was still living a grand adventure. I instantly liked and trusted this man.

I had been to the tunnel opening earlier in the day and had seen the rescue workers, the victims and finally CJ come out. All showed effects of the ordeal, none of them good. But by the time we arrived the dust clouds had settled so I could focus on the black abyss I was about to enter. Somehow, this made matters worse. My initial hesitation at the mouth became stagnation when I realized what I was about to do. I told myself that workers went into this place every day, but it didn't matter. I felt intimidated, scared and alone.

CJ and Napy, who sauntered happily along continuing to get to know one another, finally noticed that I had fallen behind. It was CJ who walked back to fetch me. Considerably shorter, he looked up at me, smiled and all but whispered,

"It's not as bad as you think, miss. But I do confess that there's a squirrel running around in my gut too. But Napy's the best. Do as he says and we'll be alright. Don't forget, it's a murderer we're here to catch."

I appreciated what CJ was trying to do but I had seen him in action earlier that day limping out of that hell hole, after searching for survivors... the last to leave. I knew almost verbatim the details of his exploits; of his boundless courage and leadership under fire during the war. But now I had seen evidence of it personally. Amazing.

When we finally entered the tunnel it took a few moments for our eyes to adjust to the reduced light. Napy led us to a long wooden bench on the right side. Backlit by the early afternoon sun I could see it held a disheveled array of tools. Long star bits, huge sledge hammers, leather bands with small lanterns like those I had seen the rescue workers wear around their heads and large lanterns like those carried by railroad workers. Evidently at the end of a shift workers didn't want to carry their tools any farther than they had to and just dropped them here before leaving the work area.

"I think the brakeman's lanterns will serve our purposes best. They're 'evy but give the strongest beam." Impassively he added, "Don't forget to check the fuel and 'ze wick. You don't want 'zem winkin' out when you're six 'underd foot in."

When we all had lit our lanterns and pointed them into the tunnel. I was startled by the amount of detail revealed. Jacks and timbers seemed to be all that kept the mountain from crashing down on our heads. Remembering what Mr. Northkutt had told us about the nature of the stone here gave me very little comfort. Behind these wooden supports the extremely rough surface of the rock lining had icicle stalactites hanging from the ceiling and what looked like streams frozen in time and space flowing from the walls for as far as the light beams allowed us to see. Clearly this tunnel was far from stable… far from secure.

As we proceeded, the sounds of activity outside were replaced by the crunching of our six feet and the periodic pinging of CJ's cane on the gravel floor. My feelings of isolation became quite palpable. Only my trust in the courage of Sergeant Mulcahy and the experience of Napoleon Blais kept me going.

We followed the set of narrow gauge tracks which ran down the middle of the tunnel floor leading us farther and farther into the darkness. On them were three mining carts each large enough to hold a considerable amount of rubble but small enough to be pushed by two men. After we negotiated our way around them, the going became much easier. I sensed more than saw that the tunnel floor actually followed a gentle incline. In a short time I became quite used to it and in fact learned to ignore it.

The most unnerving effect though, was an optical illusion that the tunnel tapered into a pinpoint of darkness that I swore I could reach out and touch. However, no matter how far we walked that pinpoint of darkness never got any closer. Any feeling of spaciousness perceived when I first entered the tunnel was replaced by a new sense of increasing confinement.

We had gone on for what seemed a considerable time when the silence was broken by Sergeant Mulcahy.

"I was quite charged up this morning and didn't pay attention to how far we'd gone but I think we're almost there."

I appreciated that when he spoke it was about his own uncertainty, not to utter some patronizing claptrap asking how the poor fragile lass was bearing up. I had already decided that if I was to be treated as an equal I would need to act that way. I was ready to take care of myself and I wanted them both to know it. What I didn't want them to know was how frazzled my nerves actually were.

Napy then said,

"Oui, look into the darkness. When we get close your beam'll bounce back off of 'ze blast bench because for the most part 'zat's where the tunnel ends. But it'll 'stel be as black as before at the top because the heading bore 'zere goes quite a bit farther in."

"That's where the sorry amadons died and that's where the evidence is," CJ prodded. "So that's where we need to go, Ginger."

When I responded to him with a curt,

"I  KNOW  THAT, Sergeant." he looked up at me with a head tilted quizzically, but said nothing more.

I immediately regretted both what I had said and even more how I had said it. Was CJ simply sharing information about where we were going and I saw condescension where none was intended? In my petulant effort to demand equality, had I in fact conveyed a very foolish air of unearned self-superiority?

*Seanmháthair, help me. Your granddaughter is a gobshite.*

When we reached the tunnel's end a few minutes later we held our lanterns high and looked up. To call the cliff looming some fifteen feet above us a bench was about as appropriate as calling Mt. Greylock a mole hill. When I said as much to Napy, he laughed heartily and said,

"The name actually came from how it looks on Mr. Northkutt's blueprint. Just an engineer's joke, I guess." Continuing to chuckle he added, "They draw 'zer pretty pictures, we dig 'zer very big holes."

On the tracks we had followed and flush against the blast bench wall was a contraption that could best be described as a medieval wooden siege tower on railroad wheels. Its top platform was level with the heading bore opening. A wide sluiceway attached to its rear led down on an acute angle. A mining cart at the sluiceway's mouth and nearly full of rubble mutely testified to the tower's purpose.

Leaning against the tower was the only apparent way to the top, a rickety looking ladder. CJ went over and gave it a shake while looking up. He then turned his head over his shoulder and looked at me with a penetrating glare and said,

"This way up, *Miss* O'Leary."

Then… he winked. His eyes softened and the corners of his mouth turned up slightly. And that was that. Turnabout was fair play and I was grateful for his understanding and forgiveness.

"Thanks, CJ," was the best I could do returning his almost smile.

And up I went. Bolstered by CJ's encouragement, I was completely unconcerned about the show my petticoat and the skirt of my dress were giving. It was as though I had received validation that fear was to be expected. It was in leaning on each other that we overcame it and got the job done.

I remember reading in the *Transcript* just last year that the vulnerability of our soldiers exposed to dangers perceived as mortal forged an unexplainable group trust. Such a group could face down situations that would terrify the individuals if alone. It was the reason why although military groups were *assigned* numbers by the Army for identification they always *adopted* their own names for identity.

I felt extremely lucky to belong to *this* group. I was one of the guys.

When we trained our lanterns down the heading bore I saw just how claustrophobically small it was. This extremely rough excavation may have been six feet high at the ceiling's center, but its turtle back shape made the tunnel much lower as it reached its edge. It was about twenty feet wide and quite deep but our lantern light revealed a finite end. Both Sergeant Mulcahy and Napoleon entered it easily, but when I crossed the threshold I felt the need to duck.

CJ's gait was painfully slow. He seemed to be scrutinizing every rock and pebble. We had meandered in this fashion for quite a way when CJ tossed me his cane, crouched down and maneuvered to his left until he reached the tunnel sidewall. There he knelt down, reached into a crevice and pulling on a leather strap detached a rectangular wooden box from its hiding place. The box was about a foot high and wide by sixteen inches long.

He slung the strap across his shoulders and while the box dragged along the floor CJ crawled on hands and knees back to where we waited. Once back, he sat upright put the box on the floor between his legs and opened it. This revealed that it was actually a lead lined box with a smaller metal box inside which had its own lid. Between the two boxes the packing ice was almost gone. The space was full of what looked like slushy water. When CJ lifted the inner lid we saw that four empty clear glass bottles were occupying the inner box. Each bottle was bell shaped on top and had a ground glass stopper closing off its rather small raised pouring spout. When he lifted one of them out of the box he said,

"It's still cold."

He held it up for us to see, beamed and said,

"Hello, hello what have we here?"

Etched into the glass bottle was:

```
┌─────────────────┐
│                 │
│   DANGER        │
│                 │
│   NITRO         │
│                 │
└─────────────────┘
```

"Well, Napy, what do you think?" I asked.

"Well…The box is about the right distance from the blast site. Ya don' want it so far that that liquid hell has a chance to warm up, but you don' wan' it so close zat it might be affected by the blast and go up too. That would kill everybody and collapse the entire heading bore."

And a few seconds later he added,

"But why hide the box like that? Surely it would have been safe left where we are now. And why were ALL of 'ze bottles empty? That blast couldn't have used more than one bottle. It's almost as if … well, as if only one had been filled to start out because someone knew that 'zer was only going to be one blast."

"Those are two very good questions." CJ said. "I can't wait to hear how Mr. Northkutt will answer them.

You weren't at our meeting with him, Napy, but the account he conveyed as being almost certain isn't looking too good right now."

I muttered under my breath,

"I'd say it's a load of crap."

*At least I'm least I'm gettin' a bit better.*

CJ evidently heard me because he tweaked my ear from behind with his finger and told me,

"Close up the box and take it out ta' the tower platform, Miss O'Leary?"

I swiped back playfully and smiled, but wasn't fast enough to slap his already disappearing hand.

When I returned evidently CJ was filling in Napoleon about everything we knew so far, so I just quietly observed.

"Kelley was still quite shaken when I last talked to him but this much was clear; it was his responsibility to set off that charge."

"He kept saying that it went off too soon and claimed to have been lucky to be just far enough away when the blast unexpectedly detonated to be hurt but not killed. He said that he was still laying the line of powder from the charge holes along the tunnel floor when everything went up."

"Well that just doesn't fit either, mon Sergeant." Blais countered. "I have seen these men work before and 'zat is not how they operated when setting off a charge. Ned Brinkman and Billy Nash always bored 'ze holes and 'zen Kelley poured in 'ze Nitro. My point is Ned and Billy were always 'ze *first* to leave 'ze blast site for safety, *not the last*. If 'ze explosion occurred while Kelley poured 'ze powder trail *he* would have been 'ze one killed."

"Well, has Napy given us enough to get that amadon Kelley yet?" I interjected impatiently.

Pointing his lantern down the maw of the heading bore and probing the floor with his cane for solid purchase CJ growled,

"You've got that right. But we need to be thorough. Let's finish this."

"Try to stop me!" I exclaimed.

Deeply troubled by the mounting evidence that a betrayal of the most important tunnel commandment had indeed occurred, Napoleon Blais stared of into the darkness of the heading bore and whispered sadly,

"Oui."

Only a short distance farther into the heading bore the evidence of a burned powder trail became all too obvious. We followed it and it led us directly to the disaster site. There were no other trails and no other previous detonations anywhere near this site. Unless the detonation had somehow back fired the powder trail, the only way it could have burned would have been for someone to have set it. And the only person there, the person in charge of the detonation, the murderer of Ned Brinkman and Billy Nash was Ringo Kelley.

The reality of what up to now had been a disturbing vision made my head swim and my stomach turn. The pain and suffering that I had been chosen to bear witness to only last night came cascading back. The awareness Nash and Brinkman had of their impending doom, the feelings of incredible pressure as tons of rock squeezed the life-breath from their lungs, the crunching sounds they perceived more than heard as their skulls were being crushed, all preceded an instant of searing pain before their final fall into the oblivion of darkness that is death. It was at that moment that their souls screamed out to me,

"JUSTICE… JUSTICE.."

Tears streaming down my cheeks I fell to my knees and crossed myself. I begged for the intercession of my Seanmháthair to God.

*Please… grant me the courage and strength to unveil the lie that is the murder of Ned Brinkman and Billy*

*Nash. Help me find answers to the unanswered questions that remain.*

Not least of which was how Kelley convinced the lost duo to stay while he left for safety.

And then darkness overwhelmed me.

When I came to my head was still spinning and my eyes struggled to regain focus. Both CJ and Napy were looking down on me their brows deeply furrowed with concern.

"Ah, there you are, miss. Glad to have you back with us. Now, I've seen even seasoned soldiers have bad reactions to seeing a scene such as this for the first time."

I almost laughed. For all of Sergeant Mulcahy's concern I was once again grateful. There was no way he was going to say that which was on his and Napy's mind, "This is a hell of a place for a girl."

What he couldn't know was that it was reliving the scene for the *second* time that knocked me off my pins.

The return walk to the world of sunlight and fresh air was as uneventful as it was quiet. Each of us had our own reasons:

With every ungainly step CJ was preparing the presentation he was going to give Da… and the questions he was going to ask Mr. Franklin Northcutt. At our earlier interview had Northkutt simply tried to absolve himself of blame? Or could he be involved in some more sinister way? How could we use what we now knew to catch Kelley in his lies?

I was lost in the quandary of what I was going to say to CJ about my seeming failure of nerve in the face of danger. He came with his parents from Eire as we had. But what of the second sight? Seanmháthair's letter said that it had been an enigma of Irish mysticism for centuries. I know he would *understand*. But would being American as well as Irish make him more, or less likely to *believe*? And most importantly, would he accept that I was truly one of the dark ones? Twelve hours ago *I* didn't know it.

Although Napoleon Blais' thoughts were less convoluted they were even more tortured. His walk time was spent taking stock of what he now believed to be a lost twelve years of his life. His adventure was ruined. His faith in honor among men had been crushed. His innocence was lost.

And don't ask me how I knew their thoughts.
*I just did.*

# Chapter 6

## Now We Are Two

Going into that bloody pit was like a descent into hell. With each uncertain step we walked deeper and deeper into a black hole we could never reach out and touch. The darkness became a symbol representing the evil we sought to investigate, that place of destruction where lives were stolen, that place of death.

When we began the odyssey of retreat from this awful place, I could detect an equally untouchable pinpoint. But in this direction it was the light that grew ever larger with each step. As we chased that symbol of salvation I was tempted to run. Escape this underworld. Reclaim my life. However, as soon as this thought crossed my mind I dismissed it. We had entered this hell hole together; we would emerge from its bowels together. CJ and Napy had accepted me, and that's the way I liked it.

Finally inhaling deep lungsful of fresh cold dry air I was quite surprised at how much time had passed. When we first crossed the tunnel's threshold it was just past noon. Now the sun was well on its way to its hiding place for the night behind the Taconics. It was late afternoon. As our eyes adjusted, the light which at first seemed brilliant became quite dim. Long shadows originating from the base of every object pointed to the northeast affirming that it was nearly dusk. I was reminded that even though it was almost spring, living in the cradle of two mountain ranges caused night here to literally fall. And it would be dark again all too soon.

I felt as though I had been robbed of a day. I can't imagine how these tunnel workers did it. For much of the year, they went to work in the early morning darkness and worked at dangerous back breaking jobs holding four foot long star-nosed bits or swinging the twenty pound sledge hammers that drove them into unyielding granite; shoveling spoil or pushing the mining carts that carried it away; all while seldom standing upright because the area of excavation in which they toiled was less than six feet high. And then, after finishing their ten hour shifts they headed home in the late afternoon dimness. The taste I had had of it was more than enough for me. At that, I bowed my head and said a prayer for the safe keeping of each and every one of them.

The constant din that had been created by throngs of workers both angry and scared was gone. They were gone.

The relative silence was quite deafening. I don't know what I expected, but only Da and a shivering Franklin Northkutt were there to greet us.

Suddenly, Napy walked to the forefront of our group and confronted Franklin Northkutt. His movement was so decisive that the totally startled man took a step back. Napy raised his hand and pointed his finger directly at Northkutt.

"Tu es un salaud couché." was all he said.

*You're a lying bastard...That just about says it all.*

Just as suddenly Napoleon Blais turned his back to Northkutt, nodded to CJ and me and with great sadness in his voice said,

"Au revoir, mon amis."

Then with his head and shoulders still bowed, this twelve year survivor of the deadly travails in the bloody pit; this gentle, gentle man headed down the tunnel access road toward South Church Street. I felt a lump come to my throat. CJ and I exchanged knowing glances. There was no doubt in our minds that we had seen the last of our dear friend Napoleon Blais.

We had become two.

# Chapter 7

## So that's How It's Done!

Even though I had met Napoleon Blais only a few hours ago, I felt a deep sense of emptiness now that he had chosen to walk out of my life. And I blamed one Franklin Northkutt, Head Engineer of The Hoosac Tunnel Bore Project for it. While my heart had already convicted him of deep involvement in the murder of innocents and betrayal of the tunnelmen's most revered tenet; in the back of my mind I knew that my rage was not based upon logic. At this point the evidence we had discovered pointed to no one other than Ringo Kelley. The only reason I suspected Northkutt at all was because his high handed explanation of the blast seemed designed to point the dimwitted constables and the Amazon away from the truth. His condescension had insulted me. And Napoleon Blais no longer trusted or respected him.

CJ's reaction to Napy's outburst and departure was quite different from mine. Sergeant Conal John Mulcahy reported to Constable Captain Charles O'Leary in a most officious manner that he'd a few questions he'd like to ask

Mr. Northkutt. And that was all. By the time I had begun to recover from my confusion at CJ's seeming coldness Da was addressing me.

"Virginia, it's near time ta' head for home. D' ya' think ya' could lend a hand gettin' our horses and Sergeant Mulcahy's road cart set ta' go?"

Da had seen it, the fury in my eyes. And clearly, he now didn't want me anywhere near the follow-up interview. Being relegated to getting the horses ready had given me time to take stock of why I was here and not back there talking to Mr. Northkutt.

Each time I had approached a situation based upon "I" trouble resulted. I was exposed as a child attempting to pass herself off as a woman. Recalling each episode of petulance, arrogance or self-importance had reignited the intense discomfort of the heat that had blistered my face at the time. I told myself over and over, *"Learn your lesson, girl. See the big picture. A seeker of truth must be an instrument of justice, not part of the story."* And wasn't Da right ta' send me? Imagine how I would have mucked up that meeting.

*Da, don't I love ya', though. Ya' mightn't have An Dara Sealladh, but right now it's your intuition I think I'd rather be havin'. Ya' read me like a book.*

The trip home was slow. Da and I on our horses, CJ on his single horse road cart. This time we followed the longer, but more refined path of South Church Street and then up the west shaft road. By the time we came over the last swale toward home a half hour later it was nearly dark. The last embers of sunlight had winked out also extinguishing any of its residual warmth. Daytime's gusting breezes which shot and swirled off the mountains this time of year had also subsided.

Sounds now seemed to travel forever. The huffing of the horses which had served us faithfully during this long and trying day and the squeaking and creaking of CJ's horse cart were no longer part of the ambient background noise. They were brought to the forefront and in a strange way represented the exhaustion we all felt.

I inhaled a deep breath of the cold crisp air and was rewarded with the rich, pungent smell of the wood fires burning in the kitchen stove and the great room fire place. The amber light which shone through the windows in our farm house served as a beacon directing our final hundred yards home. As we got closer I could see Ma through the windows setting the dining room table.

Upon our arrival the farmhouse front door opened and our head farmhand Stanley Woszniak stepped out to greet us. Puffing on his trusty ever present pipe he said in his uniquely Polish-Irish accent,

"Looks like ya've had longk day, folks. Would ya' like me ta' be tay-king'ah care of your mounts for ya'?"

And Da replied, "Thank you, Stanley. And will ya' be breakin' bread with us this evenin'?"

"Tank you, sir. But da' missus fed me earlier. Anyhow, time I'm headed off ta' my rack. Cows'll be needing'ah my attention soon 'nough tamorrow. And I'll be leavingk a lantern burning'ah for ya' on da' porch, Sergreant Mulcahy. A bed's all set for ya'."

Stanley's "rack" was anything but. After he had been with us for about a year Da was so impressed with Stanley's ability to run the day to day dairy operations that he parceled a small lot for him in the corner of our property. Together he and Da built the four room cottage he called his rack.

As Stanley led the horses away I recalled once asking him why he called his cute little house a rack. He turned to me countenance darkening and replied,

"Miss, tiz' a way ta' remind meself how lucky I am. In Poland a rack in a barn is the best I could ever have hoped for."

The aroma of the evening meal Ma had prepared caused my knees to nearly buckle. It was then that I realized just how hungry I was… starving really. The last thing I had eaten was the rashers and toast at breakfast.

Crossing the threshold Da became ensconced in the warm cocoon that is home and his persona reverted to match the setting. The commanding presence of Constable Captain Charles O'Leary was packed away for the night. He was again husband, father, friend.

As Da took off his policeman's hat he swept it across his body, bowed and said, "So, me lady, have ya' prepared a repast for the three famished wandering souls ya' see standin' before ya'?"

"Just sit yourselves down and I think ya'll be pleased when ya' find out." was Ma's reply as her mitt covered hand struggled to lift the cast iron Dutch oven containing our supper off of the stove. Da quickly intercepted her and took over the task of setting the cooker onto a trivet protecting the dining room table from its heat.

When Da removed the cover from the pot steam wafted out of it revealing the luscious stew Ma had labored over all afternoon. Dark rich gravy, praties, Florida mountain turnip, celery, carrots and onions accompanied cubes of succulent beef.

As was our custom, Da sat at the table's head. He ladled the stew into each of our bowls and passed them around while Ma served fresh brown bread and butter that had been churned this very day. I poured each of us tall glasses of tangy, hard cider from the pitcher already waiting for me on the table. I took great care to not get any of the sediment from the bottom into any of the glasses, lest we spend tomorrow in the outhouse.

These tasks completed, CJ led us in saying grace to the Lord thanking him for our meal.

As we supped and dined we all unconsciously uttered the sounds of folks thoroughly enjoying a most pleasurable experience. The events of the day and our condition because of them enhanced the aromas, flavors and textures of the meal. It was a good thing we thanked the Lord before we dug in because right now our praise and appreciation were offered only to Ma... sincerely and often.

When we all pushed back from the table completely satiated, Ma got up and went to the kitchen. A moment later she returned carrying a serving dish. On it was a number of irregularly stacked hunks of spicy, nutty, aromatic cake-like confections...apple brownies. My favorite winter dessert!

We all feigned groans and Ma laughed,

"Ya' don't want 'em? Not to worry. I'll just save 'em for the farmhands tomorrow." And with mock sarcasm she added, "I'm sure *they'll* appreciate 'em."

Da, CJ and I rose from our chairs in unison. We chased after Ma as she retreated toward the kitchen and either reached over her shoulder or around her to snap up our portion of this tasty treat.

"Coffee pot's on the stove. Cream's on the side board. Get your own."

She then put down the serving plate on the kitchen table so we could get seconds if we wished and went to the great room to sit in her favorite chair and enjoy the fire there.

I brought Ma a small plate with an apple brownie on it and CJ brought her a cup of coffee. I curtsied and CJ bowed as we presented them to her. Ma smiled and bowed her head to acknowledge us.

Returning to the kitchen we saw that Da had already heated a kettle of water, poured it into the sink and added the washing soap to it. On the counter next to the sink was a rinsing basin full of cool clean water. With hardly a thought each of us fell into our expected task. Da washed and rinsed, CJ dried and I put things away.

Thus enjoined, Da initiated conversation when he said,

"My talk with Doctor Sam went just as we expected. When I asked him about Kelley's injuries his response was, 'What injuries? All Kelley had were superficial cuts and scratches on 'is face and hands.' Doc also said that there were absolutely no embedded rock fragments in any of the wounds he did have… and that the cuts were lateral incisions like scrapes you'd see on a child's skinned knee."

"When I asked 'im if Kelley could have gotten such injuries by being thrown forward while trying ta' escape the blast, he said yes. But if he had there would 'ave been puncture wounds ta' his back and there were absolutely none of those. In fact there were no cuts or abrasions of any kind to his back."

"So what do ya' think, Cap, Kelley cut himself up a bit?"

"I surely do, CJ. And after my little visit with him he's not gonna' be able ta' bug out on us either. I have 'im sittin' in stir for safe keepin'."

Hearing this I nearly dropped the plate I was putting on the kitchen cupboard shelf.

"You mean you arrested Kelley… on just what Doc told you?"

Da turned to face us and smiled like the cat that swallowed the canary.

"'Course not. I convinced 'im we were protectin' 'im from friends of Ned Brinkman and Billy Nash who've vowed ta' kill 'im. I told 'im we'd guarantee his safety by keepin' his cell locked, have a meal sent over from the Old Black Tavern and keep Doctor Briggs on call ta' help him cope with his *grievous* injuries."

"So you, you lied.?"

"Naw…I simply played on the sympathy he was lookin' for, Virginia. Right now he thinks I'm the best friend he's got. And after all I don't know that what I said *isn't* true…do I? In fact I'd be surprised if it wasn't."

"Anyway, I want 'im nice and relaxed so that when we confront him with all the evidence we now have he might just brick it and confess. If he doesn't, we still have enough ta' bring 'im up on charges. Although it'll be harder ta' find out if he did it for revenge or was bought by someone else."

"Like our patronizing friend Mr. Northkutt?" I added.

"Ya', like Franklin Northkutt, Ginger."

"But what could be his possible reason, Da? How does causing a stoppage of work on the bore benefit *him*? It doesn't seem ta' make sense."

"Actually it does," CJ broke in.

"Northkutt sees completion of the tunnel as his ticket to fame and future fortune. He's made promises to some very powerful people that no man could guarantee. Progress has improved since he got here but it still lags far behind the east portal bore."

"I also get a sense that the pressure's crumbling him from within just as the porridge stone crumbles the tunnel walls. Bit off more than he could chew, he has, and needs to find a way out...or to at least delay the state shutting down the excavation. A tragic accident such as this certainly gains sympathy of those political forces biting at his heels."

And after a deep breath,

"I've seen it before, Ginger. I try to stay clear of such people because they think nothing of taking you down with them. One thing is certain... Failure will never be their fault."

Yes, CJ *had* seen it all before. And from reading about his service in the war I could guess where. General Cousins, the last general under whom he had served, exhibited the same tortured quest for fame. And quick to buy success he was, by ruthlessly and needlessly using up people below him.

Da added,

"Yes, Ginger, Northkutt blusters with hollow arrogance. But by the time we were through with 'im he knew his bluff 'd been called. He attempted ta' dismiss our questions with a wave of his hand and actually said we were ignorant and uneducated."

I felt my face flush but caught myself before my temper could get the better of me. Good thing I *wasn't* there. Uneducated? The amadon obviously doesn't know CJ's background.

"How'd you both manage to keep from belting him a good one?"

"Not hard at'all at'all." An impish smirk crossed his face as he winked at CJ.

"We actually had a fine ol' time eatin' the head off a' this gobshite."

*What divils me Da and CJ are.*

"He counted on very few people other than himself knowin' with certainty how a detonation should take place and why."

"He denigrated Napy's account o' the appropriate proximity of the box ta' the detonation site. He said, 'How can a mere tunnel rat know or understand the complexities of using nitroglycerin.'

CJ said,

"I asked Northkutt how many detonations of the stuff he had taken part in or witnessed. When he squirmed to come up with an answer I reminded him that *Mister* Blais had observed every single nitro detonation conducted in the tunnel so far."

"His answer to this was to simply mumble that Kelley's group *must've* left the ice box too far away."

"When I told him where I had found the box hidden and that there were three empty bottles in it, he replied that Kelley would certainly do something like that for added safety. The box was designed to carry three bottles and one bottle would be extremely dangerous because it would rattle around."

"Very true, but he was purposely missing the point. Just to let him know that we knew it, I reminded Northkutt of his earlier charge that Kelley, Brinkman and Nash were lazy and careless."

Da then took the floor,

"I do believe that at this point we had Northkutt about as uncomfortable as we cared ta' make 'im. After all, it was clear to us that although an accident might garner sympathy for him in the right circles, murder would serve ta' only accentuate his problems. It's clear to us that Northkutt's an opportunist simply trying ta' turn events ta' his advantage and had nothing t' do with the murder of Brinkman and Nash."

"Yeah, Cap. But wasn't it fun to see the shock and I do believe little bit of fear in the git's expression when two simple, ignorant constables such as us saw right through him?"

"Right ya' are CJ. That was good enough for me."

The last of the supper dishes clean and stored, we now went to join Ma in front of the great room fire. CJ and I sat in arm chairs. Da went to the tall walnut display cupboard standing against the wall that enclosed the stairway that lead to our bedrooms. His back to us, Da opened the glass doors of the upper cabinet, removed the crystal carafe stored there and poured a bit of the creature into matching crystal glasses. Completing his ritual, he gave the first jar to Ma and the second to CJ. Finally he returned with not only his glass but also one he presented with a big smile… to me.

"Virginia O'Leary, my dearest daughter. Today tis' a woman you've become and tis' proud of ya' I am. Féadfaidh an Dia, Naomh Pádraig argus ár sinsear dul in éineacht leat I gcónaí.

Ma with a tear in her eye and CJ expressing a bit of surprise both raised their glasses and translating Da's toast reiterated,

"May God, St. Patrick and our ancestors be with you always."

Just last night Da's distribution of the nightcap had been my cue to adjourn to my bedroom for the night. But on *this* night… this very special night, I had my own jar of the beautiful golden fluid that is Jameson's whiskey. I held my glass up to the fire light and the contents seemed to glow. Da had been often known to brand it the nectar of the gods.

And so, I took my first sip.

My reaction was instantaneous. The burning of my palate caused me to cough so violently that the "nectar of the gods" streamed out of my nose.

Da, Ma and CJ raised their jars, laughed hysterically and chanted,

"Sláinte, sláinte."

Watering eyes now accompanied my hacked response,

"Wow, Da. This is really good. Thanks...I think."

Upon recovering I took my second sip. Wiser, it was miniscule and had a chance to mix with moisture in my mouth before it hit my palate. Did I taste it or smell it? I'm not sure it mattered because indeed this stuff was the nectar of the gods.

For a long time nothing was said. We simply relaxed and watched the fire dance in the hearth. When the solitude was finally broken, Da leaned forward, rested his elbows on parted thighs and dangling his glass between his knees said to CJ,

"Virginia bein' with me this mornin' was no accident. I needed her and I assume you may have some inkling why. Her... *eccentricity* has been well known about town for some time now. Anyway, 'tis a hell of a tale we have ta' tell ya'."

"Can I pour ya' another jar, CJ? I know I need one."

"Maeve, me' love, will ya' start us along?"

# Chapter 8

## March 21, 1865

Oh God, it can't be morning already. Haven't I just closed my eyes? My body feels like it belongs to an overworked dray horse and my mouth is filled with cotton.

But the clank-banging of Ma working at the kitchen stove is informing me otherwise. I decided to risk that painful reality and cracked open my right eye. The dim but discernible light that invaded my bedroom window penalized me for my choice.

Growing more alert by the moment now, the humming sounds from downstairs became the voices of CJ, Da and Ma quietly talking. Wonderful aromas summoning me to breakfast had diffused upstairs and, and, and… holy shite. CJ has already come over from Stanley's cottage. Da's already passed Ma's inspection. Breakfast was being served.

*"I'M LATE!"*

Jumping out of bed I jammed each foot into a slipper, threw on my robe and cinched it around my waist.

*"Oh God, CJ's here."*

As I ran to my dresser I pondered why I felt the need *this* morning to look in the mirror and brush the tangles and knots from my hair. CJ has stayed over many times in the past. Then I flushed...

*Oh.* Brush.

*Oh, oh.* Brush, brush.

*God. No.* Brush. Brush.

*No, no, NO!* Brush, brush, BRUSH!

*Well... maybe...* B-r-u-s-h...

Having made sense of this conflict between mind and emotion, sort of, I slammed my brush down on my dresser, took a deep breath and emerged from my bedroom. I padded down the stairs with as much dignity as my slightly hung over seventeen year old self could muster and said,

"Morning everyone. Sorry I overslept. Did I miss anything?"

"Wellllll, if it isn't Sleepin' Beauty," Da chortled. Ya' look like ya' bin' kissin' a frog."

"Charles!" Ma scorned as she slapped Da's shoulder. "You should talk."

"Virginia, ya' shoulda' seen *these* two before they had their mornin' coffee and washed up. It was more than a *couple* o' jars they had after you went upstairs last night, I'm here ta' tell ya'."

"And anyhow, ya' daft man, ya've got your Grimm's mixed up."

Then a chair scraped over the kitchen floor drawing our attention to it. Rising, CJ smiled,

"Good morning, Miss Virginia. To me you look fine, just fine."

Ma and Da glanced at each other with surprised looks.

Caught completely off-guard I blushed, but managed to respond demurely,

"Thank you, Sergeant."

As I sat down it all came back. Ma had told Conal everything. Ev-er-y-thing. She even gave him Seanmháthair's letter to read and shown him her daguerreotype.

Last night with the creature to bolster me I'd only felt relief that CJ had learned the deepest truths of my being. I felt absolutely no resentment of what Ma had done. In fact, at that time I wanted to shout to the world and get it over with. Right now, though, I felt completely naked. But strangely enough I was unashamed. Conal had "seen me" and *still* his morning greeting had conveyed not just acceptance but... affection?

Whether my stomach churned because of this realization or primal pangs of hunger, it was Ma who knew what to say and at exactly the right time.

"Tis a bit late ya' are, dear but I've hoarded a servin' o' hash browns from these vultures and I can fry ya' a couple o' sunny side up. Coffee's on the stove and the cream's on the table here. It'll be just a minute."

Da and CJ quietly sipped yet another cup of coffee and munched on some toast while Ma's tasty breakfast helped me de-quease my gut. As I wiped my lips with my napkin Da's patience had reached its limit and he spoke up.

"While you were gettin' your beauty sleep Sergeant Mulcahy and I were talkin' over our plans for the day. We think that if we all play our cards right Ringo Kelley will not only confess, but also spill the name or names of anyone else involved."

"We thought ya' might like ta' join in on the fun so we'd like ya' ta' give us a listen."
I had absolutely no response...nothing. So I looked to CJ who just shrugged. Then I looked back to Da who also shrugged.

*I guess it's up to me.*

"OK, what have you two cooked up?"

There was such pride in Da's smile that I thought he'd pop a button. Then he leaned toward me conspiratorially and began,

"First I'll go into Kelly's cell and reinforce the notion that I'm 'is best friend. Ya' know, inquire about how he slept... ask the poor man if he would like me ta' call for Doc. Unbeknownst ta' Kelley, CJ will be waitin' just outside the cell area listenin' ta' me every word."

"When Kelley's softened up enough CJ'll come stormin' in makin' an awful ruckus about new evidence and pointin' his finger at Kelley, accusin' him of bein' a murderer. CJ'll try ta' get by me ta' get at Kelley but I'll stop 'im... pullin' rank, ya' know?"

"I'll play the advocate and get inta' an awful row with CJ about how wrong he is. I'll force CJ out of the cell to an area where Kelley can't see us. Then CJ and I will talk in hushed tones but still loud enough for the shite head ta' hear. As we talk CJ'll run down the evidence we've got and I'll let 'im convince me he's right."

"It's at this point I'll let *my* anger come out. We'll both storm back in ta' his cell and I'll turn over his bunk with him in it. When Kelley pulls himself ta' his feet the worthless gobshite'll find 'imself cornered by two furious

Irish coppers. But I'll stop short a' throwin' Kelley around the cell. I might, or might not cuff him one dependin' on how shocked we can make 'im."

"CJ'll then threaten 'im with the reality of his situation. Tell him he's gonna' swing, all right. But he may pray for such a quick end after the two of us get through with 'im. Then we storm outa' the cell, slam the door and make a big deal about janglin' the keys while lockin' the door. We need him ta' really believe he's not leavin' this cell in a vertical position for the next step ta' work. "

Da then looked at CJ, laced his fingers together behind his head, leaned back in his chair and grinning ear to ear said,

"CJ, why don't ya' tell Ginger here *her* part in this sordid little conspiracy we've hatched."

Conal didn't return Da's smile, however...or his enthusiasm. Instead he turned sideways in his chair and stood up. He picked up his cane which had been hanging on the chair back and using it walked to the kitchen window, gazing out. "Cap, on second thought I'm not so sure we want to involve Miss Virginia. If we lean on Kelley, I mean really lean on him, we can get him to spill it. If someone bought him we'll find out."

The tone of Da's response exposed that he was more than a bit exasperated by Conal's comment:

"C'mon, CJ we've already been through this. Do it your way we won't be able ta' trust the information he gives us. My way, he'll give it up and all we have ta' do is listen. Why the change of heart anyhow, CJ? It's not at'all like ya'."

After a painfully long moment of silence with no answer forthcoming, Da softened his delivery and said,

"Look, Ringo Kelley's gonna' swing. That's sure, just on the evidence we compiled yesterday. All we need ta' know is whether he'll have company on his scaffold. He goes ta' trial all dinged up with black eyes, busted ribs and such, we just might be the next ones in the dock. And don't forget his *lack* of injuries is part of our evidence against him."

Sheepishly now, Conal answered,

"I just think we're asking an awful lot of …"

Good God, but I'd heard enough. I stood up so suddenly that the backs of my legs sent the chair I'd been sitting on skittering away from the table. Placing my hands on my hips, I stamped my foot and bellowed,

"Hello…HELL-O- O.. It's me, here. Don't you two think you ought to stop arguing and tell me what you need me to do? If I don't think I can pull it off, I promise I'll tell you."

Well, that did it. The tension in the room was broken and sucked right up the fireplace flue with the smoke. CJ and Da turned to face each other and began laughing... tentatively at first and then with huge belly laughs. No further apology was required between these two soul mates. Both were ready to move on.

*Aaggh, men.*

"Do you two think you might knock it and finally just... TELL ME...WHAT...YOU WANT ME...TO DO??"

Conal walked back to the kitchen table and resumed his seat. He put his cane on the table holding it with both hands like it was a rung of a ladder.

"It's OK, Cap. I've got it."

"Miss Ginger, you already heard that the Captain is first going to relax Kelley and make him feel comfortable and secure. Then I come in and shake him up a bit. Next the Captain will scare the shite out of him. For this to work the amadon needs to be more scared of your Da and me than he is of whoever paid for this despicable act to be done."

"After Kelley sits alone with his thoughts contemplating just how deeply he's in, an angel appears unannounced and rescues him from the brink of despair."

"That, by the way, is you. You see, Kelley only got to town about a month ago, so he doesn't know you."

"Another constable will open the cell door, unlock it and leave. We want you to bring him his afternoon meal from the Old Black Tavern. Tell him it was ordered last night by the Captain. Make sure it's comfort food, you know; something hot, aromatic and swimming in gravy. A couple beers to go with it would be a nice touch... maybe help loosen his lip a bit."

"Mention how upset he looks. React to the condition of his cell. Help him put the cell back in order. Tell him you can't let him eat in such a mess. While you're doing this show him some sympathy... Get him talking about what happened. Tell him how awful you think those coppers are. Offer to stay with him while he eats. Get him to drink both of the pints as quickly as possible. Then casually mention that if he's still thirsty you can get him more."

"But, now comes the dicey part."

"Introduce the idea that anyone could understand if he was under orders of a powerful man, what else could he do? After all, it was either them...don't mention the names of the two men he killed... or him. They were all just pawns caught in some larger game. Keep stroking him. Keep using terms like: understandable… anyone would do the same…really no choice. And best of all… if it was you, you'd do the same. Surely even the coppers would understand if they just knew what he'd been through. Introduce the idea that it seems clear right now it's either Kelley or the people who set him up to take the fall. Encourage him to not let that happen. After all, why protect the people who put him in such a spot?"

At that Da broke in displaying that huge impish grin of his and said,

"And, me beautiful colleen, da ya' think ya' can manage ta' shed a tear or two? Could ya' maybe even casually reach out and touch his arm or hand while ya're workin' 'im? That'll help ta' open his flood gates, sure, and get 'im ta' spill it... poor abused soul such as he is."

CJ then added,

"And don't worry about a thing, Miss Virginia. We'll be just out of sight listening to his every word."

Just then we heard Ma chuckling from across the kitchen. She had just finished putting the breakfast dishes away and was drying her hands with a towel when she exclaimed,

"Tis' the divil 'imself y'are...both of ya'."

"And you, Virginia O'Leary, bein' the offspring of such a conniver, I suppose ya' can't wait ta' sucker this poor lost soul."

The smile I had shared with everyone else was slowly erased from my face. I guess listening to Da and Conal had been like enjoying a good story up until Ma spoke. It was fun to listen to, but I was detached from the reality of it. It was about somebody else.

Ma's comment had injected me into the middle of it. I was being asked to use my womanly wiles to gain the trust of this man in order to assure not only his death, but also that of some other person or persons unknown to any of us right now.

*Womanly wiles? What womanly wiles?*

In my entire life Jeremiah Colgrove had been my only boy friend. And that was a friendship based upon a mutual love of all things academic. We met in the first grade and our friendship grew stronger every year of elementary school based upon this love of learning new things. When Jeremiah went on to Drury Academy after eighth grade and I did not because girls weren't allowed, he "secured" extra textbooks for me every year. We met either at his parents' mansion on Church Street in the heart of the village or at my house at least twice a week to discuss the lessons of the week. But now my dear boy friend Jeremiah was at Harvard College studying law and gone from my life.

But a *boyfriend*? None. Zilch. How could I seduce a fully grown man? Well, Conal and Da were waiting for an answer. Could I do this? I promised I would tell them if I didn't think I could. What am I going to...

"Ginger, dear."

It was Ma.

"We're gonna send these two on their way. We need some time ta' get ya' ready. When I get done wit' ya' ya'll have that Ringo Kelley person ready ta' confess ta' makin' the leaves fall off a' the trees in autumn."

Conal and Da were no sooner out the door than Ma was already at the foot of the stairs summoning me to follow her.

"Let's go, Ginger we don't have all day."

When we both had entered my room at the end of the upstairs hallway Ma closed the door and put her back against it. The look on her face was that of a human spider who had just trapped a juicy fly in its web.

"Sit down at your dressing table, dear and I'll finish brushin' out your hair. Then we're gonna' have a little talk … woman ta' woman."

As Ma began I looked into the large mirror that was in front of me and watched her. She middle parted my red, curly, very long hair and used a combination of comb and brush in a way I never had. The improvement she'd managed after just a few minutes was quite amazing. My ever-present frizz had disappeared into the curls and my hair took on a sheen I'd never seen before. It no longer hung like weights attached to my scalp. My hair looked, well… it looked terrific.

When Ma said she'd "finish brushin' me out" she was being much too kind. What I called brushing out my hair was to just work at it long enough to get out all of the snarls. Next I'd gather all of it to the back and loosely braid it into a plait that would swing around from shoulder to shoulder as I moved. I laughingly told myself that it was my way to counterbalance my movements much as the huge Catamounts hereabouts used their tails when trying to match the agility of the whitetails they hunted so relentlessly. After all, my day, every day, was taken up helping Ma with her housework and cooking. In my spare time I read, and I read, and I read. It was the only way I could assuage the constant frustration I felt because the doors of high school had been closed to me. I had no time to care about more. I had no reason to either.

"There, Ginger. Whata' a'ya' think?"

Ma further declared her job done by holding her two hands out palms up with the implements of magic still in them.

I swiveled around in my chair to face her. Somehow, I didn't believe my degree of appreciation could be conveyed when reflected off the looking glass.

"Amazing. Why haven't we done this before?"

"You're right, Ginger. We should have. All I can tell ya' is that a mother thinks of her little girl as a little girl... always. But, over the last couple o' days I've been forced ta' see ya' as ya' really are. You're a beautiful, brilliant woman. That plait I gave ya' every mornin' when ya' were a little girl will no longer do."

"And ya' know, I think that once I put my mind ta' it I'm gonna' really like treatin' ya' as the person you are. 'Tis long overdue. Your Da is certainly expectin' ya' ta' act that way. He's actually expectin' ya' ta' seduce that reprobate Ringo Kelley inta' bearin' his soul to ya'."

Then Ma paused for a second and as she continued I caught just a hint of a smile,

"Although, I'm not so sure Sergeant Mulcahy's so pleased about anyone oglin' your charms, if ya' take me meanin'."

*Oh, oh there's that feeling of heat rising from my withers to the top of my head again.*

"Honey, don't be embarrassed. You're comin' of age, and that's a fact. Real adult love may be right around the corner for ya'. Be happy. There's no more wonderful feelin' in the world."

"So what say we give 'er a whirl and begin our chat."

Ma sat on my bed across the room and made herself comfortable by hugging my pillow across her lap and leaning forward.

"First off, all men are really little boys. I don't care how old they are, ten, thirty or sixty. They're still the same. They want ta' be flattered about how strong they are…how smart they are… how good they are at what they do. They want ta' feel like they're in control… like they're makin' the decisions."

"Second, if a man likes what he's lookin' at, a crafty woman can get 'em ta' stop thinkin' with his brain altogether because it's another part of his anatomy that'll be engaged. If ya' can do that, he'll be yours."

At that Ma and I both burst out laughing.

*Maybe this would be fun.*

"Virginia, stand up for a second and take off that horse blanket ya' call a robe. Now take a good look at yourself in the mirror. Twirl around a bit. Try to see what others see. If that wasn't you in the mirror but some new woman in the village, what would ya' think?"

*Holy Saints Patrick and Colmcille. Why hadn't I noticed before?*

"Darlin', you've got the whole package. Now just what is it ya' think it'is that Kelley's gonna' be lookin' at when you go into that cell?"

"What you're goina' be doin' today isn't like all those times ya' wrapped your big bear of a Da around your finger."

"You're a woman and ya' need ta' use that ta' close the deal… a coy smile… a shift of your hips. Make that amadon fantasize about what ya've got that he *can't* see."

"And your Da was absolutely right when he said that a well-timed tear ta' demonstrate just how sympathetic you are ta' his plight could be very powerful. This Kelley is no relative and you've sure got what he would like ta' have."

"And I don't mean he'd just want ta' kiss your hand."

Ma then stood up and playfully tossed my pillow at me to emphasize her point. We again laughed as one. Then she said,

"You stay right here, I'll be right back."

While she was gone I had time to reflect upon this most recent event of the surprising series which had taken place in my life over the past thirty-six hours. It now made sense to me how Da and Conal, though separated by years and experiences, had become such close friends. Ma had invited me to chart the same course with her and I really, really liked that idea.

*I love you more than ever, Maeve Daelyn O'Leary, my mother, my friend.*

My bedroom door suddenly opened banging against the wall. Standing in the doorway was a headless torso on caster wheels. Ma was standing behind it stretching to her full height so she could peek over its shoulder grinning ear to ear.

"Surprise."

The headless wraith was actually Ma's dressmaker's frame and it was wearing a beautiful new day dress. The sheer length of it meant that it had been designed for me. The look on my face probably said it all. Anyhow, I still said,

"Oh, Ma…it's wonderful."

The fabric was a rich, airy cream colored challis which was butter soft to the touch. The print was a floral design. Thin green bamboo shoots waved back and forth vertically along the entire length of the dress. Distributed along these waves were flowers of wild strawberries as well as tiny pink and blue-violet anemones.

I had never before owned such a dress. Sure, I had nice dresses for Sunday Mass and special trips into the village, but my usual day wear consisted of simple dresses in both style and fabric. After all, the sort of work done on a farm allowed nothing else.

But this… this was a dress such as you'd see the finest young ladies wearing in the cities. It had a neckline that scooped starting at each shoulder and plunged deeply enough to tantalize but not scandalize. The mutton sleeves were banded above the elbows with green satin that matched the color in the fabric pattern and blossomed from there only to be gathered at the wrists by satin cuffs.

The bodice was fitted to hug the torso and belted at the waist with the same green satin as the sleeves. Emerging beneath the satin belt was a lined skirt of the most modern style.  It touched the hips just enough to let everyone know you had them and flowingly hung down from there ending just above the floor.  The stiffness of formal dresses was nowhere evident in this dress.  No stifling corsets or hooped, scratchy petticoats were needed to wear it, just my Sunday chemise and drawers.

"Well, get on with it, Ginger, try it on."

Once ensconced, I proceeded to spin and dance to show off Ma's creation to her.  As I did the skirt almost floated on the air and moved as if it was a part of me.  It revealed just a hint that there was a real woman under this fabric.

"Perfect." Ma exclaimed.  "That dense eejit'll think you're his guardian angel for sure. 'Tis the hard way he'll be findin' out it's an avenging angel ya' *really* are."

*This IS going to be fun. I CAN do this.*

"Ma… I don't know what to say… our talk, my hair… and this dress. If I … no… *when* I get Kelley to spill his guts, it'll be because of you."

"Get along wit ya', Ginger. Y'ave a date with the divil."

I was fortunate to have a nice hooded woolen cape to wear over my dress. When I opened the door to leave I wasn't surprised to be greeted by the type of incongruous weather for which the Berkshire County early spring is known. As soon as I stepped down the porch stairs, big fat flakes of snow like those which had already covered the ground with cotton proceeded to softly fall on me.

As I looked out to the eastern sky the sun appeared only as a dim white disc trying desperately to burn away the late morning overcast. The summits of the Hoosac Mountains were hidden from me by the same shroud, while trees of the lower mountains appeared covered with glistening sugar. The west, not having the benefit of being backlit by the faint but toiling sun, was only a white curtain.

The paradox lay not in the early spring snow but in the accompanying air feeling so warm and calm. If the day continued as it usually did on most days like this, within one hour the snow will stop and the overcast will give way to startlingly clear blue skies. Within two, all evidence of the snowy morning will have disappeared.

*Gosh, this is beautiful country.*

The snorting of the two horses pulling the family carriage up the small knoll leading from the horse barn to the house broke my reverie. At the reins of the harness was Stanley, coatless, hatless and gloveless. He even had his sleeves rolled up. To look at him was to believe it was summer. No sooner had he "whoa'd" the horses than he jumped down from the carriage and greeted me with a smile warmer than the morning sun.

"Morninga, Miss Virginia. My, you lookin' very nice… yes, very nice. Your Dada thought it woulda be nice for you to arrive at the station in style."

Stanley held my left hand in his in an effort to assist me taking the step up into the carriage. I appreciated his kindness, but it would have been easier to get into the carriage by myself. Anyhow, once elevated to my perch in the front seat I said,

"Thank you, Stanley. That was very nice."

Quite pleased with himself, Stanley almost vaulted to his seat on the other side of the carriage.

During our ride into the village very little was said other than the usual pleasantries. And as usual when not otherwise occupied, my mind wandered. This time my affection for this tough, lovable bull of a man brought me back to the time Ma told me about how Stanley came to be part of our family.

Stanley Henry Woszniak was a Polish immigrant who arrived in America about the same time as my parents. After disembarking in New York he found the city dominated by large Irish and Italian groups. Unlike my parents, Stanley was poor. His only skills were those of a farm hand and so he found himself unwelcome in the city. He roamed north through towns along the Hudson River taking itinerant jobs on the many farms there. Eventually he made it to North Adams, again looking for acceptance as well as work.

On his very first night here Stanley was arrested in a bar fight. Drunk and tired of being rejected he nearly killed the man taunting him because of his inability to speak English. After terrorizing two officers attempting to arrest him, my Da, then a young constable, arrived. He was the only one able to calm Stanley down.

Later that night, Da came by Stanley's cell to check on him only to find him head in hands weeping like a child. Stanley's situation so moved Da that he took him home to the family dairy farm and gave him work. Within a year this powerfully built and tireless man improved operations so dramatically that Ma gave complete charge of the farm to him. At that time Stanley asked that his pay be a percentage of the profits. Hat in hand he offered, "Missus, iz simple; no profit, no pay."

Our trip down Church Street close to the center of town never ceased to impress me. Giant elm trees that had been planted on both sides of this stretch had matured to towering height and now formed a canopy covering the street with their crowns. In summer they provided cooling shade. In winter the ice and snow covered tree skeletons glistened in the sunlight and provided a crystal cathedral defining this half-mile area as someplace very special.

This is where the most ostentatious homes of the village had been built. Most had three stories. The first two provided ornate and spacious living quarters for the owners and their families. Huge windows taller than a man faced the street so that passersby were able to catch glimpses of the richness of the interior. Crystal chandeliers hanging from twelve foot ceilings, massive brick fireplaces in every room, life-sized oil portraits of family members on the walls and heavy embroidered window treatments made of the finest brocade produced at local textile mills defined the interiors of these homes. Without question, each of these edifices was designed to impress; not just the gawking public, but also each other with just how important the family that resided here was.

Ah, but then there was the third floor of these homes.

It seemed that no matter what the style: Mansard, Greek Revival, Stick Style or Victorian, window sizes on this floor were greatly reduced and occupants were forced to live under the rafters holding up the roof. The third floor was clearly designed to provide basic living space with functionality in mind, not comfort.

This was where the domestic service staff was quartered.

It seemed that all of these homes had a neat semi-circular gravel carriageway leading from the street to the foot of a large covered porch or portico attached to the house and back out. No walking from the street for these folks or their visitors.

As we passed my friend Jeremiah Colgrove's family manse I reflected on the many hours I had spent there while growing up. I never got used to how the family was pampered by the domestic staff. I found the demands put on them to be extraordinary and was always uncomfortable when they performed even the simplest daily tasks for the Colgroves. These people rose early and retired late…every single day of every single week. And their living quarters were in the in the attic.

When I asked Jeremiah how he could tolerate such pampering his answer was simple and direct. "We feed them, house them and pay them. This is what they do, so I let them do it."

More than a bit dismayed at Jeremiah's attitude I shook my head. Except for the pay, this is how I would have described our milk cows back at the farm. I just never dreamed that my beloved Jeremiah would refer to *people* in a similar manner.

"Quincy Street's comin' up soon, Miss. Would ya' like ta' take it-a or go a ways further ta' Main?"

Stanley's question brought me back to what had become a beautiful late morning. The sun had indeed beaten the overcast and was doing its job of melting away the early morning snow. Because the sun was almost directly overhead, shadows which crisscrossed the street were created by the giant Elm framework.

Stanley's offer to take us to Main Street before we went left was tempting. This route would pass by the very ornate and beautiful Blackinton mansion which stood in the distance on the corner of Church and Main. But we needed to get to Constable Station post haste.

"Stanley, I know we don't get into the village center very often, but the Captain is waiting for us. Could we please take the left onto Quincy?"

With a slightly disappointed nod Stanley complied.

Directly in front of us not more than a quarter mile away stood the village hall. Not one tree shaded it. Not one shrub beautified it. Only mud surrounded it. This building was a stark contrast to the opulence and richness of the mansion row we had just left. It certainly reminded me that North Adams was first and foremost a mill town having all of the ugliness that that implies.

Two and one half storeys of naked brick sat on a dull gray granite foundation that itself protruded a half storey above grade. The windows were large and uniformly spaced four over four on each face. The roof line was straight, pitched steeply in the simplest manner possible and shingled with dismal gray slate. Clearly, this was a building of protection and containment, not beauty. Neither flood nor fire would claim this village's records as it had in so many other towns.

Stairs facing toward Main Street carried visitors from ground level to the first floor. Two thick, eight foot tall oak doors guarding the entrance made me laughingly think of the old saying, "Despair of salvation all ye who enter here."

The granite foundation also had windows. But these were much smaller and had thick iron bars preventing either ingress or egress through them. On the back side of village hall there was another set of stairs. But these did not lead up. Instead, they were cut into the grade and led into the foundation cellar which could easily have been mistaken for a dungeon. This was Constable Station. We had arrived.

As I turned to thank Stanley for the ride he was already on his way to assist my descent. No sooner had my toe touched the ground than the Constable Station door banged open followed by an enraged Constable Captain Charles James O'Leary.

"How could that gobshite do it? He may run Adams, but I'll be boiled in oil before he'll take charge here. Damn it... Damn...it... all... to... hell."

"Stanley, get on back up there. We're goin' ta' Adams... Now."

Stanley abandoned me and leapt to his driver's position in the carriage. I don't think he even touched the step. Da brushed by me without so much as a word. When he grabbed the sides of the carriage and used the step to ascend to his seat, he gave the carriage such a yank the whole contraption yawed in his direction. It looked like even the carriage was bowing in deference to Da's power to command.

Within seconds, they were gone. There I stood; alone at the top of the stairs to the station, bug eyed, mouth opening and closing like a newly landed trout and wondering what in the world had just happened.

Just then a grim faced Sergeant Mulcahy appeared in the doorway at the bottom of the stairs.

"Miss Virginia, come in out of the cold. Wait 'til you hear this."

I closed my mouth and descended into the station and entered what should have been the stage for our two act play: "*The Slicing and Dicing of One Ringo Kelley.*"

The first thing I always noticed upon crossing the station threshold was how bright it was inside even though it was located in the cellar. The second was that all of the interior walls were made of the same brick as the outside of the building. The impression I had was that this building had to be America's version of a European castle.

At a desk located to the right of the doorway sat Constable Sergeant Elisha Smart. When anyone entered the station, he was the first person you talked to. He ran the day shift, assigned every constable his beat for the day and managed the station. On this day though, there was not a hint of his usual swagger. Constable Smart appeared quite despondent, his eyes glassy and vacant.

CJ, not reacting to the scene to our right quietly ushered me to the left and into the twelve foot brick box that served as Da's office and closed the door.  Neither of us sat.

"Ginger, there'll be no fun with Ringo Kelley on this day, or any other.  At six this morning constable Smart received a telegram from Adams Police Chief Simeon Eldridge.  Now, you know that he's the only person your Da technically has to answer to.  Well, the telegram instructed that we immediately release Ringo Kelley. No explanation was given."

"And that's what Constable Smart did."

"Ringo Kelley is gone."

# Chapter 9

## December 20, 1865

Although it has been nine months since the day Ringo Kelley disappeared, the aftermath of the circumstances of his departure hung like a pall over Da, Conal and me. Not only had the slippery, conniving sleeveen escaped the hangman's noose he so justly deserved, he was prodded to run by the only man within sixty miles who could give the order. Time and again Da, CJ and I tried to make sense of it.

Chief Eldridge had his hands full overseeing the Adams Police department. He and Da have had their disagreements, but overall they trusted and respected each other. Not once had he interfered in village business since Da became Captain of the village constabulary. Moreover, Chief Eldridge was a good, honest man. So what happened?

There was only one account that was plausible. But, Da hated it. Someone with power…real power… had gotten to him. But who? This man who Da liked and trusted had undermined his authority. And he not only wouldn't say why he did it, he clearly resented the question having even been asked. But the unanswered question that really tormented Da was how? How did Eldridge even know Kelley was "in custody" because technically he wasn't. Da had very quietly convinced Kelley that he'd be safer in a locked cell than loose roaming the village. Very few people knew what Da had done.

No telegrams were sent to the Adams Police by anyone in North Adams. Was someone watching Kelley's movements? Did that person go to Eldridge personally? Did he have the connections that could turn up the heat? Were there eyes inside the constabulary reporting directly to Eldridge? Da didn't know… and all efforts to find out thumped to a dead end. This is what drove Da 'round the bend. Whom could he trust? Right now he was sure of only three people.

And so, here I am. The Christmas season is nigh and Ma has made it quite clear that our home would be the sanctuary from all of this. Brandishing her rolling pin to emphasize her point Ma looked up at her two resident giants and grumbled,

"Bring any nonsense inta' this house and ya' will suffer most dreadful consequences."

And because of the unfathomable love Da and I have for this wonderful, resilient woman… it is so.

Ma used the season of Advent to refocus our attention from consternation over Ringo Kelley to the coming of our Savior. The candles of Hope, Bethlehem and Joy already stood lit on the fireplace mantle; one for each of the previous three Sundays. Only the Angel's candle waited to be lit upon our return from Mass this final Sunday before Christmas.

The Nativity scene was positioned on a table in the great room so that it could be seen from everywhere. As was our family tradition, the manger remained unoccupied. Only when we descend the stairs on Christmas morning will a swaddling infant Jesus will be laying there. Then we will join hands, bow our heads and say a Christmas prayer of rejoicing.

Nothing will put life in perspective; nothing will lift the spirits of an Irish Catholic more than this.

Along about mid-morning Stanley came clomping through the great room door with a big smile on his face dragging this year's arboreal sacrifice to the holidays behind him. As he erected the beautiful evergreen in front of the big double window facing the porch, he quietly sang his favorite Polish carol:

Przybiezeli do Betlejem pasterze,

Graja skocznie dzieciateczku n lirze.

Witaja dzieciatko, male pacholatko,

Pasterze, pasterze.


Dzieciatko sie do pastuszkow usmiecha

Jako Jesus czystem sercem oddycha,

Chwala na wysokosci,

Chwala no wysokosci,

A poloj na ziemi.


When Ma and I joined in Stanley burst into full song and the sweet melody filled the house. I strung the popcorn chains around the tree and Ma began hanging the iced gingerbread cookies of all seasonal shapes on the branches. The star of Bethlehem would have to wait until after supper tonight when Da would crown the tree.

As we sang my spirits lifted even more when my mind drifted back to the first Christmas Stanley was with us. Ma and I heard Stanley murmuring the tune while helping to decorate the house. Only eight or nine at the time, I mimicked him and eventually was able to sing along. When Ma made note of the song's beauty, Stanley flushed, surprised that anyone noticed. He explained in the best way his limited English allowed that this was a Polish carol about the shepherds coming to Bethlehem. When they visit the Holy Family, the baby Jesus smiles upon them and they rejoice. Stanley burst with pride when Ma asked him to teach her the carol too. Ever since, the trimming of the Christmas tree in this *Irish* home has been accompanied by a *Polish* carol.

When the tree was completed we sang, "*The Shepherds Came Running to Bethlehem*" one final time. As we backed off to admire our work there came a familiar sound at the door not heard here for over a year. Tap, tap, tap…thud, thud, thud…tap, tap, tap. Tap, tap, tap…thud, thud, thud…tap, tap, tap. That code. Our code.

I ran to the door and opened it so quickly that the latch slipped from my hand and the door rebounded off the wall. There, standing on the porch directly in front of me was a very tall, very handsome, very well dressed young man. Impetuously, I lunged forward wrapping my arms around "Adonis'" neck and exclaimed much louder than my proximity to his left ear dictated, "Jeremiah."

"Hi, Ginger. Aren't you going to invite me in?"

Upon entering, Jeremiah hung up his overcoat and placed his John Bull top hat on a side table. When he turned, the visage before me was so familiar… but so very different. When Jeremiah Colgrove had departed for Cambridge and Harvard College he was a skinny, callow sixteen-year old. The young man who had returned was broad shouldered and refined.

The shock of coal black hair that used to constantly fall into his eyes was replaced by a side-parted, neatly cut style framed by side burns that ended at the bottom of each ear lobe. No longer in casual clothes such as school agers in the village wore, Jeremiah's suit was of the latest style and finest material. An open tailcoat with black velvet trim was worn over a crisp white shirt and red paisley ascot. A gray double breasted vest tied the look together. His brushed cotton trousers were pin striped and had legs cut so narrow that his legs looked twice as long as his torso.

But it was those brown eyes… and that impish smile. *He* hadn't changed…this was my Jeremiah…this was my friend.

"Well, Mrs. O'Leary, don't I get a hug?"

Jeremiah reached out and wrapped his arms around Ma, her head barely reaching his shoulder. Backing off she continued to hold his hands and said,

"Jeremiah, or should I say *Mr*. Colgrove, What a wonderful surprise. Now, you and Ginger head on inta' the great room and sit down by the fire. I'll bring ya' some eggnog."

We both headed for the sofa and sat down in the same manner we had since we were children. Jeremiah positioned himself obliquely so he could face me directly. His right thigh was positioned across the seat with the calf bent by ninety degrees so that his boot dangled over the edge. His right arm was stretched out along the top of the sofa. I mirrored Jeremiah, except I kept both hands clasped and on my lap smoothing my skirt.

The conversation immediately flowed freely and easily as is only possible between the best of friends. Jeremiah patiently answered all of my questions about Harvard law school, Boston, and even about rowing on the Charles River. He added in anecdotes about classmates that had us both laughing.

I filled Jeremiah in about the challenges of the past nine months, from my second sight vision to the unexplained order by Chief Eldridge to release Ringo Kelley. In recounting this history I needed to tread lightly because I certainly did not want to suffer Ma's "most dreadful consequences."

Jeremiah's expression clouded with concern.

"My gosh, Ginger. You really foresaw the murder of two men by this Ringo Kelley character? I mean, when we were still in school you used to find lost objects and discompose some of our classmates' parents by predicting innocuous events. But murder? And your account of the event sounded as if you were actually there…almost as if *you* were dying. How in heaven's name did you deal with it?"

I had forgotten how overwrought I had been that night. I had long since accepted visions such as these simply as part of who I am… part of my destiny. But the retelling had clearly unnerved Jeremiah and my friend deserved an answer. So I went to the mantle, brought back Seanmháthair's small chest and set it down on the sofa between us.

The only reaction to what Jeremiah saw and what I told him was an incredulous,

"Whew."

Jeremiah's exclamation was followed by a silence so complete that the crackling of the fire sounded like gunshots. So finally I shrugged and said,

"Well, you asked."

I had forgotten that although the Colgroves were of English heritage, their forebears arrived on these shores well over a hundred and fifty years ago. They now considered themselves first and foremost American. Stories of mysticism and the Druids were merely fairy tales told to children. As we grew up Jeremiah had been aware of my developing second sight. But pragmatic to a fault for as long as I've known him, he dismissed the stories told about me as intuitive guesses of an extremely perceptive friend.

He got up from the sofa and paced back and forth. Pinching the bridge of his nose he queried,

"Ginger, are you quite sure that you weren't dreaming and this whole thing wasn't just a case of deja vu?"

I wasn't surprised by Jeremiah's question. In fact, it was only in second guessing *myself* that I had finally found peace. I had analyzed not just the vision, but also my gift so much over the past several months that I was more than ready for the challenge.

"Absolutely. First, dreams retreat into your subconscious when you awake only to be eventually lost. When I awoke this vision became *more and more* vivid. I actually believed I was in the tunnel. I felt the pain of being pierced in a hundred places by rock shrapnel, immediately followed by the pressure of being crushed by the falling boulders. I sensed the despair of imminent, inescapable death."

"Second, it was temporal. There was a definite place tied to a series of events that were ordered very specifically. Third, I told Da and Ma about it *before* anyone arrived at our house to inform us that the disaster had occurred. So, there is no way that I used events to create a vision I convinced myself had happened at an earlier time."

Perhaps less skeptical, but still unconvinced Jeremiah's eyes were drawn to the mantle.

"Is this a picture of your grandmother?" He picked up the daguerreotype and examined it. "Holy smoke, Ginger… she's beautiful, almost regal. And she looks just like you."

"Yes, and you read the letter she wrote for me. An Dara Sealladh has been in my family for over a thousand years. Some have used it for personal gain and were destroyed by it. Others, like Seanmháthair, saw the gift as a tool to help others and achieved great things. I've accepted An Dara Sealladh, Jeremiah. And the first thing I'm going to do is see that these murders are indemnified."

Jeremiah replaced Seanmh'athair's daguerreotype on the mantle and turned to me.

"Well it sure makes my study of business law sound trivial doesn't it?"

Despite his kind words, I still wasn't sure Jeremiah would ever accept the existence of mysticism. Certainly, it wasn't going to happen today.

Just then Ma came into the great room wringing her hands dry on her kitchen towel.

"Well, Jeremiah it's so lovely ta' have ya' home. Would ya' care ta' take supper with us? I'm sure the Captain would love ta' see ya'"

*Good 'ol Ma. Once again she knew when to appear. She said exactly the right thing at exactly the right time.*

The tension between us broke and we smiled at each other. I was now able to perceive the wonderful aroma of this evening's repast which triggered my stomach to grumble. Up till now my subconscious must have dismissed it. Looking at the grandfather clock in the corner I was shocked to see that it was already 4:30.

"Actually, Mrs. O'Leary I'm expected home, but thank you for the invitation."

As Jeremiah buttoned his overcoat he said,

"Wait right here, Ginger. I have something for you."

Jeremiah went to his carriage and returned with a very large package wrapped in brown paper. He placed it under the tree and said,

"Merry Christmas to you, Ginger. You are and will always be my best friend."

I was so moved I was speechless for several seconds. Finally, I said,

"But Jeremiah, I didn't know you were home. I'm sorry, but I didn't get you a present."

Jeremiah then smiled broadly and answered,

"It's only some more books, Ginger. I just saved some postage fees, that's all. But if you'd *like* to give me a gift I'll tell you what I really want."

There's that impish smile.

*He's up to something.*

"OK, Jeremiah. Do tell."

"Well, you know that New Year's Eve is coming up. And this year my parents are having a huge formal ball. And I know how you feel about the whole life style my family has. But…"

"Jeremiah, will you just get it out?"

"Alright, will you allow me to escort you to the ball?"

"What?" I squeeked.

"Well like *you* said, Ginger… You asked."

# Chapter 10

## The New Year's Eve Ball

To say that a spirited exchange next occurred would have been a gross understatement. When Ma took Jeremiah's side my fate was sealed. When he challenged me to open my mind to a new experience I accepted it.

Early the next day the Colgrove's day-carriage pulled up to the side door of our house. Miles, the family's groom assisted Mrs. Colgrove's lady's maid, Martha descend from the carriage. The package he carried for her later turned out to be the most beautiful ball gown I'd ever seen. While hanging it up for display she confided that this gown was of a most contemporary style; and also let slip that Jeremiah had purchased it in Boston just before he came home.

*That dodgy git, he knew I'd acquiesce...HE KNEW... Oooh, I'll get him...um, later.*

A tuck here, a hem lengthened there and a quick ironing; seeing myself in that gown, I no longer just accepted my fate.

I craved it.

So here I am. The biggest hypocrite of the nineteenth century impatiently waiting to be whisked away to an evening of pampering, gaiety and, dare I say it…fun? Da and Ma were clearly being entertained by my pacing back and forth.

"The ball is set to start at 8 o'clock. It's already 7:45. Where can Jeremiah be? It takes nearly an hour to get into town from here. My first formal and we're going to insult Jeremiah's parents by arriving late. Where is he?"

My steadily elevating anguish prompted Da to speak up,

"Ya' need ta' put a right puss on ya', Virginia. Trust Jeremiah. He knows what he's doin'. The rich are always late…even for each other. An hour late *should* be just about right."

I was looking out of the window at 8 o'clock when sure enough Miles pulled in… right on time. However, he wasn't driving the Colgrove's day-carriage. Instead the conveyance he skillfully maneuvered was a very upscale carriage pulled by two horses. While Miles was positioned on a bench exposed to the elements, Jeremiah emerged from the completely enclosed coach by opening a side door. The contrast between the conditions under which Miles and he travelled irked me no end. But this was not the time for the class versus class argument Jeremiah and I were sure to have yet again. After all, I'd promised to keep an open mind… and a closed mouth.

Tap, tap, tap. Thud, thud, thud. tap, tap, tap announced the "prince's" arrival.

"Let him wait, Da. I waited an entire hour. Let him wait."

Da's head tilt and pursed lips made me regret my completely infantile behavior; I took my hand off of the knob and allowed Da to open the door.

There he was, completely aware of his strikingly good looks. Jeremiah presented himself for inspection. If he was a peacock, he'd have spread his tail. Lacking said tail he spread his arms and turned a lazy pirouette instead.

White gloved hands peeked from the sleeves of a charcoal gray wool topcoat opened its entire length. Collar turned up. White cotton scarf dangling from around his neck. Crisp white shirt, white cravat, low cut white vest. Black formal suit. Shoes buffed to a bright ebony shine. Jeremiah certainly had turned out in the pinnacle of sartorial splendor.

Bowing at the waist he said,

"Greetings, Virginia. May I have the pleasure of your company this evening?"

When he added that rascally grin to his bow my discomfiture with Jeremiah for not educating me in the temporal habits of the rich melted away. Clearly Jeremiah was playing a role… a haughty, arrogant one that he also saw as ludicrous. I had forgotten that he never enjoyed playing the socially correct son. But his presence was expected. His absence would set tongues wagging and socially embarrass his parents. So, because of the love he had for them, he would perform most convincingly. And because of the deep affection I had for Jeremiah, so would I.

I stuck my nose in the air and took my turn at having my style of dress and coiffeur scrutinized. Jeremiah pronounced me, "Spectacular." We both laughed while he helped me don my cape and off we went.

The Brougham carriage proved to be much like Jeremiah's world; quite fancy and attractive from outside but cramped and restrictive when experienced from within. Our seats faced forward and once the doors were closed there was so little room that our shoulders rubbed when ruts in the road caused our carriage to jostle. Our body heat quickly filled the coach causing the side and front windows to frost over only increasing the claustrophobic sensation.

Regardless, the trip was made enjoyable by our banter. Jeremiah ran down a quick list of the dignitaries who would be in attendance while I responded with a list of faux pas I would let slip during the course of the evening. He countered that it was a long walk back to the west shaft road...and all of it uphill.

Before we knew it we could sense Miles slowing the Brougham and turning right. The carriage rocked back and forth a few times as he brought it to a gentle stop. Light from the brightly illuminated Colgrove estate penetrated the frosted coach windows filling it with twilight.

When Miles opened the curbside door and we stepped down, pleasant orchestral music escaped the entrance of the front door being tended by a footman I had never seen before. As we got closer the murmuring and laughter of prior arrivals was added to the ambiance.

We ascended the stairs to the porch and passed through the entrance of the very large richly wood paneled foyer I had walked through hundreds of times before. But this time was different. This time I wasn't a visitor *to* Jeremiah's world. I was part *of* it. This time my stomach turned over and I was afraid...afraid I wasn't up to playing my part...afraid I would let Jeremiah down. My near panic manifested itself in a huge shudder followed by the wan smile I offered to Jeremiah and, as is my wont, an open mouth.

"What'n the name of St. Paddy have ya' gotten me inta'?"

Jeremiah took my trembling hand in his and calmly whispered in my ear,

"You sound like you just got off of the boat. Do you know you always do that when you get scared?"

Then he added,

"Wait until you meet some of these people. You'll find that money can't buy class…or intelligence. They are crass opportunists who got rich simply because they got here first. Any ten of them couldn't make one of you or any member of your family."

"But there *are* a few who have both…and trust me; they'll recognize them in you. Now, stop worrying and open yourself up to the possibilities of the evening, not the least of which is fun."

I took one last deep breath and with its exhalation tried to convince myself that Jeremiah wasn't just saying anything that would keep me from fleeing the scene for home. I stood dead still, closed my eyes and shuddered. When I opened my eyes back up I dropped my hand from

Jeremiah's, put a smile on my face and strode the rest of the way into foyer like I belonged.

To the center, rear of the foyer was a grand staircase leading to the second floor. Large doorways to both our right and left opened to large rooms prepared for the evening's festivities. Upon our arrival two of the service staff who had been waiting against the back wall of the vestibule on either side of the staircase rushed to greet us.

"Good evening, Master Colgrove," Francis, the page bubbled. "May I take your topcoat for you sir? And Sharon will assist Miss O'Leary to remove her cape, if that serves, sir?"

Whenever visiting the Colgroves in the past I always spoke to members of the service staff, calling them by name. This would constantly annoy Jeremiah's mother because she felt my manner overly familiar and diverted the staff from their assigned tasks.

Tonight, though, Jeremiah had already warned me. So I smiled warmly at Sharon and turned my back to her so that she could remove my cape without disturbing either my hair or my gown. Fortunately, Sharon was fairly tall and accomplished this feat without incident. While performing her task she almost inaudibly whispered, "You look beautiful, Miss Virginia." I had to bite my tongue to not say thank you.

"The gentlemen's lounge is the tower office off of the refreshment room to your left, sir. Miss O'Leary, the ladies lounge is up the stairs in the front room on your left. You'll be given your dance card there."

Francis bowed, Sharon curtsied, and the two servants quickly withdrew through a door at the back of the vestibule to store our outerwear.

Jeremiah turned to me head tilted, left eyebrow raised and smiled,

"Now don't forget, being taken care of by servants is part of the experience. Please, just… allow… them."

When I didn't respond he continued,

"I'm going into the men's lounge to say hello to father. Martha will be in the ladies lounge all evening. She's supposed to help all of the ladies; but I know for a fact she's very excited that you're going to be here. If you head on up she'll not only give you your dance card, she'll also go through it with you so you'll be sure of what to do and when."

And so here I stood…abandoned and alone. Poor, defenseless me, I laughed to myself.

*Oh well, all y'ave got ta' do is make it up to the ladies' lounge without causin' a commotion. D'ya' t'ink ya' can manage…*

Sure enough my ascension of the grand staircase had reached only the fifth stair when three ladies, looking radiant and very, very rich in their gorgeous ball gowns also began descending…side by side… laughing and quite enjoying each other's company. The stairs were easily six feet wide, but the four of us passing abreast of each other just wasn't going to happen.

*What do I do?*

*You belong as much as they. Keep going.*

I decided to continue and see how things played out. I expected that by the time we reached each other we would make eye contact, laugh and compromise a way to pass without colliding. We might even exchange greetings and names.

Then again, we might not. In fact we didn't. By the time our collision was imminent my beaming smile… hell, my existence went completely ignored.

*Grrrr.*

And so we met. And so we stopped. Surprise! Even though I was on the lower stair, I was still taller and looked down at this self-absorbed trio of gits. Copious flaming hair and piercing green eyes accompanied my playfully mischievous smile and was returned with expressions of startled shock. Soothing orchestral music played in the ballroom just below in irony to the confrontation at hand.

*Don't ya' dare tangle torsos with the banshee.*

"Good evening ladies. That must have been some conversation you were having to not notice *me*."

Feeble hellos were croaked by them followed by curt nods as they decided to skirt gingerly around me.

*My gosh, but don't they sound like the frogs they are.*

Reaching the top stair without further incident I was greeted by Jen the upstairs maid who was clearly working to suppress laughter of her own.

"Good evening, Miss O'Leary. Ladies lounge is to your left."

I nodded in acknowledgement, and headed for Mrs. Colgrove's bedroom which had been converted for the occasion. When my back was turned to Jen there came a murmur, "Way to go, Miss Virginia." That was validation enough for me.

As I entered the "ladies lounge" it hit me that I had never before been on the second floor of the Colgrove mansion, let alone in the private bedroom of the lady of the house. To use one word, it was huge. It must have been twenty-four feet on a side and would have looked out on Church Street through windows as large as those on the first floor. But on this evening the view was denied by lavish heavy drapes drawn tightly closed.

Although Mrs. Colgrove referred to this space as her bedroom, clearly it was her domain. For although a white ornately scrolled wrought iron bed occupied one quarter of the room on the right, another quarter to the left held a huge white French style wardrobe, matching mirrored vanity and full length oval floor mirror. A marble topped white low boy dresser completed the dressing suite.

The entire other half of the room took its full width and was located in the front of the house. This area was anchored by a magnificent wool Persian rug. Arranged around its perimeter and facing back toward the door I had just entered was a lavender velvet chaise lounge, a violet brocade sofa and a matching side chair. The end tables and kerosene lamps were of the same French style as the rest of the room.

As I proceeded farther into the room I became aware of the laughter and punctuating exclamations of women who had arrived earlier. They seemed to be everywhere. One gingerly sat at the vanity in front of the mirror having final touches put on her hair while two others hovered around. They expressed compliments and patiently awaited their turn to receive theirs.

Two more stood in front of the floor mirror turning to and fro while holding their skirts out to simulate their motion as they would dance.

Curiously, the comfortable sitting area remained ignored. Not one woman wanted to risk wrinkling her gown or messing her hair with such frivolous behavior. Worse still, no one wanted to risk exposing her "delicates" because sitting upon her crinolines would open her skirt and reveal her legs like dangling clappers of a bell.

As I reached the sitting area another room to my right revealed itself. It was the second floor turret room which had been set up as Mrs. Colgrove's sewing room. When I poked my head in I was relieved to finally locate Martha. She was armed with a tape measure hanging around her neck, scissors in her right hand and threaded needle clenched between her lips. She had just finished mending the hem of the gown of a handsome middle aged lady who said it was torn when she had stepped out of her carriage.

Ebullient with praise, the lady thanked Martha for saving her evening and set to depart. As we met at the doorway we each turned to yield passage for the other. She encouraged me to enter first and as I passed she quietly confided, "That Martha is a saint," smiled and was gone.

*This must be one of the good ones. Her I must meet later.*

As I approached, Martha was still looking out the doorway enjoying her mind's afterimage of this kind lady. Pink cheeks betrayed her abashment but she quickly recovered when she noticed my presence.

"Nice lady, that Mrs. Blackinton," Martha said.

Less bewildered than I would have been a half hour ago I still shook my head but kept my comments to myself.

*Damn it, common courtesy dictates that kindness* should *be reciprocated with… SHUT UP, Virginia. Let it go.*

"Jeremiah said that I should see you, Martha…"

"Oh, yes miss. I've been expecting you."

As she talked Martha turned to the sewing table, picked up an elaborate card and returned positioning herself side by side with me so that we could both examine the writing on it.

"This, Miss Virginia is the dance program for the evening."

# NEW YEAR'S EVE 1865

| ❖ Set 1: | Gentleman |
|---|---|
| Grand March | _____ |
| Schottische | _____ |
| Spanish Waltz | _____ |
| Reel | _____ |

| ❖ Set 3: | Gentleman |
|---|---|
| Lancer's Quad. | _____ |
| Waltz | _____ |
| Schottische | _____ |
| Reel | _____ |

| ❖ Set 2: | Gentleman |
|---|---|
| Gilderoy | _____ |
| Polka | _____ |
| Waltz Quadrille | _____ |
| Waltz | _____ |

| ❖ Set 4: | Gentleman |
|---|---|
| Polka | _____ |
| Rustic Reel | _____ |
| Gallop | _____ |
| Last Waltz | _____ |

"Jeremiah will dance the entire first set with you. So we won't worry about that. But take a look at the rest. Any there you're unfamiliar with?

To my surprise I had been doing all of them since I was a little girl.

"Gee, Martha these are the same dances we do at the church get-togethers and community dances. But why should I be concerned with not knowing a particular dance. Can't Jeremiah and I just sit that one out?"

"Um…you could. But the actual reason for your dance card is so that other gentlemen can sign up ahead of time to dance with you. All of the ladies are expected to accept the offer of any polite gentleman and allow him to sign her card. It's considered quite an honor to have a full card. If you didn't know a particular dance we could have put Jeremiah in that place to protect you. But it's much better if you're free to dance with others. By doing so you actually do honor to Jeremiah and his family."

My hackles were immediately roused.

"Let me get this straight. I come to the ball with Jeremiah, but the best thing that can happen is that I spend most of the evening in the company of other strange men? This does him and his family *honor*?"

Flustered by my vehemence, Martha responded,

"It may seem so, miss. But you *do* dance the first set with Master Jeremiah. And, and there *are* the three intermissions between sets. And there are strict rules that no gentleman may get overly familiar with you during your dance. And, and the Last Waltz will be with Master Jeremiah."

"Please, Miss Virginia…just for tonight…could you…"

Martha's final halting imploring words triggered my complete empathy for the situation Jeremiah had put her in. I turned toward Martha, took up both of her hands and looked down on her our eyes meeting.

"Don't worry, Martha. I'll not shoot the messenger. This must not have been easy for you. But when I get my hands on that gobshite Jeremiah alone…"

"Yes, miss. He is rather good at being among the missing when the axe falls, isn't he?"

I gave her an impulsive hug and said,

"Let's keep that between you and me, Martha. Rest assured, turnabout *will* be fair play…I'll get that amadan …for both of us."

Martha feigned fluffing the skirt of my gown and brushing my shoulders as she escorted me back to the bedroom door. In actuality she was doing her best to ignore the throng of ladies who all seemed to call her name at once. She evidently wanted a piece of Jeremiah as much as I.

And speak of the devil, there he was leaning against the door jam, arms and legs crossed with that shite eating grin of his plastered on his mug.

But the glower he got from both of us in return straightened him up and wiped away any of the residual smirk that had greeted us. Sheepishly, he entreated,

"Thank you, Martha…I think. What say, Virginia; ready to dance the night away?"

"When this is over, Jeremiah Colgrove, you owe Martha one huge apology.  As for me…let's just get this over with."

At that I stormed by the slack jawed Jeremiah. When I was a few steps ahead I turned back to him and said,

"Are you coming?"

I actually enjoyed the image of the six foot two inch Adonis trailing me like a chastised puppy.

When I reached the head of the staircase I had only a second to wait for Jeremiah's timely arrival. I offered my arm to him, placed a sparkling smile on my face and together the most striking, but also most oversized couple at the ball descended to meet the guests of the Colgrove family.

*Not to worry, you git. I'll play my part and I'll play it well. But, this one's gonna' cost ya'. Ya' knew how I'd react so ya' put Martha in the middle. Yeah, this one's gonna' cost ya' alright; not for me, but for Martha.*

When we reached the bottom of the staircase and made the left turn into the formal parlor I found that all of the furniture had been pushed against the walls creating half of tonight's ballroom. The orchestra was ensconced in the huge bay window area in the front of this room. The rest of the ballroom was through the huge twelve foot doorway toward the back of the parlor and normally served as the Colgrove's dining room. I had earlier seen its furniture in the drawing room which had been set up as tonight's refreshment room.

Most of the guests were in the ballroom. Women were arranged around the perimeter in small or large cliques which seemed more or less fixed. Men milled around frenetically paying respects to ladies they considered attractive. The game seemed to be to appear polite enough to sign her dance card, but also to sign as many cards as possible.

The biggest clique, by far, had at its center the three gobshites I was forced to confront on the stairs. They were holding court and I was clearly the subject of their attention. One by one members of the group turned to offer looks of disdain.

I was so intimidated by this attempt to make me feel uncomfortable that I excused myself from Jeremiah and began strolling over to the group to have a chat.

I hadn't taken more than a couple steps when I heard Jeremiah say,

"Whoa there, Ginger... please?"

When I turned to face him he said,

"OK, what's up with them? They're the most poisonous shrews in the village."

As I had apprised him of the altercation on the staircase I could feel my face warm. At that Jeremiah raised a single finger to his lips as if hushing himself would work with me. Well, it did.

Jeremiah spoke loudly with his deepest bass voice which I'd like to believe resonated across the room to their ears,

"They're sour, stupid, mean and not worth your time or effort. Forget them."

Jeremiah took my hand and began to lead me away when behind us we found a veritable line of gentlemen had queued up.

"Master Colgrove, who is this vision of beauty. Would you introduce me so that I might beg her leave to sign her dance card?"

And so it went until the trumpet sounded announcing the Grand March to begin the first set.

Jeremiah, who had faded away after his first introduction, was suddenly back to reclaim me and quietly said,

"Well, Ginger, still want to throttle me?"

"I have to concede, attention like this is pretty heady stuff. Is it like this for all of the women?"

"Unfortunately not. It's my father's responsibility as host to poke, prod and otherwise bribe his closest friends to sign the dance cards of women who would otherwise be ignored. It's a wise host who procures such accommodations ahead of time. The hypocrisy of such action is all forgiven because in the end everyone gets to dance."

Jeremiah then chuckled and added,

"Sons, by the way, are first to be tapped for this duty. That's where I was while you were becoming the bell of the ball. So while you may be suffering the ignominy of dancing with strangers, I'll be…well let's just say I'll be honoring my father."

I gave Jeremiah a jab to his upper arm and recounted,

"I'll still not forgive you for putting Martha in the middle. You owe her, you know. Why didn't you just explain this to me?"

Jeremiah looked down at me wittingly,

"Come on, Ginger, you don't know…really?"

And after a pregnant pause I succumbed and responded,

"Yeah, I guess I do."

*Damn, he's infuriating. How does he* do *it. He's turned the tables on me again. Aggghhh.*

Mr. Colgrove took his place as marshal of the Grand March in front of the orchestra while Jeremiah's mother ceremoniously strode across the ballroom to take his arm. Other couples immediately jostled for a position to be close to the Colgroves in the queue. We, however, found this amusing and accepted any available place that opened up. Thus, we found ourselves nearly at the line's end.

Pecking order established, the orchestra broke into the "*Japanese Grand March*" and we were off. First in an anticlockwise circle that paraded everyone around the ballroom's perimeter chained together by intertwined hands. Then Mr. Colgrove led the line in a serpentine route which allowed all present to politely nod while passing friends and acquaintances. Next we strode down the center of the ballroom toward the orchestra. Upon reaching it the Colgroves went right and the next couple went left establishing the pattern of two perimeter circles wheeling in opposite directions around the ballroom. When couples met in the rear they formed four by four ranks and again sauntered proudly toward the orchestra. As Mr. Colgrove's rank reached the front everyone stopped and bowed to the orchestra. When the band finished the tune they stood and bowed to the crowd. Everyone clapped and cheered. The ball had officially begun.

A second explosion of revelry erupted when the orchestra announced the Schottische. Unexpectedly, I found myself among the noise makers. The Schottische has always been my favorite dance.

*What? Virginia, what're ya' doin', girl. Are ya' havin' fun?*

*Shut up and go wit' it.*

As the music began Jeremiah and I began the freewheeling 1, 2, 3, hop; 1, 2, 3, hop; spin step hop, spin step hop, spin step hop about the outside of the ballroom. After early negotiations Jeremiah and I hit upon an interpretation of the basic steps which allowed us both to flow with the music.

The other couples had also personalized their steps. The result was the usual laughing and near collisions that typified this dance. If you wanted to get to know everyone on the dance floor, dance the Schottische. During its course you will have said, "Pardon me" to everyone. This night was no different. When the song ended the exchanged smiles and nods conveyed a palpable sense of good will throughout the room.

The individuality and liveliness of the Schottische proved to be a perfect prelude to the Spanish Waltz. It prepared couples for a dance in which partners were exchanged with just about every other couple at some time during the course of the dance. The dainty melody and polite formality of its steps also calmed the ball to the elegant event little girls envision a Victorian ball to be.

So it was in grand spirits we were as we began our "Spanish" journey around the outer reaches of the dance floor in waltz spirals to the music's three-quarter time. Since I knew more of the estate staff than I did the guests I was not surprised that the first couple the second stanza paired us with was unknown to me. We bowed and curtsied our greetings to each other.

But as we took approaching steps in preamble to our first partner exchange light surrounding the gentleman I was facing suddenly dimmed. A translucent black mist seemed to waft from his body and as I got closer it engulfed me. My stomach turned, my knees buckled and I became strangely disoriented. But I still managed to complete the next dance steps which backed us away to our original positions. The gentleman's smiling countenance returned to normal and my symptoms disappeared as quickly as they had appeared. I hoped it looked to our foursome like I had merely stumbled.

Nevertheless, it was with great unease that I danced back toward him because this time he and I would join hands in a partner exchange and dance a waltz pirouette together. As I approached, his black mist returned and when I re-entered its clutches my symptoms recurred. When our hands touched all light was extinguished and I became ice cold. I suppose my body was still dancing, but I wasn't aware of it. I wasn't there. Instead I found myself observer of a play that flashed through its scenes so fast I was hard pressed to keep up with the action.

And then the light returned. It hurt my eyes so much that I crossed my left arm over my face to shade its intensity. As I became more and more aware of my surroundings I was certain that wherever I had been was gone and I had returned to the here and now. I was still shivering from head to toe and writhing back and forth on the floor in anguish and discomfort that I no long felt.

When my eyes had accommodated themselves to the brightness above me I removed my arm only to see the terrified face of my angel Jeremiah.

# Chapter 11

## A Moment Of Truth

After a few moments I got my bearings, rolled onto my side and propped myself up on one elbow.

"Well, that was interesting," I said in a strong, composed voice.

Jeremiah, who had been genuflecting by my side when I returned from my trip to the netherworld now rolled around to sit back on his haunches and ran his hands through his hair. Shock and concern alleviated, not just by my proclamation but also by my posture, his relief quickly spread throughout the room. Whispers, titters and exhalations confirmed the passing of apprehension which had evidently gripped everyone when I initially went down.

As I sat up I noticed that Dr. Briggs had also been down on one knee, Jeremiah's bookend brother on my other side. How long he had been there I can only guess. I had seen him earlier in the evening and remember being surprised he'd come to the ball. Tonight his ever-present cigar may not have been lit but it was rolling back and forth from one side of his mouth to the other.

"Now don't you dare try to get up until I have a chance to examine you, Miss O'Leary."

My return was calm but combined with a willful smile,

"Now, Dr. Sam, I'm sure my spell has passed. Really, I'm alright."

I rose with ease and had completely regained my full stature before Dr. Briggs could rustle his considerable girth back to what height he had…which, by the way, was not considerable.

"OK, OK, young woman, I take your point. But I'd still like to give you a quick check," Dr. Briggs huffed.

Jeremiah who had also returned to the vertical took me firmly by the arm,

"C'mon, Ginger, this way."

More than a bit surprised by Jeremiah's instant change in attitude I still managed to say,

"Well, it doesn't look like I have much choice, now does it?  Anyhow, I'd like to talk to both of you privately."

Jeremiah said nothing but quickly led us through a door I had never entered before. It was off the side of the dining room and opened onto a utility corridor which ran behind the Colgrove's living spaces.  It first took us by the kitchen on our right which was frantic with activity as Mrs.

Neville supervised preparation of hors d'oeuvres for guests of the ball. As we passed this cacophony I saw cook's room was adjacent to the kitchen. The servant's stairs emptied into the corridor on our left and the butler's pantry was next to them. The butler's room was at the corridor's far point straight ahead before it turned right and led to the rear service door.

Neville, who I had always called Mr. Matt, was waiting for us and held his keys in hand ready to open his room for Jeremiah.

"All set, Master Jeremiah. My room will provide you with privacy and comfort."
Neville's offer of his only private space in the world was most unusual and Jeremiah made sure Neville knew how greatly he appreciated the gesture. I was left perplexed as to why Jeremiah thought we'd need it and could only guess how Jeremiah and Mr. Matt had come to this arrangement while I was visiting that other place and time.

After showing us into his sanctuary and lighting a kerosene lamp Neville withdrew to resume his duties and quietly clicked the door shut. I sat on the edge of Mr. Matt's bed and as Dr. Briggs began his examination I asked,

"How long was I out, Jeremiah?"

He ignored my question only to ask his own:
How is she Doctor?"

When Dr. Briggs declared me, "Sound as a dollar," Jeremiah impetuously roared,

"What in hell happened out there, Virginia?"

Quite taken aback by Jeremiah's harsh tone I ignored his question and tersely fired back,

"That man I danced with…who was he?"

"He was a guest in my father's house. That's enough. When you got done with Mr. Johnson he gathered his wife and left without a word. My mother is furious. She's not sure whether it's at you or Johnson. Either way, I'm the one who caught her wrath."

"So, that's what this is about? You're afraid of your mommy." I responded derisively.

I was getting on a roll and continued,

"You mean to tell me that she's blaming *me* because my fainting scared a guest so much he left the ball?"

"Fainting…fainting. Is that what you call it? I was damn glad when you *did* faint. It put an end to your performance. You scared the hell out of *me*."

"What are you talking about, Jeremiah? This man…Johnson? He has an evil soul and murder in his heart."

"What are you…" was all Jeremiah got out before I cut him off.

"His shade was black, Jeremiah. When I approached him his physical being disappeared behind a black mist that oozed from him and reached out to me. The first time it touched me I weakened and nearly passed out. I almost fell. When we exchanged partners I touched his hand and was engulfed by this dank, empty essence that permeated my very soul. It was as though I'd been shot. There was…a jolt, and then everything went black. There was no *performance*."

"Are you trying to tell me you don't remember what you did?"

"You don't remember backing off Johnson and striding around him, pointing your left index finger and aiming your arm like a rifle? It was as though you were looking down a barrel at the poor man. But instead of firing bullets you screeched and then bellowed at Johnson like you were…two different people."

"I'll not soon forget what you said: 'Could have stopped it! Why didn't you stop it! Didn't need to happen!

We would've made the tunnel fail! We wouldn't have talked! We'd have kept quiet... Murderer! Murderer!' Then you went down so hard the floor shook. People stopped dancing. The band ceased playing. Everyone stared. At first I thought you were dead. But then you started to roll around on the floor flailing with both your arms and legs. It looked like you were trying to fend off blows from some source. After about ten minutes, Ginger, you came back to us."

"Listen, Jeremiah, I don't remember doing anything like that. While I was in the darkness it was as though evil sought to displace me from my body and claim me as its own. I was terrified and fought like I'd never fought before. I kicked and pushed and twisted so that it would release me from its clutches. I ran toward a light I saw in the distance and the emptiness left me more and more with every step I took. I thought I had won. But when I reached the light I found I wasn't at the ball at all. Instead I was hovering above a wood paneled office. I don't know where. Johnson was there sitting behind a desk designed strictly for function. An engineer's square, scale ruler and slide rule occupied its top. Just like Mr. Northkutt's desk."

"Ringo Kelley was sitting in a chair in front and a third man was circling Kelley, arms behind his back. This man was fairly tall and while he wasn't handsome, his sharp features etched a spot in my memory. He had the bearing of a man who was used to being in charge. His suit was neatly tailored and his shoes shone as if they were polished that very morning."

"I couldn't really hear what he was saying, but it was clear that he *was* the man in charge. As he circled he bent at the waist speaking into Kelley's ear. Part of the time he was smiling at Kelley and patting him on the shoulder. Each time he touched Kelley it appeared he'd jump out of his chair and bolt for the door. Clearly the third man wanted Kelley to agree to something and Kelley wasn't really going for it. But it was also clear that Kelley didn't feel free to refuse."

"Exasperated, Johnson rose up and walked to the low boy chest next to the side wall of his office. He poured a glass of water from the decanter there and brought it over to Kelley offering it to him. Johnson then assumed a relaxed posture, resting his haunches against his desk, legs crossed at his ankles and arms folded across his chest. His head nodded slightly toward Kelley and he smiled broadly. Whatever he said, it must have convinced Kelley because he nodded back and slouched in acceptance. The third man may have brought the idea to this meeting but Johnson was the one who sealed the deal."

"It was then that the scene faded into darkness. The next thing I was aware of was the blinding light in my eyes. At first I really thought I'd died. When my eyes finally adjusted I realized the light was coming from the ballroom chandelier and I thought I was looking into the face of my best friend. Instead I returned to be greeted by an inquisitor who treated me as though I was on trial."

Jeremiah was on the verge of saying something but instead chose not to. He loudly emitted a deeply pent-up breath and his confrontational posture deflated along with it. The finger he had pointed at me instead reached out and gently stroked the side of my head. He turned away put both hands in his trouser pockets and proceeded to pace back and forth in what small space there was in Neville's room.

Jeremiah and I had been so focused on each other I think we both received quite a jolt when Dr. Briggs ended his mute observation of our scene.

"Do you three always talk to one other this way?"

Both Jeremiah and I both said in unison, "Three?"

"Yeah, three. T-h-r-e-e, three. If you two will calm down for a second you'll realize that there's something pretty strange going on here. There's you, Jer, my boy. And then there are the two personalities you assumed, Virginia."

Jeremiah started to say something but Dr. Briggs cut him off at the knees.

"Quiet, Master Colgrove. You've already said quite enough."

"Now, you and Jer have been inseparable friends since you were both tykes, haven't you?"

Not daring to incur Dr. Sam's wrath I meekly nodded.

"And you've always loved this young man in spite of his insufferable matter-of-factness and constantly scheming ways?"

Again, I nodded.

"Now, Master Colgrove, do you realize that some see you as the reincarnation of your father because of these...attributes? People fear that you will soon be capable of the same ruthless decisiveness as your father... and it scares the hell out of them?"

"But Dad is one of the most respected men in the county, Doc."

"Yes he is, Jer. He's honest, fair and can be quite kind. But he's also brilliant. And in business he's a most terrible enemy to cross."

"My point is that you've supported Ginger ever since she was first branded by folks as one of the dark ones. She gives the willies to those who believe and even people who don't tread lightly around her, just in case. But so do they around you."

"*Both* of you intimidate by just being yourselves."

"Now, I'm not really sure what happened tonight either. But unless you think Miss Virginia is a liar and consciously set out to ruin your family's damn party you need to open you heart and mind to the notion that what she has seen could be true."

"And you, Miss Virginia need to apologize for the cheap shot you took at Master Jeremiah for reacting the way he did to the mortifying dressing-down he took from his mother."

"It's only then that we can start to figure out just what the hell happened."

Jeremiah and I argued all the time. Our parents and teachers learned long ago that the yelling, flapping of arms and stomping of feet meant nothing. It was a way we tested each other and actually had fun. On the few occasions that one or both of us crossed the line from intellectual dual and digressed into the morass of willful hurt, that person had lost. It was then that an apology was required. It was a system that had served us well. Tonight was no exception and tonight both of us were guilty.

And so Jeremiah began in the manner that was our custom. As eighth graders Jeremiah and I decided to teach ourselves Latin. We used an old dog-eared copy of Latin grammar we found gathering dust in the school's library. We challenged each other by seeing who could translate passages of Caesar's Gallic Wars faster. Father Lynch mediated our disagreements and explained the ablative absolute, which nearly drove us crazy. He also taught us the Latin pronunciation rules so we could speak correctly. Declaring our war armistices in Latin is a remnant of that time. It instantly reconnected us to a happy time we shared and extinguished any residual anger.

"Ego sum remux, meus sanctimonialis. Pacis vobis."

And I responded,

"Ego sum remux, meus frater. Pacis vobis quoque."

Dr. Sam stood up, gave a resounding belly laugh and said,

"'I am sorry, my sister. Peace to you?... I am sorry, my brother. Peace to you also?' I won't even ask where you two learned Latin."

"Anyhow, let's take another look at tonight's events. Everything that happened seems to hinge on Lemuel Johnson. Now, Miss Ginger, his effect on you seems obvious. You can believe Jeremiah that you put on quite a show out there."

"I was just entering the ballroom so I could watch the Spanish Waltz…Very elegant to watch it was. Anyhow, my attention was drawn to you and Jer because of your striking presence. The dance had just started when you shoved Mr. Johnson away from you with what I can only call great force. At first I thought he had said or done something untoward and you were responding to his insult."

"But, my God Miss Virginia, the way you towered over the poor man. Your hair fell from its set and bushed out nearly covering your face. Mrs. Johnson screamed and I thought her husband would dig a hole right there and jump into it."

Dr. Sam being Dr. Sam, paused a moment and chuckled at the image of the much older Johnson cowering at Virginia's feet.

"So, what you said struck a chord with him. He understood. Do you? Think about it for a second. Jer, what was it Miss Virginia said again?"

This time when Jeremiah recounted my tirade I wasn't engaged in self-protection and heard what he said.

I shot off of the bed and shrieked,

"My God, Ned Brinkman and Billy Nash."

"Who?" Jeremiah inquired.

"The men who were killed by that terrible blast in the Bloody Pit last March. That's it."

Doctor Briggs' eyes lit up but Jeremiah looked thoroughly confused. So I invited him to sit down because I had a tale to regale. When I finished Dr. Sam's eyes told me that he'd also had an Archimedes moment. What amazed me was that there was no skepticism in his demeanor. This man of science had accepted my story as fact. But I guess the ensuing evidence we'd gathered and Ringo Kelley's disappearance didn't hurt in convincing him either.

Dr. Briggs actually stated what I already knew:

"Ned Brinkman and Billy Nash spoke through you. They hate Johnson and want him to join them in hell."

"That's right, Doc. And it was Brinkman and Nash who dragged me to the scene in Johnson's office. I didn't escape evil. Their evil souls released me to observe the genesis of the conspiracy that put them in hell. And they not only want Kelley and Johnson to join them. They want that third man too."

# Chapter 12

## Happy New Year, For Now

There was very little celebrating going on when the grandfather clock in the corner of the great room chimed midnight to announce the turning of the New Year. In fact the two carriages that had spirited me, Jeremiah and Dr. Briggs away from the Colgrove manse arrived at the O'Leary farmhouse just in time to hear its faint resonance reach out to us.

As the three of us stepped onto the porch landing I realized how spent I was from the evening's events. I had shivered nearly the entire ride home and was now leaning heavily on Jeremiah. I was heartened though, when I looked through the window and saw my parents snuggling on the sofa.

As Jeremiah opened the door, warmth from the fire conveyed its greetings nearly floating us inside with its soothing effects. Ma and Da also seemed mesmerized by it, the dancing of the fire light and probably a jar or two of the creature because they didn't rouse until Dr. Sam purposefully closed the door.

Trying not to seem startled, Da rose to greet us. Hair tousled, braces hanging down to mid-thigh and just a tad glassy eyed he said,

"So, me fine young couple, how'd it go?"

It was Ma who, as usual, sensed our uneasiness and immediately rose. Nearly tripping over the blanket that had been covering her lap she shot over to us and took me by the hand.

"Come. Sit down and tell us all about it."

Her look of concern turned to trepidation when leading us to the sofa revealed the much smaller and up to now hidden Dr. Briggs. Ma began to tear up and exchanged a quick glance with Da. Now alerted and alert he growled,

"Spill it, Doc, and spill it'all."

"Virginia is fine, Captain. She..."

"I saw something, Da." I blurted, cutting off Dr. Briggs. "But this time it was more than a vision. This time it was so strong..."

Dr. Briggs cut *me* off and clinically reported,

"This time, her trance was so strong it appeared to all of us that she'd fainted. Crumpled right to the floor, she did. Whatever she saw... wherever she was... well, it lasted over five minutes."

Now striding back and forth, hand clasped behind his back Dr. Sam continued,

"When she came out of her torpor she was clear headed and coherent, not at all like someone who'd fainted…"

"I know who did it, Da." I know who convinced that slug Ringo Kelley to kill."

"I danced with him, Da." And with a shudder I added, "I…I touched him."

"ENOUGH." Ma screeched. Then she whispered, "Enough."

"We'll speak no more of this tonight. No more, I say. 'Tis off ta' bed we'll be goin'."

With that being said, Ma began giving stage directions leaving no question that we had any choice but to comply with her orders. Pointing to the stairs using her right index finger, arm fully extended she said,

"Captain, show Dr. Briggs ta' the spare room at the top o' the stairs."

Approaching Jeremiah, both palms below her waist and facing him, Ma shooed,

"Jeremiah, you'll bunk in with Stanley. I'm sure he's only just finished beddin' down Dr. Brigg's horses. Go find 'im. And let Miles return home. I'm sure Bess'll be waitin' up for him."

Left arm crooked at the elbow, Ma this time summoned me with a wagging index finger,

"Virginia, you come wit' me."

Ma then gave a quick clap, clap of her hands and issued her final command to everyone,

"Go!"

Jeremiah, who was mute during this whole interchange, was the first to respond. He rose from the sofa, took two steps toward her and bending at the waist gently kissed Ma on top of her head.

"Good night Mrs. O'Leary."

Ma being Ma stood there, put both hands on her hips and glared up at Jeremiah. Then a tiny curl at the corners of her mouth softened her countenance but her eyes still demanded compliance.

So with a click of the gently closing door, Jeremiah was gone.

While that was going on Da treaded warily over to the walnut cabinet at the foot of the stairs and quietly poured Dr. Sam two fingers of the Irish he always kept stored there. Dr. Sam, who never saw a vice he didn't like, smiled and cheerfully accepted this symbol of hospitality.

Da gave Doc the shush sign as he delivered the measure of golden ambrosia. The Doc returned the "shush" sign, smiled and off they went up the stairs.

Then Ma looked me right in the eye.

"'Tis a heavy burden, ya' bear, dearest daughter...terrible heavy."

""'Tis fine, Ma, 'tis fine. I have understanding folks around me...and Grandma O'Leary will show me the way. 'Tis fine."

"Nevertheless, I'll be wantin' ta' have a word with ya' before ya' wink out for the night. Do ya' think ya' can manage ta' slither out a' that gown and put on somethin' warm? I'll be right along after I turn down all of the lamps."

I rose from the sofa, gave Ma a scrunching embrace hoping to transmit how much I loved her and headed up the stairs, last of her subalterns to comply with her orders.

I meant to wait for Ma, I really did. But once my head hit the pillow and I became ensconced in my cocoon of warmth my last conscious thoughts were:

*"Oh, Ma, 'tis amazin' y'are. 'Tis so very exhausted I am. Ya' always know. Thank ya', Ma."*

When I woke up I was uncertain if it was truly morning. All of the usual cues defining it were missing. No tantalizing breakfast aromas filled the house stimulating my stomach to rumble with emptiness. Ma was not rattling dishes or banging the cast iron skillet on the stove top as she cooked. No combination hum –sing of an Irish tune by Da as he shaved at the kitchen sink. No slamming of the front door as Stanley's foot closed it, arms laden with the next installment of the morning's wood supply.

Furthermore, the light coming through my bedroom window was so dim it didn't seem possible that the sun could yet have cleared Hoosac Mountain. Yet awake I was, obviously the first riser. Yes, morning it had to be.

I slipped on my calf skin slippers and what Ma calls my "horse blanket" of a robe and went to the bedroom window to investigate. As I looked at the sky I groaned. What I saw was the worst kind of Berkshire morning. A thick blanket of steel gray clouds capped the entire valley from the Berkshires to the Taconics preventing any but the most diffuse of sun rays from reaching us. The frigid air that was Canada's periodic gift to us rolled in last night and would be with us the entire day.

The good news was it wouldn't snow today. The bad news was the reason it wouldn't snow was because it would simply be too cold. It was a quirky phenomenon of the Berkshires that it actually had to warm up to snow.

What does that say about a typical Northern Berkshire day in deep winter? Your choices are cold and cloudy, even colder and clear or warm and snowing. Sometimes even a clear cold morning would warm too much; the surface of valley snow would evaporate, form clouds and sure enough by mid-afternoon…snow.

As soon as I opened my bedroom door the sonorous wheezing and snorting emanating from the other bedrooms confirmed that I was not only the first riser, but also likely to be so for some time to come.

*Ah, the creature. How many "two finger" jars had you and the good doctor snuck after Ma went ta' bed, Da? Seems you and Ma had a good start by the time we got home. Not ta' worry, though, not ta' worry. 'Tis clear as a bell I'll be needin' ya' both when I tell ya' MY tale. God's given us the break we've been hopin' for. I can't believe I'm sayin' this…but it'll wait.*

Yes, my sleep had been so deep and restful that I awoke feeling calm, almost serene. For the first time in months I could help alleviate Da's pernicious frustration. That meant the world to me. And I knew that CJ would arrive by noon to celebrate New Year's Day as well. His chagrin over these past several months had been second only to Da's. He deserved some peace as well.

*Oh, Seanmháthair Saorla I'll finally be able to use my gift for good.*

So, indeed, it *could* wait.

As I reached the bottom of the stairs it became obvious just how soundly I *had* slept. A neatly placed stack of wood had been delivered to the great room hearth. I then swung open the kitchen door and peered in. Another small, but adequate wood bundle had also been arranged next to the stove. Either the little people had been at work or Stanley had somehow survived last night's celebration unscathed and managed to quietly make sure we weren't inconvenienced.

The tightly banked, still glowing coals from last night's fires expedited restoration of both hearth and stove to their purposes. A scant few minutes later the pleasing aroma of hot coffee permeated the kitchen. After cinching my robe against the outdoor chill I filled two tall mugs and set out to thank that wonderful burly bear with an offering of the steaming elixir he made possible.

Closing the porch door with my backside I noticed that the residual measure of the morning's wood had been stacked against the house. I smiled and nodded appreciatively,

*Stanley Woszniak, what ever did we do ta' be entitled ta' the likes o' you?*

The only redemptive thing about my bone chilling trek to the cow barn was that its interior would be warmed by the body heat and activities of those sheathed within. The problem was that my arrival was also assaulted by the sweet almost combustible fragrance of bovine flatulence provided by the constant plop, plopping goo of the cows as they defecated.

Seemingly unaware or completely habituated, farm hands sat on tiny stools methodically squeeze-yanking cow teats. Metal pails rang from the squirt, squirt… squirt, squirt of the theft calmly being perpetrated. And during the entire time placid, almost catatonic Ayrshires relieved themselves of their mother's milk while witlessly consuming sustenance at one end and expelling the refuse of making it at the other.

In the middle of all this were two figures with their backs to me: the first of average height but broad dimensions, the second very tall and very lanky. Both were coatless and had their sleeves rolled to the elbows. Both had mud splatters covering their boots and climbing their pant legs. Both labored almost constantly to fork the requisite raw materials fast enough to keep the whole system running. Both turned to face each other when they were satisfied with a job well done.

The first, as expected was the person I wished to repay for his consideration. The second... the second? I broke up, hysterically laughing, drawing their attention.

"Jeremiah? Can this really be? Is this the Harvard lawyer in training? Is this the heir to the Colgrove fortune?"

"Stanley, how'd you do it? I didn't believe Jeremiah would ever pass within ten feet of a mud puddle. And yet here he is, in formal slacks, standing in it up to his knees."

Stanley, too polite to laugh and seemingly flummoxed that he should be expected to, shrugged and walked over to accept his cup o' coffee. Smiling, Jeremiah posed to swing his pitch fork at my rear end until he saw my outstretched arm and the steaming peace offering at its terminus. Under the circumstances, I could wait for my own cup until he and Stanley returned to the house with me for breakfast.

"I'm sorry, Jeremiah. But you must admit this was quite a surprise."

"Yeah, I am quite a sight at that. But Stanley has been so gracious... and we hit it off so well... it just seemed natural to pitch in. It's pretty obvious that holidays are just like every day on a farm. So if I can make today a bit easier for him…"

Never able to pass up an opportunity, I offered this friendly jab dripping with false sarcasm,

"Really? Whatever happened to the chap who once told me, 'We feed them, house them and pay them. This is what they do, so I let them do it.'"

Obviously embarrassed that Stanley might have heard, Jeremiah contritely answered,

"Let's just say my new life has caused me to reassess that position."

I wasn't sure what Jeremiah was talking about, but I didn't really care. Jeremiah had always displayed a heart too kind to actually believe the drivel his mother and her pompous friends professed. However, this was the first time he'd admitted it to me.

It surprised us both when I spontaneously lurched forward and affectionately kissed his cheek. That was all there was to be done or said about it, now or ever.

Although Jeremiah had put on his fine woolen topcoat and my robe really *had* been fashioned from an old horse blanket I'd particularly liked, the best that could be said about our walk back to the house was that Jeremiah and I survived it.

Oblivious to our discomfort, however, Stanley ambled happily along enjoying the morning, coatless and with his sleeves still rolled to the elbows. Whistling a lively tune his warm breath condensed to form small, puffing clouds in front of him the entire way.

We both shuddered just watching him.

Stanley and Jeremiah sat on the steps of the porch scrubbing their boots with brushes while I clanged around the kitchen: wood to stoke the stove, new pot of coffee on the back, butter in the two cast iron frying pans on the front and two freshly pumped gallons of water into the kettle warming on the side for hand-washing.

I hoped to create enough turmoil to roust the dream weavers still snorting away upstairs. I knew I'd make no friends by forcing them to face the day, but CJ would be here by noon and it was nearly 9:30 already. I hadn't seen him in weeks and I wanted to look especially nice. That would take time.

So, I continued: dicing, seasoning and tossing potatoes into one frying pan, slicing bacon and laying the strips into the other, cracking a dozen eggs into a bowl and scrambling them with milk. I thanked sizzle and aroma for conspiring with me. Opening the kitchen door I urged them to climb the stairs and slither under the bedroom doors. I was assured that it would only take a moment to get there.

The first to come hither was Ma. As soon as she entered the kitchen she looked about for something to do, some way to proffer assistance. But everything was done: coffee was made, breakfast was cooking, the table had been set by Jeremiah while I prepped and Stanley had added more wood to the great room fire. So around and around she flitted unable to relax.

I brought the coffee pot to the table and filled a cup,

"Would you like a cup 'o, Ma? Why don't you just sit yourself down and enjoy. Let us serve you for a change?"

"Yes, Mrs. O'Leary, it would be our distinct pleasure to attend to you and Mr. Woszniak on this fine New Year's morning," Jeremiah said as he pulled out a chair for her and a second for Stanley.

Reluctantly, she complied. But once she'd taken a deep sip of the steamy brew and inhaled its nutty bouquet she sat back and finally began to really fancy her unusual position.

I led the perplexed Stanley by his hand to his seat. Jeremiah, standing behind Stanley, put one hand on each of his shoulders and encouraged his descent into the chair.

Jeremiah and I hadn't planned this. Without saying so we both seemed to agree that on this day we wanted and needed Stanley with us.

It was not unprecedented for Stanley to partake of a meal with our family; but only when *he* was ready to call it a day.

"I can have cup 'o coffee, but's a work day an' da' men…" an unsure Stanley offered.

"Now, Stanley, don't worry about the men or your responsibilities. Isn't there someone out there we can 'promote' for the day?" asked Jeremiah.

"Well, Simeon is good'a man. Works hard… is'a respected by all."

"Good, I'll see to it," said Jeremiah, already putting on his top coat and half way out the door.

There was no doubt in my mind that Jeremiah couldn't wait to grease the wheels of Simeon's 'promotion' for the day with the transfer of a shiny silver dollar when the two shook hands. The other workers would not be jealous because they would never know. In fact, Jeremiah would plant the seeds of sympathy with them for Simeon's extra burden.

*Ah, Jeremiah, but aren't ya' too slick by half. You'll soon be comin' back proud as all get out, bustin' ta'tell me*

*what a dangerous, clever man y'are. And me knowin' this*
*the whole time. Will ya' pardon me when I laugh?*
*Somehow I doubt it.*

I was at the stove giggling to myself while plating up mounds of tender potatoes and crispy bacon when who should straggle through the kitchen door but the Irish drinkers from the night before.

"Cawwwwffffeeee... cawwfffffeeee." Da pleaded. "For both of us, Ginger, please. And be quick." Da plunked himself in a chair, put his elbows on the table and cradled his head in his hands.

Doctor Sam, on the other hand sat bolt upright. A thumb and forefinger of each hand tugged his braces at chest height and through a clenched jaw holding an unlit cigar he politely requested coffee.

"Good morning, Miss Virginia. Yes, I would love a cup of coffee. May I have some cream to go with it?"

As I filled their cups I could only marvel that the good Doc had either not partaken of the creature last night as I'd believed; or because he did it every night had somehow immunized himself from the effects. His reputation convinced me it was the latter.

On the other hand, I'd only seen Da in this condition on a couple of other occasions. Da was at best a poor drinking companion, I'm happy to say.

In any case, there was absolutely no sympathy to be had from Ma who surveyed Da's condition over the rim of her coffee cup and recited,

"Charles James O'Leary y'are a bloody eejit… you should know better." And that was that. Ma returned to enjoying her coffee as though Da was not even there.

The next thing I knew Da winced, his chair shot across the kitchen floor and he made a break for the porch door; I'm sure on his way to the outhouse. I didn't think grey was a possible skin color until I got a good look at Da escaping.

I was still processing the scene which had just transpired when a quite unconcerned Doctor Briggs hinted,

"Well, Miss Virginia, breakfast smells luscious. Do I see some eggs there ready to go?"

At that even Stanley guffawed with the rest of us, though he looked quickly from Ma to me checking that it was appropriate for him to join in the reverie. Ma's wink to him conveyed the answer. The ensuing banter fostered a pleasant ambiance throughout the kitchen while I scrambled up the mess of eggs.

We had already begun chowing our breakfast down when a much more human looking Da returned to be with us.

"I don't suppose I might …"

Using potholders Ma brought back from the stove's warming shelf the plate she'd prepared earlier.

"Pull up a chair, me darlin'. Nature's retribution has exacted a toll fine enough on ya'."

Da took a loud slurping sip of the coffee I'd just poured for him, closed his eyes and deeply exhaled,

"Ahhhh."

Doc Briggs chuckled,

"Well, Captain O'Leary, looks like breakfast has a much better chance of staying down now."

Closing one eye and holding a piece of bacon like a stiletto he was going to zip at the good Doctor, Da retorted,

"'Tis in league with the divil himself ya're, Doctor. No human can drink like that and survive… no one."

When we all calmed down from the merriment Da's good natured jab at Doc Briggs' had instigated the serious business of finishing off the food which produced a silence broken only by utensils hitting our plates. Looking around the table, however, reminded me of the real reason this eclectic group had been assembled in the first place.

# Chapter 13

## A Day to Remember...Always

I had to laugh at myself.

*Ah, 'tis so like the ladies at the ball I've become...showin' off and enjoyin' the show.*

Here I am standing in front of the full length mirror I'd borrowed from Ma's room, preening and sashaying back and forth. It was the first occasion I'd had to wear the wonderful day dress Ma had given me since the plan to entrap Ringo Kelley had fallen through last March.

`And I couldn't wait for CJ to see me fill it out.

The hair styling artistry Ma had shown me had again worked its magic. I was now able to transform the brassy rat's nest on top of my head into wavy, chestnut colored silk any time I chose to put forth the effort. This was surely one of those times.

*'Tis a woman I am, Conal John Mulcahy and ya'd better notice if ya' know what's good for ya'.*

As I was putting the final touches on my coif a knock came at my door. It was Ma.

"Virginia, 'tis past noon, dear. Everyone's waitin' for ya'… and Sergeant Mulcahy's cart just pulled in."

*Already? Is this why the rich are always late? Lost in myself, I am.*

*Get a grip, girl and put a little giddy-up in your git-along.*

When Ma and I reached the bottom stair Jeremiah and Stanley were at the great room hearth tending the fire. Jeremiah was crouched, poker in hand, attempting to arrange the logs for maximum efficiency. It appeared that all he was accomplishing, however, was to generate sparks which were immediately being sucked up the flue. Stanley, leaning against the fireplace stonework with arms crossed, laughed at Jeremiah's ineptitude while all the time offering encouragement.

To my mind, Jeremiah was taking his new found immersion in custodial duties one step too far. From the looks of the fire, he'd have us all freezing to death in no time at all.

Da was reclining on the sofa resting a mug of coffee on his chest. His two meat hook paws surrounded the mug nearly concealing it in mock prayer. I couldn't see for sure but I'd wager Da's eyes were closed and the only prayer being offered was that his headache would subside.

Doctor Sam, on the other hand, was standing in the kitchen doorway with a big smile on his face. Ma's bib apron he was almost wearing barely covered half of his rotundness. This and the towel he was using to dry his hands told me that he wasn't playing dress-up, but instead had been helping Ma prepare the New Year's Day repast.

I didn't get to ask him whether he found Da's pain or Jeremiah's inability to maintain the hearth more amusing because just then the door opened and in stepped CJ, I think. It was the right time and the stature was about right, but who could be sure.

The effigy before me was completely clad in black and covered with glistening frost. The only other clue to this figure's identity was a small slit of exposed flesh around two laughing steel gray eyes. The hat had ear lappers; mouth and nose were wrapped in a wide woolen scarf. A thigh length coat had its collar upturned and was buttoned to the top. Leather gloves protected his hands. Knee high boots hid the trouser legs which were tucked in them.

My analysis came to an end when the muffler was removed and the smile linked to those eyes caused my heart to skip a beat. I hadn't seen Conal for quite a while and it was only now that I realized how much I missed his company.

"Happy New Year, Miss Virginia."

The gentle almost insecure way CJ greeted me was one of his most endearing qualities. Member of the Massachusetts Bar, larger than life war hero, Da's most trusted colleague and he greets *me* with all of the nervousness of a schoolboy.

*'Tis you who's actin' the schoolgirl. He's a man and you're barely a woman. Don't be readin' anything inta' his politeness.*

*Still I can dream. And I will, damn it…I will.*

I almost ran, but didn't. Instead I casually strolled over and gave him a polite hug.

"Wonderful to see you, Sergeant Mulcahy. Can I take your things?"

So, one by one: hat, scarf, coat, gloves were shed and handed over. And then I noticed. I guess it must have been all of the interference of his outerwear that did it. But, I finally noticed.

"Conal, where is your cane?"

CJ gave me a broad smile but his eyes glistened, "Don't need it anymore, Ginger…don't need it."

He straightened his sleeves, tugged on his suit jacket and strode confidently into the great room. There was only the slightest residual limp to his gait.

*Da, wait 'til I get ya' later. Ya' never let on. Ma, you never said a word either. How could ya'?*

Now it was my turn for glassy eyes. There was no way I wanted to ruin this moment with girlish tears. Still I knew, even though he'd never said, that using that cane... displaying that weakness... symbolized all of the horror of that damned war he wanted so much to put behind him. His body had finally mended. Now he had a real chance to salve his soul.

Greetings were offered all around and I introduced CJ to Jeremiah. The sight of the six foot-two inch, broad shouldered Jeremiah's effusive admiration for the short and slight of build Conal made me chuckle. I guess we naturally envision our greatest and bravest to be George Washington on a white steed not a rumpled earth bound U.S. Grant smoking a stogie.

CJ who clearly saw himself as neither was withering under acclaim he neither wanted nor felt he deserved. He had seen too many of the bravest and greatest die terrible and anonymous deaths...just one of a hundred who died on any day, almost every day.

Polite to a fault CJ patiently waited for Jeremiah to take a breath so he could tone down or at least divert the conversation to a different topic.

When CJ noted that Jeremiah was studying law the spell was broken. Common ground had been established and they were soon laughing and gesticulating as they told stories of law school to each other. I just stood there and enjoyed the show for some several minutes.

*Ach, thank ya', Lord. I don't know what I'd do if... I love them both so dearly, these two dear, dear men. 'Tis friends they'll be. I can just tell.*

*Shoot, a blind man could tell.*

"Penny for your thoughts, Ginger."

Startled, I turned to see Ma had arrived with a tray carrying three cups of steaming hot mulled cider. Ma and I exchanged the kind of almost-smiles only a mother and daughter could share. They communicated the entire story without a single word being spoken.

"Snacks are ready as well."

Ma's idea of "snacks" was, well, impressive to say the least. Spread out on the low boy against the wall just outside of the kitchen were three platters, each with a distinctive cheese. Next to these was a calico lined woven basket overflowing with thinly sliced toast points. Two jars: one containing coarsely ground mustard, the other a horseradish spread that past practice has taught me will set fire to your nose hairs. To the right of this collection was Doc's contribution of two stuffed roasted chickens surrounded by delicately sliced root vegetables. He'd obviously been very busy this morning. Everyone knew he could eat; no one figured he could cook.

"Come on, everyone gather around so we can say grace," Ma announced.

"But before we do, today's feast needs to be afforded the honor it deserves."

"Charles' parents were both remarkable people. But, this story is about Charles' da, Padráig and how we need ta' thank him for these wonderful cheeses on our table."

"Padráig O'Leary was handsome, imposin' and quite ambitious … Why, I do believe I had a bit of a crush on him meself."

At that Da gave his best startled look followed by a most fake jealous stare. Everyone broke up.

"True, too true," Da interjected. "But so did the bloody English."

Laughs again.

"No, no. My dearest is right. His gift o' the blarney charmed them no end. While they were met in pubs with growls and veiled threats by most o' the Irish, Padráig greeted them with a pat on the back with one hand and a pint ta' offer in the other."

"Clever man that he was he knew that business success in Ireland meant gettin' on with the bloody English. And so, he did what he had ta' ta' establish an export business in Cork City."

"Still, Da O'Leary always resented British graft and taxes, both o' which stole easily half o' every Irish punt earned. How often I remember him wishin' that rather than pattin' an English back he had a knife in his hand ta' plunge inta' it."

"In only a short time wealth blessed the O'Learys. In fact, O'Leary Exports grew so large that Padráig operated pretty much as he pleased. Shuttin' him down or even interferin' with him would not do. The economy of Cork City depended on him."

With a scornful sneer Da weaved in, "And a' course it would also have made the blood suckin' British governor a much poorer person."

Ma wrapped herself around Da's right arm and continued:

"The people o' Cork City may have been flourishin'. But the farmers a' County Cork were growin' poorer by the day. The prátaí bein' grown appealed ta' no one but the Irish. And that was only because the poor, rocky soil allowed little else to be harvested. It was a matter a' survival for them, not commerce. Harvest after harvest had failed and entire families were starving."

"But grass and clover we could grow, ach we could grow them. Dairy farmers produced enough milk for everyone. But few in Ireland could afford ta' buy it. And exportin' it didn't work because milk spoiled so quickly."

"So dairymen switched ta' makin' butter. Most exported their products through Padráig's company. Although Irish butter was the sweetest and purest in the world, the British taxed it so heavily the dairymen were barely able ta'survive. British repression also nearly extinguished production o' the symbol o' the dairymen's pride, cheese. Churnin' butter took such time and effort that cheese makin' simply became a luxury no one could afford."

"But Padráig, ever ta' see opportunity where others groveled and complained, encouraged every dairy farmer ta' produce as much o' their favorite family recipe cheeses as they could and promised ta' buy every single wheel at a price the farmers could not resist."

"He enlisted the waggoners ta' collect these products along with butter the farmers produced and added enough extra ta' their purses ta' ensure buttoned lips. At the port he labeled the cases, "IRISH BUTTER" but also added a tiny distinguishin' message in Irish. Unwittin' English duty men grouped these cases with the butter and taxed them at that rate."

"Padráig's business partners in America and France were in on the game and quietly culled these crates and distributed the wares. It gave them great pleasure ta' give the British government slivers when they stuck their fingers inta' these Irish tills."

"At first things went slowly. But it wasn't long before Irish farmstead cheeses became a popular delicacy in both countries. The Cork Dairymen saw their standard a' livin' rise because prices o' their black market cheeses rose dramatically."

"The irony was that they had ta' limit cheese production because butter was the secret o' their success. The British needed ta' continue ta' rape Irish dairymen o' butter profits for the whole thing ta' work. If London saw tax revenues decline or they found out there was more ta' steal, I guarantee you, the Irish dairy farmers would've been right back where they started."

"But they didn't."

"Da O'Leary's black market went on for years. I can't say for sure, but I'll wager that key Englishmen controllin' the port o' Cork were slipped more than a few punts by Padráig ta' remain dumb ta' the whole operation."

Ma paused and looked quizzically toward the ceiling.

"Ya' know, I always wondered how he got away with it because even the English couldn't have been that stupid."

"Hey," Jeremiah exclaimed. "I resent that comment."

Everyone laughed heartily because we all knew that although the Colgrove forebears came from England, Jeremiah's entire family proclaimed loudly that they were Americans first last and always.

Still smiling, Ma resumed,

"So, Da's father had found a way ta' help the County Cork families, as well as stick a shiv inta' the backs o' the British he so thoroughly hated."

"With pride restored, farmers competed ta' produce the finest farmhouse cheeses. Cheddar, gruth, mulchan, milsean, tanach, and tath appeared on the O'Leary black market. The distinct textures, flavors and aromas of these cheeses could not be obtained anywhere else. Many County Cork families survived the potato famine because a' these black market profits."

"Some o' these families back in Ireland still send wheels o' their prize cheeses ta' us at Christmastime. Irish appreciation runs deep."

"So let us bow our heads in remembrance o' Padráig O'Leary and in thanks to our Lord God for the bounty we are about ta' enjoy."

At that I found myself suppressing a strong desire to giggle.

*Grandda Padráig the black marketeer and the Deity hand in hand is it, Ma? He must really have been something. I so wish I had known him.*

As the celebration proceeded the roasted chickens mysteriously became carcasses, bowls of cider and apple jack emptied and wheels of cheeses reduced to slivers. Stories were told, toasts made, and glasses clinked. But all the time there was a certain... a certain disquiet that hung over the room. As the afternoon began, it nibbled at me. As it waned it consumed me. All of the revelry became so much noise and I finally withdrew alone to a corner and relived events of the previous evening. I don't know if it was minutes or an hour, but I'd held my peace as long as I could.

"Enough. I've been patient. I've waited long enough."

Silence was instant and complete. Everyone knew why I had exploded. Everyone, that is except poor CJ who quizzically scanned each person in turn for any cue he might glean. Finally our eyes met and he knew. He knew it had happened again.

Ma ardently walked to my corner, took my two hands in hers, smiled at me and announced,

"To the kitchen, everyone."

During my time alone in the corner I recalled CJ's report of our tunnel investigation. Full of hatred and confused emotion I wanted to hang Franklin Northkutt on the spot. But CJ had calmly and dispassionately reported observations and facts. At the time I couldn't understand how he did it. I also recalled that not being able to relegated me to readying the horses for the trip home. So this time I was determined to do it right.

Once I started my story flowed and was punctuated like the north branch of the Hoosic River riffling over rocks into the village. Ignoring the fear and anger I felt at the time and the hurtful and puerile way Jeremiah and I had argued I was able to complete my narrative in far less time than it took to live. It was clear and concise; almost as if I was reporting events that happened to someone else.

When I finished Ma beamed with pride. CJ picked his jaw up off the floor. Jeremiah applauded. Dr. Sam snuck a quick snort from his pocket flask. Stanley stood up and paced. But Da did nothing. Eyes cast downward his countenance darkened as I had never seen before. He withdrew within himself looking at no one... speaking to no one.

It was Ma who broke the tension.

"Soooo...whata' we do next?"

The question proved to be rhetorical because before anyone could offer a response she continued,

"Doc Briggs, ya' may not have Ginger's second sight. But ya' do know just about everyone a' means in this part o' County Berkshire. Ya' know how they connect ta' one another. Ya' know who can be trusted ta' help us bag this Johnson and more importantly, who can't."

"Stanley, don't ya' still go inta' the village on Saturday night for a bit o' socializin' at the pubs and ta' find a bit o' feminine companionship? Kelley has slithered inta' a hidey hole and I'll bet ya' can loosin' lips the

Constabulary can't. Someone knows where that might be.
"

"Jer, my boy. Ya'll be returnin' ta' Cambridge in a couple a' days. I'll just bet ya' know somebody who knows somebody who might know who our mystery man might be. Da' ya' think ya' might be able ta' do a bit'a' diggin' on your end?"

"And as for you, Constable Charles James O'Leary. The last time I saw that look on your face we had ta' leave Erin. Snap to it and do your job. Murder isn't part of it. Stand for the law. Use the law ta' hang these gobshites. Get'all of 'em, me darlin'. Get'em all."

"Coffee, anyone?"

And so we talked, planned and plotted well into the early evening before exhausting ourselves. But we were satisfied that some very powerful people would be very uncomfortable very soon.

Laughs, back pats and hugs accompanied departures. We were a team and we were ready. CJ was last to leave. As I walked him to the door he opened it, took me by the hand and ushered me through it into the crisp, cold air of the porch.

Suddenly, and without preamble Conal whispered,

"My God, Ginger you looked beautiful today."

At that he brushed my cheek with a kiss so gently offered as to barely touch, turned and walked to his carriage. As I stood there stunned and watched him leave the stars seemed to twinkle especially bright and I swore they warmed me to the core.

# Chapter 14

## March 20, 1866

The only way my reputation could have grown more exaggerated over the past months would have been to fly about the village on a broom. The gruesome trio from the Colgrove's New Year's Eve Ball had seen to that. But, I simply didn't have time or the inclination to care what the intellectually bankrupt, idle tongue-waggers of the village thought.

The kind of support I had received from the people in my life who meant the most was a fair trade. It was important to me how *they* felt.

I could not only count on Jeremiah's continued friendship but also his acceptance of An Dara Sealladh. When we were younger it was easy for him to dismiss my second sight as the ability to solve problems without consciously thinking about them, an interesting parlor trick. The seriousness of events of the recent past had changed that for good, although he did still shake his head in wonder.

CJ confessed premonitions he'd had during the war, especially the night before the battle of Port Walthall Junction. At the time he'd dismissed them as his mind's response to the fear and panic he felt for so long but dared not show his men. The morning of the battle he'd decided it would have been so much easier if he *were* killed. It would be over. Seeing his mangled body lying on the turf in that dream actually gave him peace. So Conal understood and cherished this special connection we shared and felt closer to me because of it.

And it also turns out that "Briggs" is an ancient Scottish family name that dripped in the mysticism of the highland Druids. I had always wondered why Dr. Sam never doubted the truth of my visions. I was the first true manifestation of An Dara Sealladh he'd ever encountered and the scientist in him found me fascinating. I may have felt like a lab rat at times, but I knew he couldn't help himself. I also knew that he cared for me very much.

However, that's not to say I had not been rattled to my core by the experience of coming into contact with Mr. Lemuel Johnson and the souls of Brinkman and Nash. As children, we Catholics are taught that our lives are a constant struggle against succumbing to the seduction of evil. And it's only our vigilance through prayer and the reconciliation of confession that prevent our eternal damnation.

We have personified this evil which constantly dogs our heels and he is called Satan. As a little girl I believed this so completely that it was easy for me to see his face. God was three people, each with a job to do, so Satan must be a man too. On New Year's Eve that long forgotten icon was dashed.

The evil that sought to rip out my soul had three names: Ned Brinkman, Billy Nash and Lemuel Johnson. It was they who terrified me. The former two committed themselves to destroy and ruin. Johnson's choice had been far worse. He enticed another already blemished soul to cross the line into damnation by trapping Ringo Kelley to kill for him. Somehow this reality seemed so much more treacherous than a lone figure with horns and a pitch fork running around the world seducing vulnerable personalities.

Instead the truth was that the potential for evil already existed *within* each of us. And offered the proper enticement each of *them* had adopted it.

Even so, I was certain of three things: Brinkman and Nash were dead and could do me no physical harm. The limit of their influence was an attempt to enlist me as the vehicle of their revenge. Ringo Kelley was a fangless snake that had slithered into some hole to save his own skin. That he was alive was of no consequence because he was a coward. Furthermore, he didn't even know I existed.

Then there was Lemuel Johnson. Johnson was already responsible for at least two murders. It was clear that he was capable of anything and that he saw me as a threat. Certainly, the longer I stayed out of sight the less Johnson would worry about me.

Then why am I posting my trotting Hessie big as life down Main Street this bright Monday noon?

Simple.

I am not going to hide in a cave until this is over. If I've learned one thing these past months it's that life is dangerous. And no one can protect me but me. I actually have to thank the three big mouthed dingbats. In planting the seeds of apprehension and fear throughout the village they handed me a powerful tool.

So, in spite of a churning stomach and anxiety of my own I've embraced this challenge. I'm going to find Ringo Kelley *and* I'm going to serve him to Da and CJ on a silver platter. He is the key to not only exposing Johnson, but also identifying the mystery man of my vision. And I have this strange feeling that bringing *him* face to face with

CJ is critical. It doesn't make sense. I can't quite see why. But I know it's true.

So in preparation for my downstreet adventure this morning I chose riding togs. There was no way I wished to present to the village a demure, vulnerable young girl who needed to be chauffeured by a man. I wanted to capitalize on my reputation and dress to intimidate... to be someone feared.

I'm close to six feet tall in stocking feet; the heels on my knee high riding boots put me just over. Jodhpurs made my legs look endless. The shoulder pads on my cold weather riding jacket had the desired effect. My white blouse buttoned to the top accentuated my wind-blown flaming tresses. The visage now displayed to the lunchtime traffic of a crowded North Adams was that of a wild Irish banshee...l'il 'ol me.

Mothers didn't exactly whisk their children away to safety. But I did glean pointed fingers, stopped traffic and startled looks. As I pulled Hessie up in front of the Wilson House and made her fast to the post ring, I greeted passersby with warm smiles, but penetrating glares. No one made eye contact.

Some scurried away while glancing over their shoulders to see if I was still looking at them. I responded with a smile punctuated by giving my riding crop a slap, slap against my thigh.

I paused for a second to take in the majestic edifice that was the Wilson House. Rising four full stories it was situated on the corner of Main and Holden Streets and occupied a full block in both width and length. The first storey was constructed of native granite and provided space for six stores as well as the two main hotel entrances which projected proudly from the front of the building's face. Their rectangular shapes continued up the entire height of the building, rose above the roof line by a full storey and were capped by room sized cupolas.

The overall effect was that the Wilson House appeared a granite and masonry castle protected by two huge towers. But somehow, the ornate roofline fascia and huge windows that pock marked the street facing sides reminded everyone that the Wilson House was in reality a Victorian structure.

As I gathered my thoughts and focused on the Corinthian columned entrance, I was startled to see a cigar chomping Dr. Briggs beaming down from his perch at the top of the stairs.

"Never ceases to impress, does it?"

I simply smiled and said, "Well, at least I can see why you wouldn't want to live in one of those Church Street mausoleums."

Doc flicked an ash from the tip of his stogie and chortled,

"Yeah, all the comforts of home and none of the problems."

I began my ascent to join him, but Dr. Sam instead came down to join me.

"Let's take a walk, Miss Ginger. The guy we need to talk to is persona non grata here. But, he's got a hell of a story I think you need to hear."

As we began our walk back up Main Street I couldn't help but be struck by the contrast between the Wilson House and the rest of the businesses on this side of the street. None was more than more than two storeys; most displayed the tired effects of age. The difference between where North Adams had been and where it was going was on display here and totally due to the textile industry, growth of the railroads and the promise of the tunnel.

The only buildings that could rival the Wilson House in style if not size were banks on the other side of the street. In fact, one of the newer streets in North Adams was Bank Street. And not coincidentally this street led directly south to Village Hall and the Constable Station.

It wasn't long before we came upon one of the most dilapidated structures on all of Main Street. It was advertised as "Gregory's Fix It Shop." But it didn't look like a lot of "fixin'" had gone on here for a very long time.

Rusted tools spilled out of the horseless wagon that clogged the alley between Gregory's and his neighbor. The clapboards, which I guess must have been white at one time, were now dripping with a greasy film of dust that made them appear a dull grayish-brown. The store front windows were nearly occluded by this same film. The sills and frames were mildewed and cracked.

But no one seemed to be complaining. People passed by as if "Gregory's Fix It Shop" didn't even exist. Everyone, that is, except us. Dr. Sam and I were the only customers who entered or left.

As Doc Briggs opened the creaking door for me I couldn't help remarking,

"Here?"

With his other hand gently encouraging me to enter the portal, he chortled and said,

"Sometimes to get at the truth you need to enter the belly of the beast."

His statement prompted flashbacks to that awful day CJ and I had spent in the bowels of the bloody pit so I simply said,

"I understand."

Once inside, all signs of abandonment abruptly vanished. To the left of the doorway was a felt covered round table which was surrounded by card holding men. The cacophony of their enterprise filled the shop. Smoke seemed to emerge from them with each breath they took and rose in palls toward the lighted kerosene lamps above.

To the right was a "work bench" with several bottles of spirits on it. For the moment at least, the men were clearly too obsessed by their activities to even notice. When I estimated the amount of money in the middle of the table it came as no surprise to me that they ignored us as well.

The hand concluded when the player facing the doorway "called" everyone else. After all the hands were shown, he tossed his hand on the table, vigorously rubbed his two palms together and proclaimed,

"Ha, ha... Three queens."

The others either moaned or swore. One slammed his chair backwards, rose and threatened,

"I'll get you, you cheatin' prick." When he fled the scene, not one other card player reacted.

The winner was a rotund man in his sixties. He leaned back in his chair and using tobacco stained hands repeatedly slicked back his hair causing an otherwise white mane to be stained a dull yellow and curl around his ears. Stubble growing down the back of his neck merged with the bristles covering his face.

His collarless, tattle tale gray shirt was opened two or three buttons down allowing it to flap open revealing a forest of curly white hair. Wide red braces were all that held his trousers up because when he rose I could see that two or three buttons of them were also undone so that his pants flapped open at the top mimicking his shirt.

"Howser, Doc...Be right with ya'. Deal me out, fellas."

He unsteadily rose from his chair and placed both hands on the small of his back. Arching backward his bones snapped and popped. He grabbed one of the bottles off the work bench, looked over his shoulder and said,

"Foller me, folks."

We were led through a doorway into a fairly large room at the back of the shop. There were two small film streaked windows which transmitted only enough daylight to bathe the room in an eerie twilight of suspended dust.

"Have a seat."

This was tough to do because our choices were an unmade swaybacked bed, a small bench placed against a wall or a single kitchen chair.

"I guess it's past noon. Care for a snort?"

When Dr. Sam surprisingly waved off this man's attempts at hospitality, he said,

"Well, don't mind if I do, then."

Wasting no time, Doc Briggs whispered to me,

"We'd better get this going before he snorts himself senseless."

And followed out loud,

"Miss Virginia O'Leary, this is Dutchy Gregory."

Raising the bottle toward me in what I guess was a salute, Dutchy burped and said,

"Pleased to meet ya', m'am. You the witch?"

Both miffed and humored I approached this stumpy, disgusting creature. And when close enough I bent over and whispered one word into his left ear,

"Yes."

I don't know if it was my size or my reputation, but Dutchy took two startled steps back and nearly fell onto his bed. Thus positioned, his nose was only level with my thigh.

"I think I'll just put this away for now."

Dutchy corked the bottle and while never taking his eyes off of me gently placed it on the floor.

Next Dr. Briggs spoke up.

"Dutchy, Virginia needs to hear the story you told me. What do you say?"

Dutchy's eyes now darting back and forth between Dr. Sam and me said,

"Right, right'chu are, Doc. Right'chu are."

# Chapter 15

## Dutchy's Story

"Durn' the daytime I got my reg'lars, see? Soon as they get rich they come 'n see me. An' we sits down and have us a fine ol' time. I got this reputation for runnin' a clean game here. No cheatin' or nuthin'."

The smirk and raised eyebrow with which Dutchy said this hinted that he doth protest just a bit too much. What followed confirmed my suspicions.

"'Course ush'ally costs 'em a bit for this kind of honesty, if ya' know what I mean. But I always leaves a man with somethin'. Never clip 'im unless he's just plain stupid, like our friend ya's met earlier. Still, get a better deal here than just about any other place in the village."

"Anyhow, when guys come in from outa' town firs' thing they ush'ally do is go to the local. An' after they had a pint or two and found a brasser t' give their knob a ride, they's feelin' pretty good, see? So natch'ally I slips the keeps a couple a' bits ta' get 'em to suggest a small game a' chance to the fellers. Anyhow, 'nough of 'em come for a visit to keep me busy 'most every night."

"So, one night a while back, oh, I think it was middle a' January... these three guys I never seen 'afore stops in lookin' for some action. Couple of my boys 'd been hangin' around so 'afore I know it we got six guys around the table and the money starts changin' hands back and forth real quick, see?"

"Turns out they was doin' to us what we was doin' to them. Cheatin' bastards was teamin' up... sendin' signals back n' forth, ya' know? Didn't take too many hands for all 'a us to see it wasn't every man for his self 'round that table, but three on three. No one was goin' to win nothin' this night. So, rather than call each other swindlers and get inta' a fight we all starts laughin' an' I get out the hooch."

"Turned out they come up from Springfield on business an' thought they'd come in an' have a bit a' fun fleecin' the backlanders. They was impressed with us. 'A course we had to stroke them in return. When I asked 'em what their business was they serioused up real quick."

"Was pretty obvious they weren't 'aspossed to say, see? But by not sayin' nothin' I only got curiouser. So I kept their glasses full and waited for their lips to loosen. See, nothin' makes a smart guy stupid faster'n too much a' my hooch."

"Get it from the Florida mountain boys. Worth it too. Buy a few jugs ever' time they come into town sellin'. Won't let you have it 'til you let 'em stream a little 'cross the table an' light it. Always burns blue, see? They laugh an' hoot like they's impressed with their own handiwork and tell me how many times they had ta' run this batch through the still to get it that way."

We could tell that Dutchy was losing focus when his eyes glazed over like he was dreaming. He ran his tongue across his lips and smacked them while looking thirstily toward his bottle on the floor.

"Stuff'll take the paint off the walls, but boy what a jolt. Sure yous' don't want a snort?"

Doc and I shared exasperated scowls and I was about to speak out; but Doc Briggs reached out to touch my hand, took a deep breath and calmly said,

"Go ahead, Dutch have yourself a quick sip."

"Oh yeah. Right'chu are."

As Dutchy picked up the bottle and squeeked the cork out of it I couldn't help thinking that there probably weren't too many minutes of a day when Dutchy wasn't either drinking or thinking about it.

Whistle whetted, Dutchy wiped his lips with the back of his hand and replaced the bottle on the floor.

"Let's see, where was I? Oh yeah, the blokes from Springfield."

"Anyhow, we're just shootin' the breeze, see? An' wasn't long 'afore they starts braggin' on how they works for the Western Railroad an' how pretty soon they's gonna' buy up the North Adams-Pittsfield line, see?"

"Then one of 'em, real snotty like outa' nowhere says how that'll make the tunnel an antiquated waste of time, effort and manpower."

"Western Railroad? Antiquated waste of time, effort and manpower? I starts wondering just who these guys are. They talks like the gentry, see? But they sure don't look like it. They's dressed in reg'lar workman's clothes, see? It don't add up. An' why's Western Railroad guys sniffin' around here? That route runs along the bottom of the state from out east to Springfield. An' it's just in the last few years a line's connected them to Pittsfield."

"So I'm mad, see? I tells 'em, like I'm makin' fun of 'em, that the tunnel's gonna' finish. An' when it does the Western Railroad's the one'll be the antiquated waste of time. The northern route from Boston to Troy'll connect the entire string a' textile cities in the state, I tell's 'em."

"When I asks 'em, 'Who's gonna' wanna' pay top dollar to move goods eighty miles south 'afore they can go one foot west when the tunnel will let ya' go straight across the state's north and connect ya' to Troy, the third guy blows up."

"He screams at me that that'll never happen if they have anything to say about it."

"So, I laugh's in his face, see? An' I says, you know challengin' like, 'An' what would that be?'"

"So, he stands up real rickety, almost falls over an' says, 'You'll see, shithead.... you'll see real soon.'"

"The other two guys who weren't quite as far along musta' realized he'd let the cat outa' the bag. They got up an' almost carries their friend outa' my 'stablishment. That's the last I saw of 'em."

"But, when I made my rounds of the local taverns to stroke the keeps with their two bits for the week, I tells 'em the same story I told you. An' they tells me there's three guys snoopin' real quiet like around the village offerin' top dollar', 'specially to the workin' girls. They's tryin' to find Ringo Kelley. An' they want him bad, real real bad."

At that Dutchy smiled, picked up the bottle and showed it to both of us.

"Want a snort *now*, folks?"

# Chapter 16

## The Seduction of Power Is Powerful

Johnson's men.

I must really have knocked Johnson off his pins to act so quickly and rashly. Up until now Da and CJ figured that Kelley was being hidden *by* him or at least paid off to get lost. The manner in which he'd been released from the lock-up smacked of pulled strings and back room power. The order came in the middle of the night and it came directly from Chief Eldridge.

When Da confronted him, Chief Eldridge's response was completely out of character. This man who Da liked and trusted so much had completely undercut his authority. It was clear to Da that the Chief rankled at what he'd done, but had no choice. Da's conclusion was that certain very powerful men wanted Kelley gone beyond the reaches of the North Adams Constabulary or the Adams Police Department.

Instead, it was now clear that Kelley had somehow slipped *Johnson's* clutches. Initially he might have been willing to bid Kelley good riddance. But Johnson's happenstance encounter with me at the Colgrove's New Year's Eve ball had changed everything and instigated a desperate race to find Kelley. Johnson's past treachery had made it equally clear that if his henchmen finished first the outcome would not be good for one Ringo Kelley.

*At least I'd found out that there* was *a race. And we hadn't lost... yet.*

Kelley hadn't yet turned up so they must not have found him. But these were clever people and they must certainly be using their head start to advantage. They'd probably already eliminated places we haven't even thought of, let alone checked out.

*Somehow I had to get ahead of them. Time was definitely running out.*

Right now all I could do was hope that one of Dr. Briggs' tipsters knew where Kelley was and came trolling for thirty pieces of silver.

*Not exactly a winning strategy.*

And so, it was with urgency that I now cantered Hessie back up Main Street and took the right onto Bank. By the time we reached the crown of the small knoll and crossed Summer Street to arrive at Village Hall, she was snorting and woofing from the exertion.

When I clomped down the stairs leading to the cellar that was Constable Station I found Da in his office sitting at his desk. He looked up with a start from the paperwork he was attending but quickly recovered with a knowing grin.

"Well, look at ya'. I don't know whether ta' cross meself or salute ya'."

I had completely forgotten about how I was dressed. After looking down reflexively I slowly raised my eyes and gave Da my very best "she who must be feared" devilish grin.

Da's approval was obvious as he slapped his desk with both palms, let out a belly laugh and said,

"OK, OK. So what mustard ya' been stirrin' this fine day, me darlin' daughter?"

Da had visitor's chairs in his office, but I chose to stand as I recounted the events at Dutchy Gregory's Fix It Shop. When I finished, Da rose from his chair and motioned for me to take a seat. He walked around his desk and rested one haunch on its corner so that his leg could dangle from its edge.

"OK, my turn. But ya' need to calm down. I not only want ya' ta' hear me... but I want ya' ta' HEAR me."

Da crossed his arms and leaned toward me a bit to emphasize how serious he was.

"First off, you and Doc 've done fine... just fine. Lord knows the street folk aren't exactly goin' ta' knock down my door tellin' me or any of the other constables where Kelley's hidin'. Far as they're concerned he's one of 'em. They've got no particular affection for him or what he's done. But they're not as outraged as ya' might think either. For most of 'em violence is part a' life. Given the right circumstances killin' someone wouldn't be that big a deal."

"Kelley's gotta' have a bit o' money from the payoff he must've received for doin' in his mates. As long as that holds out they'll protect 'im. But, when it runs out... an' that'll be soon... rest assured someone'll be lookin' ta' cash in on the information. What they *will* do is toss 'em out first. Call it the street code, but they'll sleep well if they give 'im a fair start. Whatever happens after that is on him."

Da stood up arms still crossed, took a deep breath and with his gaze cast downward began to pace.

"I'll thank ya' for lettin' me know what ya've found out. It confirms the information I've gathered. CJ and I figured that when the time came there'd be a race ta' sell out Kelley.  What's unsettlin' is that Johnson's got deep pockets. He's got support runnin' all the way ta' Worcester. If he's an agent of the Western Railroad, an' I'm sure he is; his power may even extend ta' Boston."

"So, those three already must've put out the word of a big pay day. Furthermore, there's no reason to not go to them first.  Especially since dealin' with me would definitely rub 'em wrong."

"But, as I see it we don't have a whole lot a' choice but ta' wait and hope."

At that Da stopped pacing, turned and looked me squarely in the eye.

"Now listen, Virginia Maureen.  As a lark Doc may dabble a bit, but the gutters o' North Adams are a terrible dangerous place ta' go snoopin' around. These folks play by a set a' rules you know nothin' about.  They may be superstitious, but they're also concerned about where today's meal will come from. An' they'll do whatever they have ta' ta' get it... an' worry about the hereafter later."

Then Da went down on one knee directly in front of me, took my two hands gently in his great paws and said,

"I'm sure that today you made a powerful impression on the downstreet folks. Even now I'm sure that word is spreadin' about the image you've put in their minds.

"You're no longer the Captain's strange little girl. You're an adult now who's larger than life. An' I'll bet ya've intimidated a lot of 'em. But remember this, my dearest. Your Seanmháthair always dressed ta'... ta' calm folks. Her influence over them came from within and radiated out."

"Now, ya've got 'em scared, sure. But remember this. Saorla could walk down any street of the warren that was the back streets o' Cork City, twirlin' a parasol over her shoulder like she hadn't a care in the world."

"Ginger dearest, I want ya' to think about why that was."

Da's words hit me as if a brick had fallen on my head. My face immediately flushed a shade to nearly match my hair... and I started to tear up. I wasn't embarrassed. I wasn't sad. I wasn't angry.

I was stupid.

*There ya' go, gobshite. Tinkin' o' YOU instead a' THEM. Ya' still haven't learned that arrogance is the worst attribute... The WORST. Will ya' never learn?*

Da rose gently escorting the effin' Queen from her throne. I found myself on the verge of telling Da what I was thinking, but instead just nodded and gave him the tiniest hint of a smile. Then I instinctively kissed him ever so lightly on the cheek.

"Thank ya', Da."

My entire ride home was so fraught with conflicting thoughts that I hardly noticed the left turn Hessie had taken onto the carriageway that told us both we were home. Once in the stable I began performing my routine of pampering her.

When I was a small child needing a stool to extend my reach I had fallen in love with the washing, brushing and currying of this beautiful horse. Her haunches were dappled shades of gray while the rest of her reminded me of a solid overcast sky.

I had worked her hard this day. She had served me both faithfully and without complaint. Although my head was telling me no, I could swear that the nodding of her head was her way of showing appreciation. Today more than ever I certainly appreciated *her*. Ablutions completed, I gave my friend a gentle slap on her right haunch, ushered her into her stall and said, "Thank ya' Hessie, me girl."

As I headed up toward the house I stole one last look. I laughed to myself when I saw her nod.

I shuddered as the late afternoon air reminded me winter hadn't yet released Berkshire County from its clutches. Waning but perceptible sunlight told me spring was soon to win. But it was only when I opened the porch door that I realized just how much time I had lost in thoughts that chased each other around inside my head.

Lamps already lit throughout the house, the great room hearth's fire danced before me. Clanging pots and wonderful aromas emanating from my right told me Ma was hard at work and the evening meal was close at hand.

"Ginger, is that you?"

Not waiting for a response she continued,

"D' ya' think ya' might lend a hand?"

We spent the next hour ostensibly setting the dining table and finishing the evening baking and cooking. But what really occurred was a most wonderful exchange between Ma and me that left us both laughing. She drew the day's events out of me, both good and bad and left me feeling not quite as troubled as I had on the trip home.

*How does she do it? Right now I don't really care.*

By the time we heard Da clomping his feet on the porch floor it was totally dark.

After supper we adjourned to the great room to continue the evening conversation and have our wee jar o'

Irish. Da told us about the drunks his constables had locked up so they could dry out without being rolled; the family disputes settled before the wife brained her husband with a skillet and other transgressions of the day, none of which were out of the ordinary for the village of North Adams.

Finally, the conversation gravitated to the Hoosac Tunnel. Da announced that he was now four square behind the project. Shocked, Ma and I looked at each other and then back at Da. Ma asked the question on both our minds.

"Why's that Charles?"

Da collected our glasses and as he was refilling them he began,

"Two reasons, really. The first is a matter of personal principle. The second is a matter of the future of North Adams."

"When we came to America I swore I'd never again put up with folks bein' raped a' their hard earned money simply because others could. The British taxed our countrymen inta' submission and ta' this day they continue ta' bleed 'em dry. Any prospects our people have for a better life lay in leaving their homes for distant shores. The British don't want partners, they want subjects."

"Right now in Massachusetts power rests with Boston and the state's southern cities. And the only reason for that is that they were established first. They're bigger, have more money and feel entitled ta' stay that way forever."

"But the future's with the newer small cities along the northern tier. The rivers comin' outa' the mountains along this route are bein' harnessed ta' power textile mills and furniture factories. Hardwood from the forests o' New Hampshire and Vermont and cotton from the South are flooding daily ta' these cities."

"The railroad from Fitchburg ta' Greenfield was built ta' support these businesses. North-south routes were built as well connectin' Boston ta' Springfield by goin' through Worcester. From there it's a straight shot to the South through New York City."

"These Western Railroad folks have little problem with the route that's been built from Fitchburg to Greenfield because they own the north-south routes that connect the northern tier cities to their route."
"What infuriates me are the fees they're chargin' ta' transport goods on 'em. They're no better 'n highwaymen holdin' a gun ta' the heads a' the folks along the northern

tier. The Western Railroad owners don't want partners any more than the British."

"They also know that new rail lines are bein' built west ta' Chicago an' North Adams sits plunk in the middle of the route ta' gettin' there. If the Western Railroad gets their way the route'll run from Springfield to Troy through Pittsfield and North Adams. The entire state'll be hostage ta' those bastards and North Adams will become just a whistle stop along the route."

"But, if the tunnel is finished, the whole game changes."

"North Adams becomes a major rail hub connectin' both routes to Troy and the West. Northern route cities'll have equal access and no longer have ta' pay for it. The Western Railroad'll lose a ton of money.

"Is there any wonder why they'll kill ta' have it stopped?"

I was about to chime in but Ma beat me to it:

"Charles, I thought the governor and legislature were simply frustrated by the lack of progress at the tunnel and its cost ta' the state. That's why they favored the southern route. After all, t'is nearly completed and would connect Boston ta' Troy just like the tunnel route."

To which Da responded:

"I don't doubt that this is the reasoning for some in Boston... maybe most. But, I've found out some interestin' information over the past few days.

The southern route had a whole host o' challenges that the Western Railroad haven't been willin' ta' tell folks about. There may not've been a mountain ta' go through, but southern Massachusetts is very swampy in spots. So they either had to add miles ta' the route ta' go 'round them or bring in tons n' tons o' fill ta' shore up the track beds.

There were also several deep river gorges that needed ta' be forded. Keystone granite trestles needed ta' be built ta' accomplish that task. Some o' these are monsters sixty feet high, and span deep river gorges as wide as a half mile. While none o' this is costin' the state directly, if the Western Railroad gets their way and has the tunnel project shut down they'll be able ta' pass these extraordinary costs on ta' the businesses usin' their route.

So the Western Railroad has been spendin' millions o' dollars in Boston ta' buy the poltical influence they need ta' protect their interests. It's my understandin' that that's where more than a little o' the Boston hub-bub against the tunnel is comin' from. It's got many o' the uninformed folks in the state buyin' a load o' shite and I'll not see it happen. These bastards'll not get away with it. That tunnel simply must be completed.

"We've lived isolated and protected by our valley for so long that we've become naïve. The railroads may have opened up the world ta' us but they've also brought the true ruthlessness a' power for the sake o' power with 'em."

"So, there's terrible danger in ignorance on this issue."

"I wanted ta' tell ya' all of this earlier today, Virginia. But, even in my own station the walls may have ears. It's become very clear ta' me that we need ta' not only focus on what's in front of us, but also what's around us."

"The facts are, justice for the murders and mayhem around here may be relative. I don't believe in my heart that Boston will allow us any more than that."

Da then stood up and winked at me.

"'Course that doesn't mean we won't push their limits a bit, now does it?"

Da raised his tumbler in toast and gave the last splasheen of his Irish the bottoms up. Then he winked at me and said, "Sláinte."

*Holy Saints Patrick and Colmcille.*

As Da headed up the stairs to bed I offered to clean up the after dinner glasses and shooed Ma to follow. Her askance look told me she knew it was just an excuse, but she followed after Da anyhow.

The cleanup took only a few minutes. Then I had what I wanted...to be alone, alone to talk to Seanmháthair. I walked over to the hearth's mantle as I had so many times over the past year, looked up at Saorla's image and smiled.

Ever faithful, she responded with the almost smile, frozen in time so many years ago, that said so much about her but told me nothing about myself.

*Oh, Seanmháthair. I've come so far. I've learned so much. I've finally realized that I can never be you and should never again try. Today I only made matters worse. I didn't help anyone. I didn't solve anything. Worst of all, justice seems more elusive than ever.*

*Evil cannot prevail, Seanmháthair. I must do something. What do I do? What do I do?*

As usual the conversation was one sided. It was as though Seanmháthair's silence was an answer. Not *the* answer but *an* answer.

*Look within yourself.*

I found my eye drawn to the box my grandmother had given Ma and Da to take with them when they left Ireland.

*The letter. Perhaps Seanmháthair had left some clue in it about An Dara Sealladh I'd missed or forgotten.*

But when I opened the box the first thing I saw was not the letter, but the divination stick I'd inherited. It was wedged diagonally in the box and firmly held the letter underneath. There was no way of getting to the letter without its removal.

The first time I'd handled the stick it was just one in a treasure trove of objects. In fact compared to Seanmháthair's daguerreotype and letter it held my attention least. And Seanmháthair had most sternly warned me off its use at a time I was struggling to deal with my second sight visions. I certainly wasn't looking to force any new ones.

Today, however, when I picked up the stick I felt part of me drain into it. The divination stick had become an appendage of me, almost alive. It was warm to the touch and I thought I could discern a pulse. Somehow I knew that it was ready to serve.

The problem was I didn't know how.

When I examined the stick more closely hoping to detect some clue, I noticed it was made of some gnarly wood that was straighter than twisted; certainly fashioned by a hand that embraced its imperfections rather than sought to eliminate them. This was the work of someone who deeply venerated the tree of its origin. The deep reddish-brown color and shiny patina spoke of extreme age and use, not display.

There were three lines that ran the length of the divination stick dividing the surface into thirds. Each had a series of strange symbols either originating from or cutting through them.

When I began to gently stroke the symbols light in the room dimmed around me and I felt myself start to spin. Was it me or the room? I didn't care. I'd begun a journey and I was anxious to see where it led.

Touching different symbols seemed to stimulate different effects. It was almost as though each series of symbols put me on a pathway to a different place. Soon I was overwhelmed by a sense of happiness and contentment I'd never before encountered. I became embraced by a benevolent presence that had both love for me and concern for my wishes.

I only had to make them clear.

*"I am your Baile, your spirit guide...What is it that you seek?"*

Confusion and a touch of fear filled my soul. Who was this, this Baile?

No answer was offered, only the same question,

*"What is it that you seek?"*

What do I seek? What do I seek? I wasn't sure. But the desperation I felt to secure justice for the murdered souls of the tunnel and punishment for those responsible came roaring back.

*"Why?"*

Why? Instantly anger and hatred for Johnson and the mysterious Western Railroad operative darkened me and extinguished any euphoria I possessed when this journey began.

I wanted to see them swing. They deserved to die the most painful, ignominious death I could arrange. I wanted...

*"Is evil for evil what you seek?"*

Whoa...what? Evil for evil? I'm not evil. I'm after justice. I'm after....

*"Retribution."*

At that I had no answer...nothing...blank.

*"And your other reason?"*

Glory.

The word had no sooner materialized in my mind than I felt shock and disbelief. Is that me...the person I really am?

NO. No it isn't. I'm better than that.

*"Then what is it that you* do *seek?"*

To go back.

Suddenly the fire in the hearth was before me and I was alone. My hands shook as I carefully placed the divination stick back into the box where it belonged and closed the lid.

No one to tell. No one to share. Who could understand, anyhow?

But up on the mantle was Seanmháthair, ever faithful and still almost smiling down upon me. Both of my hands now slid to grab the mantle's edge. I closed my eyes, bowed my head and rested it against the hearth's mantle.

I had no doubt I had just met Seanmháthair and she had saved me from myself.

# Chapter 17

## Sunday, April 15, 1866

I confess that my mind was wandering during today's Eucharist.

I was still reflecting on my brush with the seduction of divination. While innocently searching for Seanmhátháir's letter I had unwittingly stumbled upon the stick of strange symbols and only vaguely recalled Seanmhátháir's warning about its use.

Somehow, however, this ancient implement had sensed my need and communicated a strong desire to serve. It asked no questions at all except what I sought to know. It possessed no morality of its own, but rather depended upon my honor to direct its use.

It was fortunate for me that Seanmhátháir had interrupted the divination stick's unregulated momentum toward revealing the unknown. One would need to possess incredible wisdom to be trusted with such knowledge. The temptation to use it for personal gain ... or worse, to manipulate events was simply too great.

Just then a gentle tug at my sleeve and a quiet whisper brought me back to the here and now.

"Virginia, dearest, would you care to take a seat with the rest of us?"

"Conal... What?"

Still standing, I looked around the church only to see that everyone was seated except for CJ and me. Trying to get my bearings I looked to the altar only to see Father Lynch patiently standing at the rostrum to the left of the altar with a huge grin on his face.

I was more than a little embarrassed as CJ gently intertwined his arm with mine and we both joined the rest of the congregation.

Far too nice to publically grind me into dust for my inattention, Father Lynch began his homily as though nothing had happened.

"Last Sunday we came together to celebrate the anniversary of Appomattox. Because of the bravery and selflessness of many men sitting before me today the Union was preserved. We also prayed for the souls of those who made the ultimate sacrifice in that terrible conflict between brothers."

"Today we come together not in celebration, but in commemoration of the senseless murder of the man who held this nation together by his determination, intelligence and patriotism. As I prayed for his soul this week I couldn't help but wonder what drives any man to lead. And so, instead of my usual style homily I want to share with you these thoughts:"

"We humans are strange creatures. Without true leaders we whirligig out of control like maple seeds falling to the ground. Nature's breezes push us hither and yon with no concern for our welfare. We're simply along for the ride. We may land in a favorable place and then germinate into something new and beautiful. But the odds are heavily against it."

"And so, we pray for someone to take control. Show us the way."

"When that person does he is immediately opposed by nearly half of us. Those with jealous ambition or conflicting interests work on the fringes to chip away at him. He quickly learns that true leadership takes both courage and conviction. Somehow he must get the nearly half of us who oppose him to come along too. He can only hope his enemies haven't eroded him enough to make a difference. And…God help him if he doesn't secure the success we pled for."

"Since success of any course of action is never absolute, neither is his. Unforeseen problems always lurk, predictably robbing him of complete victory. And so, he is relentlessly vilified by cynics who focus on the shortfall. Although supporters applaud his efforts, their voices seldom match either the volume or intensity of the critics."

"Retirement from the fray does little to diminish his defamation. Only in death does our leader secure peace. But, if natural death in due course results in being seen in a quixotic light, assassination elevates him to sainthood."

"Devotees build monuments, libraries and name schools after him. They tout how proud they are to have been represented by him. It's as if they can capture a piece of the leader's so recently bestowed greatness by finally giving up the anonymity they hid behind for so long. Pretenders scurry to mitigate their incessant attacks through mellifluous praise while quietly maneuvering to improve their positions to take his place."

"I don't know if this is the way it has always been, but it is certainly the way it has been in my lifetime. Thank God for our true leaders. Let us never forget that their lives would have been so much easier had they remained that maple seed fluttering in the wind."

"Nearly all of us do."

"So why *do*es anyone choose to lead? I still don't know. Do you?"

"Now, let us bow our heads in silent prayer not only for the repose of the soul of Abraham Lincoln but also in thanks for all of those who will take his place. God bless them and keep them."

By the end of Father Lynch's parable many of the women were weeping. Men looked either at their feet or about trying to gather cues what to think from friends and acquaintances. Children looked up at their parents with looks of concern.

Murmurs became discernible. The high vaulted ceilings of the cavernous new St. Francis of Assisi church collected and amplified them.

Then someone broke out in solitary spontaneous applause. A few more joined in. Soon nearly the entire congregation was on their feet filling the church with this symbol of approval.

But more than a few families also left.

Father Lynch seemingly ignored them all by returning to the altar and resumed the liturgy by chanting:

"Dō---minus vō-bis-cum..."

The choir responded from their perch high in the loft at the back of the church, "Et--cum spiri—tu –tu-ō..."

And I whispered into CJ's ear, "Doesn't Father Lynch realize the very story he just told us is being played out right now?"

CJ looked up at me, locked his eyes onto mine and almost inaudibly whispered, "I'm sure he does, Virginia."

"But several families actually left, Conal.  How rude."

CJ broke off his gaze, looked down toward the floor and growled under his breath,

"Some people living in North Adams still sympathize with the Southern cause, Virginia. They believe that Lincoln's assassination was a legitimate outcome of the war his policies had instigated. I'm sure they took Father's homily very, very personally and were deeply offended."

At the conclusion of Father Lynch's homily the people had demonstrated the truth of his message. CJ's words had explained it.

Finally I understood how Captain Conal John Mulcahy, the man I had come to love, had nearly been destroyed by the pressures of leadership as much as that chunk of rebel shrapnel while serving the Union cause. I gave his arm a strangled embrace and could see the tears streaming down his face.

Father's words also caused me to take a new and different look at my Da. I was always proud of the respect people in the village had for him. Was this only to his face? To my face? To Ma's face? Did Da really face the sort of challenges Father Lynch spoke of every day?

I was also certain that he did yesterday and would tomorrow.

And Seanmháthair...what of her? Was this the way the people of County Cork really saw Saorla? Did she face these challenges as well?

Without doubt.

I was also certain Father Lynch knew the answer to the question he posed.

Why do people lead? They're born to it. They have no choice.

Just when I had found a bit of peace and could refocus on the liturgy, the two center aisle doors to the vestibule opened with a bang that reverberated throughout the church. Everyone reacted with a start and instinctively turned to face the source of the disruption. Standing in the entrance was a single obviously frazzled man, who gasped several times before he bellowed,

"Ringo Kelley's been murdered..."

"In the bloody pit..."

"Right where he done Brinkman and Nash."

"Was their ghosts that done it."

# Chapter 18

## Just What the Doctor Ordered

The reaction was immediate. We Irish may be Catholics on our faces but still retain residual paganism in our sinew. Cacophony nearly rattled the stained glass windows. There were even a few screams. Evil was at work; evil that the people could neither understand nor control.

A visceral fear travelled first down the spine of each member of the congregation and then spread throughout the church. This smooth sea of prayerful families had become a choppy roiling mob. A subliminal something had been exuded that had everyone on the verge of fleeing for the safety of home.

CJ and I immediately turned to face each other and shared sardonic grins.

"Those gombeen men got him." CJ spouted.

We looked around the church for Ma and Da, locating them both already at the back of the church standing next to the town crier. Ma waved to us both and we swam through the throng as best we could to join them.

Da was escorting the man none too gently down the church steps when we caught up with them. To our rear I could barely hear Father Lynch over the din imploring the parishioners to calm down. He had won over a significant number of families, but many others ignored him and had already cut and run.

"What in the name o' St.Patrick made ya' think that was a good idea. Anyone hurt inside that church is on you, ya' gobshite."

The man I did not know was cowering under Da's withering outburst.

"Is this the first church ya've visited with your...your announcement?"

The man claimed that it was but I could sense his lie. Da could too.

"There are three other churches between the dig and here. You tryin' ta' tell me ya' didn't sprinkle a little sunshine on them first?"

"Come on, man out with ya'."

The man's mute downward gaze said it all.

"Jesus. The whole village'll buzzin' by noon."

"CJ, you and Ginger get to that damned bloody pit quick as ya' can. I'm goin' ta' the station ta' organize the constables and get out word for the night shift ta' report.

We'll need a police presence downstreet here and at the tunnel as well. So expect six or seven guys ta' help with the crowd at the tunnel. I'll send 'em soon as I can."

Da then arched his back, ran his fingers through his hair with both hands, took a deep breath and growled,

"And you, ya' bloody fool...get ya' home and shut your bloody trap. Do ya' see the trouble ya've caused? If I didn't need ta' keep the cells open for what may happen today you'd be in one."

Then he grumbled to no one in particular,

"What an effin' mess."

When our carriage reached the top of tunnel road the scene before us eerily mimicked the last time we were there. That assessment, however, proved to be superficial. This time the fear and confusion of the tunnel workers manifested itself as anger and hostility. Workers were milling about aimlessly. Cliques were fluidly constructed and changed members constantly. This time they were also looking to vent their anger on someone and it looked to be us.

This time Franklin Northkutt wasn't currying sympathy for himself with Father Lynch either. Instead our approach prompted him to storm out of the engineer's hut, gait so assertive that the lower portion of his long topcoat flapped open as alternating legs pushed through. Arms flailing, mouth opening and closing, great beak of a nose, Northkutt appeared to be some huge bird of prey about to pounce upon its quarry.

Northkutt reached us just as CJ pulled up the horses; who, by the way had not reacted well to Northkutt's approach. They nearly bolted, side stepped and knocked Northkutt off his pins.

I jumped down from the carriage and assisted the crashed eagle to his feet. Fortunately he'd been tossed into a cushion of last year's leaves near the side of the muddy road and not landed in it.

He looked up at me with an accusing stare and was on the verge of saying so when I sweetly said,

"My heavens, Mr. Northkutt are you OK?"

I added my most radiant smile and batted my baby green eyes. What he didn't know was that as I beamed I was actually attempting to suppress a hearty laugh because if I knew Conal, Northkutt may have been right.

CJ tied off the horses and rushed over.

"We've just heard about what happened, Mr. Northkutt, and we're here to help. Several more constables will be here soon. What say we go into the engineer's hut and have a talk?"

Northkutt ignored his shroud of crumbled leaves and instead tugged at his coat cuffs in an attempt to recover his dignity. Unconvinced he'd succeeded, or at our sincerity he nodded and grumbled,

"Let's go."

Once inside the shed and seated, Northkutt's arrogance returned. Unable to remain seated, he shot from his chair and paced about the room. Then he began barking,

"The North Adams Constabulary has had a year to bring Kelley in and give him what's coming to him. One year. Do you see what has happened because of your incompetence? Do you see? Someone has taken matters into their own hands and throttled the bastard...in *my* tunnel."

Northkutt paused for more than a second, took a deep breath and then bellowed,

"Look at the effect it's having on the men outside. They're already superstitious by nature. Not a shift goes by that I don't lose a worker or two. They come out of the tunnel terrified that they were touched by spirits of the forbidden mountain or the ghosts of workers killed in accidents."

"You've been inside. You know how the breezes and shadows play tricks. Even if you didn't believe in such clap trap on your first day, how many incidents would it take? If you're susceptible to suggestion and lord knows most of these fellas are, there are plenty of them in every nook and cranny of the place. Sometimes even I come out with the willies."

"Those men have one day off a week, Sergeant. But news of Kelley's murder has drawn them away from their families today. Right now they're out there feeding off each other's fear. They actually *believe* the ghosts of Brinkman and Nash dragged Kelley into the tunnel and strangled him."

"If even five of them show for the whistle tomorrow I'll eat dirt."

Northkutt's engine had finally run out of steam because he pulled out a chair and nearly collapsed into it. The resulting silence was so complete that sounds of the wall clock seemed to grow louder with each swing of the pendulum. Tock...Tock...Tock.

Just then a knock came at the shack door. Sergeant Smart poked his head in.

"May I enter?"

He reported his message directly to Conal, but also showed respect for Northkutt by turning every few words to face him.

"The Captain sent me to oversee crowd control operations here, Sergeant Mulcahy. I have six constables with me. What is your pleasure?"

CJ instructed Sergeant Smart to take a seat. He explained the situation with a lot less fatalistic emotion than Franklin Northkutt had. Then he turned to Northkutt,

"How well do you know your workers?"

When Northkutt returned a look of uncertainty Conal clarified what he was after.

"Who are the leaders out there, Mr. Northkutt? And I'm not necessarily talking about foremen *you've* picked. The men I'm after are the ones that you may see as trouble makers but the others look up to. These are the men who will come to you with demands and stand proud for the rights of others."

"I need their names... the more the better."

CJ pushed a piece of paper and a pencil at the reluctant Franklin Northkutt.

"I need them *now*, sir."

Tock...Tock...Tock...

Exasperated at how long it took Northkutt to compile the list, Conal snatched what results there were from under Northkutt's hand and gave it to Sergeant Smart.

"Elisha, I need you to quickly and quietly find these men and summon them to this shack. Then group the rest of your men in pairs. Tell them that they are to circulate among the cliques and get a feel for potential problem groups. Have them talk to the folks, not strong arm them. We need to calm people, not incite them."

"And remind them of Captain O'Leary's rule: no violence, no arrests."

Sergeant Smart got up from his seat ready to go. And as he reached the door CJ emphasized,

"It's on you to enforce it, Sergeant."

Elisha nodded, gave us all a smile, a wink and with a nod was gone.

After hearing this Northkutt demanded,

"What are you up to, Sergeant Mulcahy? This is the *engineer's* hut. I don't want those people..."

CJ cut off Northkutt and said to me,

"Miss O'Leary, could you put on a fresh pot of coffee? We'll offer a cup to any man who wants it."

Northkutt attempted to interrupt, but again CJ immediately shut him down.

"Now listen to me, sir. Rumor stirred this pot and irrationality spread the fear. We're going to enlist the natural leadership that exists out there to restore sanity and end the nonsense."

"If you or I were to stand out there and address the entire assemblage about what really happened, it wouldn't work. They don't trust us and with all due respect to you, sir, they probably don't like us either."

"So we'd better hope we can convince the men we've summoned the truth of the matter. If we can get even half of them to listen they'll do our work for us when they return to their men."

"If we do this right, Mr. Northkutt, you might even have enough men answer the whistle tomorrow to run first shift. And if that happens word will get around so that second shift shows as well."

"So, Mr. Northkutt, I think you should get off your arse and greet these men by name and welcome them into the *engineer's* shed, don't you?

One by one the men entered the shack, some alone, a few together. All were wary. Clearly they had never before been in here and felt uncomfortable. One man took a look at Northkutt holding the door open and turned to leave.

I quickly intervened by smiling and offering him a cup of the steaming brew. Although he glanced askance over his shoulder at Northkutt, he returned my smile, accepted it and took a seat with the others.

After about fifteen minutes eight men were seated around the conference table. None were talking, most just fenced in their cups with both hands and stared down at them. When it was clear that no one else was coming, CJ rose from his seat and began:

"Thank you for joining us. We all know that Ringo Kelley has indeed been murdered. We also know that the rumored circumstances of this crime have been inflammatory. People are scared. And when fear grabs a community mistakes can be made. Mistakes that in the light of day everyone will regret."

"My hope is that by sharing with you the truth of both the slaying of Kelley and the circumstances surrounding it you will realize that the rumors indeed are just that. There's nothing to be afraid of. Some, if not all of you, may agree already. But in the absence of any other explanation what else is there?"

Then CJ roared,

"There's much to be *angry* about. But your anger should be directed at the *people* responsible. *People* who would rob you of your livelihood. *People* who would rob this village of its future of becoming the most important city in Western Massachusetts."

"Don't allow them to manipulate you."

And then searching for eye contact Conal said in a most soothing tone,

"The truth, gentlemen,  makes so much more sense than the rumors circulating now that paralyze your community with fear."

"I'll now ask you to compare between the likelihood of rumor and the truth."

CJ then resumed his oratory posture and volume,

"The rumor asks us to believe that two ghosts materialized and somehow found Ringo Kelley. These ghosts then dragged him from wherever he'd been hiding all the way into the bowels of the tunnel and strangled him."

CJ paused for a few seconds and strode to the stove to refill his mug. Then, with the drama intended, he resumed,

"The truth, gentlemen, takes a bit longer. Would anyone else like more coffee before I resume?"

There were no takers, but eight sets of eyes were riveted on him.

I couldn't help but applaud CJ's sense of timing and flair for the dramatic. He gave the men time to assess and put away one idea so that they could be receptive to the next. He modulated his voice and adjusted his posture to both interest and influence them.

CJ had dashed the fiction that it was shades of the dead who threatened them, and planted the seeds of skepticism. It must have been flesh and blood men. Who were they?

It took Conal another ten minutes to tell them. Then he concluded,

"We'd like to arrest the whole rotten bunch. But we can't. Our only connection to them was Ringo Kelley. Now they've killed him too. They have money and political connections, therefore they have protection. Even though we realize we may never succeed completely, we will go after them any way we can."

"But *you* can beat them."

"*You* can beat them by answering the whistle tomorrow to dig this bloody hole."

The questions they asked told me that Conal had won the day, at least within this shack. All of their queries were about the Western Railroad. Not one man asked about the ghosts of Brinkman and Nash. As they rose to return to their fellow tunnelmen each shook CJ's hand and then nearly bolted from the hut.

When the door had slammed for the last time I happened to catch sight of Northkutt. He'd been fuming off in a corner with his arms crossed since the workers had invaded his castle. But now he stood slack jawed, amazed.

*Yeah, ya' shitehead, your lookin' at a real leader of men.*

CJ must have also checked out Northkutt's response because when I turned to look at him his eyes were waiting to meet mine. His smile and wink were offered so quickly I was unsure if they'd really happened.

"It'll take a while, Mr. Northkutt...and not all of them will buy in. We can only hope that most of them do. If we go out there now we'll steal attention from the soldiers we've just worked so hard to enlist. So, let's have a cup of coffee and relax a bit. Kelley's going to still be dead later."

*Conal, 'tis a terrible sly one, you are...We. We? Northkutt?*

As we drank our coffee and sat back Northkutt didn't have much to say. I'm sure that he had no idea of either the academic or the military background of this short, unassuming constable sergeant sitting at the conference table calmly sipping coffee. I was also sure that Northkutt's social hierarchy had just been turned on its ear because he paced back and forth sneaking quick peeks of CJ every so often that asked, "Who is this man?"

Conal and I quietly waited for the "thank you" that was never going to come when the door bang, banged, nearly knocking it off its hinges. It then swung open wide enough to accommodate the corpulent girth of none other than Doctor Briggs.

"Hey, what are you folks doing in here?"

"Did you know the mob out there is starting to break up? Looks like they've had enough and are heading home."

"Do my olfactory lobes detect a nutty aromatic elixir diffused from ground roasted coffee beans placed in boiling water?"

Doc didn't seem too concerned with anyone answering his questions because he turned his back to us, walked over to the wood stove and rubbed his hands together in an attempt to get warm.

The coffee pot was right in front of him, but I was certain that this man who would cover himself in flour while helping Ma bake bread would die of thirst before he'd pour his own coffee.

There weren't any unused cups so I wiped one out with a towel and saved Doctor Sam from a horrible, painful death.

Doctor Sam accepted my offering and joined us at the conference table.

"Gave me quite a chuckle when word reached downstreet about the untimely demise of our friend Mr. Kelley. Boy, that Dutchy Gregory...best scuttlebutt in the village."

"Anyhow, I came as soon as I heard...must have been over two hours ago. What time is it, anyhow?"

Doc had up a full head of steam, so everyone ignored the question and patiently waited as he snapped a match to life with his thumbnail and lit his stogie. He lolled his head back, closed his eyes and took a deep draught.

Sure enough, Doc could've cared less what time it was because when he came back from wherever he'd been he opened his eyes, looked around the table, and continued as he exhaled a bluish column of noxious smoke,

"Did you know you can't smoke inside the tunnel? Shoot, there's water raining off the ceiling, water oozing out of the walls and they told me to put out my stogie."

There was little sympathy in *this* room for Doc either, only looks that implored Doc to get on with it.

"Anyhow, when you two didn't show I grabbed a couple tunnel rats and asked them to take me to the body."

"By the way, my compliments to you, Mr. Northkutt. I was amazed at how much progress has been made since last year. Nice ride, actually. The boys were able to take me all the way to the body by rail on this little hand car. Took these two guys only a few minutes to transport me all the way."

Finally, an exasperated CJ spoke up, "Doc, for heaven's sake, can you please get on with it?

With a wink to me and a coy smile to the others Doc divulged that he'd just been having us on.

*Damn you, Doc.*

He pushed back his chair and using the table to coax his considerable mass against the forces of inertia, stood up and began pacing around the room with his hands clasped behind him. He was once again Samuel Briggs, M.D., scientist.

"Ringo Kelley *was* strangled, alright...and none to gently either. Based upon the narrow lividity marks around his neck I'd say a thin rope was used. Hands leave evidence of differential pressure around the victim's neck. That would result in differing shades of purple girding it. The marks on Kelley's neck showed equal pressure all around. Looked like he was wearing a dark purple necklace."

"Whoever did this got him from behind too. When I examined Kelley's hands and fingers there were no defensive wounds... no evidence he'd punched, grabbed or scratched anybody. Most likely, he was nice and relaxed when the killer came up from behind and garroted him...in an extremely violent manner. He went down fast... and for good. When I perform the autopsy I'm sure I'll find his hyoid bone and windpipe were crushed. Must have been a very strong man to have inflicted this much damage."

Doc stopped strutting for a moment and glared at us one by one and then said,
"Or a well-coordinated gang of two or more assailants...say the three guys who visited Dutchy's gambling emporium?"

"I also knew that you'd want to examine the scene for evidence of a struggle or that Kelley had been dragged in against his will, Sergeant Mulcahy. Well, I'm here to tell you there wasn't any. Not one blessed mark."

"In addition to that, the condition of the body tells me that he's been dead for a while. How long, I can't say. It has been so cold out; it could be a few days... maybe as long as a week. In other words, Kelley was not throttled inside the tunnel. If he was, someone would've certainly stumbled on him before this. He was definitely killed someplace else and dumped here."

"Would have been easy for three men to pull off too. If they had knowledge of railroad equipment they could easily have used the hand car to transport Kelley's body last night after second shift went home. I'll bet they never even got off the car."

"All that was left to do was pay off a few guys to spread the rumor that the ghosts of Brinkman and Nash had taken their revenge on Kelley."

"So, there you have it...Unrest among the tunnel workers shuts it down and if it goes on long enough, costs you your job, Mr. Northkutt."

Doctor Sam then beamed, snapped another match to life and reignited his disgusting cheroot. Obviously quite proud of himself, he took several quick drags and nearly filled the room with a stinky bluish haze that burned my eyes.

I, on the other hand was rewarded when Doctor Sam commenced a staccato hacking.

*Why in the world would anyone smoke one of those things...for pleasure?*

Undeterred, Doc flicked an ash from the tip of his cigar and proudly announced,

"We have evidence, my friends; evidence of foul play by people, not ghosts."

"Impressed?"

*Just what the doctor ordered.*

# Chapter 19

## This Is Justice?

# 𝕿𝖍𝖊 𝕿𝖗𝖆𝖓𝖘𝖈𝖗𝖎𝖕𝖙

Volume LXVI     Saturday, April, 21, 1866     Page 1

## MURDER AT THE BIG DIG

By

Wells Mitchell

### News Interrupts Sunday Worship and Nearly Causes Pandemonium

Last Sunday morning, April 15, 1866, the body of Ringo Kelley was discovered deep within the bowels of the Hoosac Tunnel by Francis Parker, member of the maintenance crew.

"It was awful, just awful. He eyes were popping. His tongue was purple and sticking out of his mouth. The man looked like a strangled chicken," Parker told this reporter.

Parker and other members of the crew present reported the grisly discovery to Franklin Northkutt, head engineer of the project who refused comment.

Within an hour word spread throughout the village that Kelley had been murdered by the vengeful spirits of Ned Brinkman and Billy Nash at the same spot they died just over a year ago.

Pandemonium in the streets nearly ensued as a result.

Captain O'Leary and other members of the North Adams Constabulary were quickly on the scene and did a fine job controlling the crowd, encouraging families to go to their homes. O'Leary also ordered all village taverns to remain closed for the day.

"Downstreet was a tinderbox. The last thing we needed was the creature strikin' a match," Captain O'Leary said.

The men who started the rumor have been identified by authorities and arrested. "I want ta' know why three men independently decided ta' shout the same ridiculous tale at exactly the same time. Somethin's goin' on here and I'm goin' ta' find out!" Captain O'Leary told The Transcript.

Dr. Samuel Briggs arrived at the murder scene by late morning and examined the body. "Ringo Kelley in fact was strangled." Dr. Briggs visibly bristled when this reporter asked if ghosts were responsible. "Kelley was garroted with a rope by at least two people. And not last night either. Kelley has been dead at least a few days and possibly a week.

Furthermore, the evidence is clear that he was murdered someplace else and dumped in the tunnel. Someone's having a game with us and I, for one, am not amused."

By early afternoon cooler heads prevailed when Sgt. Mulcahy addressed key members of the work force who had gathered at the scene. "I explained to the men that forces of evil were at work here, but they were not ghosts. Men were responsible for this deed. Men who want to see the Tunnel project shut down. I challenged them not to allow that to happen, to show up for work on Monday morning."

All indications are that workers have picked up the gauntlet as work at the tunnel has resumed this week uninterrupted.

(See page 2 for more)

## Rumor Suspects Arrested

By

Wells Mitchell

### Charged as Accessories to Murder and Mayhem

Last Sunday night, April 15, 1866, three men suspected in spreading rumors that nearly caused riots in the streets of North Adams and shutting down work at the tunnel excavation of Hoosac Mountain were arrested at their homes.

It is believed that the spreading of the rumors was the final step in a plot set forth by the men who actually carried out the murder of Ringo Kelley. Authorities said that these conspirators hoped to prey upon superstitions and deeply held beliefs of many in the village that spirits have the ability to intervene in human events.

Kevin Cullen, Dennis Hill and Hayden Worth were charged with both mayhem dangerous to the public good and being accessories after the fact to murder.

When confronted with the seriousness of their crimes and the certainty of conviction, the men quickly gave authorities names of the conspirators who paid them to carry out their hoax. "All of the detainees have been citizens of North Adams for years and have never before been arrested. We are convinced that they were unaware of the seriousness of their actions, and simply didn't think things through." Constable Sergeant Mulcahy reported.

Constable Captain O'Leary, also present stated, "They gave up the names so quickly and showed such remorse when confronted with the direness o' their position I decided ta' drop all charges against them."

Captain O'Leary assured this reporter that the offenders were made aware that dropping the charges was contingent upon their testimony at the trials of those who both engineered and carried out the plot to murder Ringo Kelley.

Authorities are searching for three men in connection with the murder of Ringo Kelley and the mayhem perpetrated on the citizens of North Adams. They are believed to be from the Springfield area and are considered to be armed and extremely dangerous.

Authorities refused to speculate about what organization from Springfield may have ordered these men to the area. They also declined to discuss possibilities of why. However, they did assure this reporter that they are investigating a "highly probable scenario."

"These blokes have already done in at least one person. They've nothing' ta' lose by doin' another," Captain O'Leary told The Transcript.

Although authorities believe that the murderers may have fled the area, they remind citizens coming into contact with strangers to take no action on their own. They are advised to instead notify the first available constable.

"These men have probably fled for home. But, there's still a chance they have more work to do here; so we ask citizens to be vigilant." Sergeant Mulcahy said.

"Way to go, Mitch."

Da shook his copy of the weekly newspaper to fold it as only a man can and tossed it onto his office desk. When he took his boots off his desk and reverted his posture from recumbent to upright his chair groaned at the work it was asked to do.

"He really came through for us. Got in every point we wanted to make."

CJ who had been standing and pensively looking out the windows of Da's office added, "I'll bet Josh Marran has already sent a copy to Springfield. I'd love to be a fly on the wall when Johnson reads it."

I had arrived a little late and was just finishing my own copy of Wells Mitchell's article and needed to catch up.

"Who's Josh Marran?"

CJ turned to face me with arms still crossed, leaned against the office wall and answered,

"Josh Marran sells tickets at the State Street depot during the day and cleans up after hours to make extra money. He's a nobody who wants to be somebody. Not very smart, but does realize that the Western Railroad has designs on buying up the Pittsfield-North Adams spur. So he weasels around for things they might want to know and sends them. We think he's the one who found out the Captain had Kelley locked up and telegraphed Springfield. He's also been quite vocal at the taverns, especially the past six months; telling folks that Springfield is going to make him station manager soon...real soon."

Just then there was a quick knock at the office door. Doctor Sam poked his head through the open doorway and said,

"You're welcome."

Da and CJ both gave a quick chuckle as Da pointed to the coffee pot on the top of the wood stove just outside his office. Completely ignoring his direction, Doc plunked his considerable bulk down in the only other empty chair and exhaling a long breath waited for his coffee to be delivered.

Naturally I poured him a cup, but chose my most regal manner of delivery and in a mock pretentious tone said,

"Thank you?"

"No, no Virginia," Doc chortled. "I said 'you're welcome' because I was at the North Adams House tavern a few nights back when I heard Marran spouting off. The next day I told your Da and CJ that Marran really thinks the Western Railroad is going to promote him as payback for giving up Kelley to them. What a moron."

Doc raised his cup to me in salute,

"By the way, Virginia...thanks for the coffee."

Da added, "We knew who Marran was but had no idea that he was a direct pipeline from here ta' Johnson."

"Anyhow, let's not get hung up about him. He's really of no importance. Good ta' know what he's up ta', though. We may be able ta' use 'im later. Right now we're sure he's sent Mitch's article ta' Johnson, so we're sure Johnson's realizin' he's made one huge mistake by killin' Kelley."

Doc got up from his chair and actually took the few steps to reach the coffee pot and saints preserve us, poured his own refill. He then poured a second cup and while on the taxing return odyssey offered it to me as though it was the most natural thing in the world for him to do. Then he added,

"Johnson made a bigger mistake getting involved in this whole mess in the first place. He's just a functionary of the Western Railroad, an engineer trained to plan and maintain rail routes. He can't take a piss without Worcester allowing it."

"I'm sure the orders to shut down the tunnel originated there, your mystery man delivered them and Johnson, ever the lackey, attempted to carry them out. Fortunately for us, he completely lacked the imagination to succeed. Unless I miss my guess, when wind reaches Worcester of how botched the plot to shut down the tunnel has become Mr. Lemuel Johnson will find himself a man alone on a limb with them holding a saw. The sweet irony is that he's in exactly the same spot Kelley was in."

Grinning ear to ear Doc continued,

"Those guys in Worcester would feed their first born to the wolves to protect themselves."

Doc's gleeful guffaws added the exclamation point to his oration. He was clearly quite pleased with his summation of the pressures that now had to be consuming Johnson. This student of the human condition, Doc clearly reveled in being a member of the club.

I, on the other hand, had come into contact with Johnson's shade and experienced first-hand the evil in that man's soul. I only felt sadness at the depths to which human treachery could sink and distress that each of us possessed the potential.

"So what do we do?"

"Do?" CJ said. "Nothing actually, Ginger. I think Doc's right. Johnson's days of causing trouble here are over."

"But he set it all up from the beginning. He convinced Kelley to blow up the tunnel killing Brinkman and Nash. Then he made sure Kelley was released from Da's gaol and sent the three killers from Springfield to take care of him. He's dirty. He's evil. Aren't we going after him? Can't we arrest him? Can't we hang him?"

Da got up from his chair, sauntered to the back of my chair and soothingly placed his hands on my shoulders. As he did so, he imparted,

"Virginia, let's allow things to play out. Justice isn't always found at the end of a hangman's noose. Right now the *threat* that we're closing in on Johnson should be enough. I agree with CJ and Doc. Word will get to Worcester soon. Those people aren't going to take any chances that any of this can come back on them. They'll deal with Lemuel Johnson."

"But, Da, even if that's true, how can you be so sure? Johnson's such a snake, how can you accept it?" When Doc leaned back in his chair his jacket fell away exposing his bulging gut and he beamed in a most self-satisfied way.

"In this world shite always follows a gradient and flows downhill from those with power until some poor drudge at the bottom is forced to catch it, Miss Ginger. In the Western Railroad corporate world Johnson is the poor peon who's going to catch it. If he's anywhere near as savvy as I think he is... and remember I've sat across the poker table from him... Johnson's heading for the hills even as we speak."

To which Da added,

"Johnson will have lost everything, Ginger. His job, his home...what little power he may have had...all gone. We've at least seen ta' that. Maybe that's enough. Maybe that'll have ta' be enough. I just don't see what else we can do. We don't have one shred o' evidence connectin' him ta' either the murder or the murderers. And even if we did, you just don't waltz inta' Springfield and arrest one of its leading citizens."

CJ, abandoning his relaxed position against the office wall marched over to Da's desk. He picked up *The Transcript* and scrutinized it as though he expected new information had somehow been added to the text. Frustrated at the outcome of his examination he crumpled it together and tossed it to the floor.

"The three murderers will also have fled by now. We'll never find them. When we told Mr. Mitchell that we had their names and descriptions we were out to maximize the heat on Johnson. But of course, this was a bluff. Cullen, Hill and Worth were so drunk that night all they ever saw were the five dollar gold pieces. As things look right now it appears everyone involved in this fiasco is going to walk."

In a fit of obvious disgust CJ stormed out of the office, up the stairs and outside.

As I bolted to follow, I heard Doc's voice spill out of the office,

"It doesn't sound like it's good enough for Sergeant Mulcahy, Captain."

# Chapter 20

## Peace to You, My Brother

The succulent crust of the roast chicken was a crisp golden brown. White flesh of the baked prátaís peeked from their lengthwise sliced skins begging to be rescued from confinement. Carrots sautéed with maple syrup and just a touch of nutmeg glistened like candy. The wicker basket holding dinner rolls was filled to overflowing. The plate of butter churned just this afternoon was patiently awaiting the onslaught of dueling knives that would empty it by meal's end. The cider was cold, aromatic and tangy.

All that was missing were the laughs and conviviality normally expected at such a lovingly fashioned setting.

Then the sullen quiet was interrupted by Da.

"Bless us, O Lord, and these thy gifts, which we are about to receive from thy bounty."

And then reestablished after Ma, CJ and I answered Da in as rote a fashion as he had offered grace.

"Through Christ our Lord, Amen."

Formalities of this Catholic home fulfilled, Da carved the chicken while the rest of us offered the rest to each other. Ma noticed the paltry portions we each had on our plates and immediately took umbrage,

"Snap out of it won't ya. You've done the best ya' can. Now EAT."

Ma's orders usually resulted in instant compliance. This evening, however, an extra spoonful of carrots here and maybe an extra roll there seemed the best we could do.

However, the food was as delicious as ever and eventually worked its magic. It enticed us to not only ensure our survival, but also dig into the seconds that satisfied Ma.

CJ looked at me, reached under the table and squeezed my hand. I smiled in response and it was returned. Da sheepishly grabbed an askance peek at Ma and offered an impish wink. When the corners of Ma's mouth turned up ever so slightly they locked eyes and Da said,

"Ya' reach over here and squeeze *my* hand Conal John and I'll knock ya' outa' that chair."

My face immediately warmed and CJ's reflected what I felt.

"Supper was wonderful, Ma. Thank you."

I'm not quite sure when CJ took to addressing Ma this way, but it was clear she was pleased by this more personal appellation.

Da and I quickly followed in synchrony as the three of us rose to clear the table of dinnerware and what few dregs of food survived.

It wasn't long before CJ and Da had finalized the routine of putting the kitchen in order. I was pouring the evening coffee when Ma's voice playfully found us all the way from her chair in front of the great room hearth.

"Were ya' thinkin' I'd forget? Why don't ya' check the warmer."

If we had any notion that Ma might've taken our earlier behavior out on us, the wonderful aroma tantalizing us declared otherwise.

Permission to investigate the source given, I opened the oven warmer door and beheld a treat I didn't think possible in April. When I put it on the trivet on the table Da exclaimed,

"Maeve, how in the world did ya' ever..."

"D'ya think ya' might stop wastin' time and bring me a slice?" Ma laughed.

On the table in front of us was our favorite mid-summer indulgence, mixed berry pie.

Black berries, red and black raspberries grew like weeds throughout our property. When I was a little girl I helped Ma cultivate patches of canes of the sweet fruits so that we no longer had to compete with the critters for the harvest...just the bees.

Regardless, Ma's store of them was usually exhausted by the end of summer. To have enough left in April to make a pie was unprecedented.

We weren't complaining.

Tap, tap, tap...thud, thud, thud...tap, tap, tap. Tap, tap, tap...thud, thud, thud...tap, tap, tap.

*What?? What?? Jeremiah???*

I gave CJ a quick kiss on the cheek and smiled, "Guess who?"

"Well, answer the door..." CJ gave me a quick swat on the butt propelling me to the front door.

Before I could reach the door, it opened and Jeremiah's handsome face poked in,

"Anyone home?"

The entrance was quickly surrounded by three smiling O'Learys and a Mulcahy.

"I didn't know you could smell Maeve's berry pie all the way to Cambridge," Da joked as he shook Jeremiah's hand. "Come in, my boy, come in."

It took some effort, but we all managed to make a significant contribution to the emptying of the pie dish. While we were still savoring the experience Da poured the evening's Jameson measures and distributed jars all around. Laughs and geniality filled the great room completely eradicating the glumness of the early evening.

Jeremiah's visit had been most pleasant, but left everyone a bit shocked and with an unasked question on the tips of our tongues, "What the hell are you doing here?" Harvard's spring term doesn't end until mid-May so the final push should be on to prepare for end of year examinations. Up to now he'd given nary a hint of an answer to this question and politeness precluded so crass an invasion of his privacy.

However, when the conversation turned to recent events, Jeremiah rose as if on cue from his place on the sofa and took the few steps necessary to reach the fireplace hearth. He placed his crystal tumbler of Irish on the mantel, turned to face his audience and initiated his soliloquy:

"Have you folks any idea what a stir the murder of Ringo Kelley has caused at Harvard? *The Boston Herald* published a story last week that the Hoosac Tunnel was haunted and evil spirits were killing people. The University is all abuzz and yours truly has become an instant luminary.

I guess because I'm from North Adams I somehow must have contact with the spirit world or mystical powers."

"I tried to explain to them what the situation really was...that I had first-hand knowledge of much of it because of my friendship with you folks. In fact I told them the whole story starting with the deaths of Brinkman and Nash. I tried to explain that it was the exhaustive investigation by the North Adams Constabulary that found the answer. But that was too mundane a response for these chaps."

"You see, they've spent all kinds of money in the quest for contact with the spirit world. Tarot, séances...you name it, they've tried it. They were convinced that there had to be more. Rich they are. Foolish they are. Stupid they aren't. They sensed that I was holding back."

"Anyhow, they hounded me so much that I finally let slip how we figured out so quickly who was responsible for the problems at the tunnel. I'm sorry, Ginger but I told them about you. I even revealed your legacy and described the incident at the New Year's Eve Ball...and told them what you saw."

"You what? You bloody eejit, Jeremiah. How..."

I was just working up a full head of steam with which to scald Jeremiah when he raised both hands palms facing me and said,

"Wait, Ginger...there's more."

The crackle and pop of wood burning in the fireplace just behind him disrupted his hesitation. Then he gave me the worst of it,

"They're at my house in search of adventure, and are determined to meet you."

At this final revelation I vaulted from my seat and flung my glass at Jeremiah. It further infuriated me to see how adroitly he first dodged, then apprehended it with one hand and placed it on the mantle.

My mirthless smirk warned Jeremiah that he'd better not turn his back to me in case I found another projectile within my reach.

Two Waterford crystal tumblers glistened on the mantle side by side; one full, one dripping only dregs of its previous contents.

*'Tis a fitting image o' the state of our friendship, ya' bloody gobshite.*

I stormed to the front door and slammed it behind me as I went out on the porch. It seemed only a second later the door opened and Jeremiah joined me.

Ma and Da knew better than to attempt any intervention between Jeremiah and me. They had personal experience with how painful it could be. Even as children

Jeremiah and I had quarreled vehemently and often. Third party mediation simply diverted our ire just long enough for both of us to attack the unfortunate intruder.

So when an unwitting Conal opened the porch door ...well...let's say it was more than the mid-evening April chill that caused him to reverse course.

It was only when we were sure of undisturbed privacy that the conversation Jeremiah and I knew needed to happen could be initiated. Unable to face him, I gazed off to the starlit eastern sky.

Jeremiah went first. "Ita sum valde me paenitet, Virginia. I really am so very sorry."

For some reason I couldn't put my finger on Jeremiah's entreaty only served to further infuriate me. My unconscious thoughts shocked me.

*This time you've crossed the Rubicon, Julius.*

Before I could get control of my emotions I shrieked,

"Don't you dare spout Latin at me, Jeremiah Colgrove. I'm not some bloody freak to be put on display for your snooty Boston friends. It's not going to work this time."

And after a short pause,

"What's happened to you, Jer?"

Sensing the finality of the situation, Jeremiah quietly went into the house but soon returned wearing his overcoat, hat in hand and offered the last remnant of our childhoods together:

"Ego sum remux, meus sanctimonialis. Pacis vobis."

When I did not respond Jeremiah Colgrove walked down the porch stairs, mounted his horse and rode out of my life.

Suddenly my fury was replaced by abject loss. I turned to go in and muttered under my breath, "Ego sum remux, meus frater. Pacis vobis quoque."

*I too am sorry, my brother. Peace to you also.*

# Chapter 21

## Sunday, April 22, 1866

Wracked with misgivings and self-doubt it took seemingly hours for fitful sleep to overwhelm me. In one felled swoop I had dismissed my best childhood friend for insensitivity, rejected the man I loved for offering to me what the other had lacked and angered both my parents for my harshness toward both.

They said nothing, but the posture and frowns I saw over my shoulder as I tearfully fled up the stairs were like none I'd ever before encountered from either Ma or Da. The two taken together were devastating.

Tears of sorrow and desolation made matters only worse, but they did serve to exhaust me. I tossed and turned most of the night but it was only when I dreamed I was standing on the edge of a cliff unable to prevent slipping into a black abyss that I awoke with a start. My heart was pounding, my breathing huffy and I was covered with sweat.

*So ya' spoke your mind. You were hurt, so ya' hurt others. How's that workin' for ya', girl?*

*Did ya' even give Jeremiah a chance ta' explain? D'ya' actually believe he wants ta' use ya' for a good laugh with his friends?*

*And CJ... all he did was show affection and concern. Is it proud of yourself y'are?*

No, proud of myself I am not.

I shivered as I wrapped myself in my horse blanket robe, stepped into my slippers and stood to look out my bedroom window. Instead of the cold blackness of not twelve hours ago which served to only deepen my feelings of loss and despair, I beheld a bright blue late-morning sky which filled me with resolve to put things right.

I even laughed out loud when my gaze was drawn to the horse corral on the other side of the carriageway by the sharp sounds of a repeating "thweet-thweet." There stood a very frustrated Stanley holding a bitted bridle out in front of him attempting to entice our hyperactive yearling, Killian, into compliance. Killian, however, was having no part of it. He darted back and forth in a manner so unpredictable that Stanley's attempts to keep up looked quite comical. I watched this test of wills until Stanley finally threw the bridle to the ground in disgust and stormed out of the corral.

Now that the show was over, I returned to reality. It was time.

I found Ma sitting in her chair in the great room putting the finishing touches on a new quilt. Da wasn't home because he was doing his part working this Sunday. He didn't mind being in the monthly rotation because it not only gave his officers an additional Sunday home with their families, but also allowed Da to invite Father Lynch home for supper after offering the Eucharist to anyone unfortunate enough to be in the lockup.

We appreciated Father's efforts to keep us in the state of grace. Father Lynch appreciated one of Ma's home cooked feasts. A wee touch of the creature before heading back to the rectory didn't hurt either.

As I approached she looked up in a way that froze me in my tracks.

"Yes, Virginia Maureen?"

Bang, bang, bang.

The front door rattled so violently it nearly came off its hinges. Without hesitation, the announcement of company was followed by the door swinging widely open.

In stepped none other than Doctor Sam.

Ma and I looked at each other and couldn't help smiling at one another. Nothing had changed, but it was clear that the conversation I'd hoped to have with her was going to wait. A truce had been declared.

"Morning, folks... Morning. It *is* still morning isn't it? It was when I left the hotel. Any coffee still brewing? Had quite a night last night, I can tell you.... Can I come in?"

Guess who was already in.

"Swung by the constable's station on my way and saw the Captain's horse. Figured it was his Sunday to cover the station. Good thing too. No Mass for you folks. Otherwise I'd have had to hold off. What I've got to say he can't hear, being an officer of the law and all."

After closing the door Doc took off his coat, hung it up on the rack behind the door and raised both hands as if to surrender as he faced us.

"You folks stay right where you are. I'll get the coffee."

Doc headed into the kitchen like a man on a mission. Through the kitchen door we heard him shout, "Sugar, anyone?"

He'd no sooner asked the question than Doc's considerable posterior emerged pushing through the closed kitchen door.  When the rest of him joined us he purposefully distributed the three mugs of coffee he was juggling:  One for me... one for Ma... the last for himself.

It was a good thing neither Ma nor I wanted sugar.

When I recovered from the shock of Samuel Briggs M.D. serving *us*, not to mention the abruptness of his entrance, I got a good look at him for the first time.  He was.... well, he was a mess.  Day old beard, bloodshot eyes.  The tabs of his collar were turned up like horns on a bull.  One of his shirt tails had escaped his pants.  The contradiction between his physical condition and his behavior was startling.

It was Ma who said, "Doctor Briggs, would ya' care ta' take a load off?"

"Can't, Maeve, can't. Got a story to tell, here. Got a story."

He gulped a deep swig of his coffee and confirmed its effects by smacking his lips and emitting a long,

"Ahhhh."

Hands behind his back, head bowed slightly forward, Doc began to pace back and forth in front of the great room hearth.  It seemed Doc's pent-up story was about to commence.

"Last night I *just happened* to be over to the Old Black Tavern...they had some travelling exotic dancers ... so I thought I'd take a gander. Guess Jeremiah and his three friends from Boston decided to as well because they were at a table just across from me....These Boston chaps sure know how to whoop it up. One of them was up front whirling one of the lady's unmentionables over his head."

"Ahhh to be young."

"Well, the show was going on... hooting, hollering and such. Silk stockings were being tossed over our heads like kites. A couple guys were tossed as well...out on their ears, that is."

The memory evidently amused Doc because he paused with a hearty belly laugh.

"They had...um... let's just say they got tossed."

"Anyhow, I thought I'd check out the rest of the crowd to see if I knew anyone else who'd escaped the clutches of Victorian propriety for the evening."

Doc paused, impishly smirked and hushed his tone as if he was slowly telling us a secret:

"You just never know when information like that might come in handy."

Chuckling, he resumed like he couldn't get it out fast enough,

"Anyhow, I just happened to glance at a table off in a dark corner and there was Johnson hunched over a table talking to this other guy."

I had sat on my hands as long as I could. I vaulted up from my seat and confronted Doc:

"Johnson... in North Adams? No offence, Doc, but you *must've* been drinking weren't you? Johnson?

Doc waved his hand at me and said,

"None taken, miss, none taken...hear me out."

"Remember, I've sat across the poker table from this slime ball. I was drinking then too. I've seen him win and I've seen him lose. I took an instant dislike to him...and I always remember a man I hate. Chances are he's none too happy with me either. In my world it's more than prudent to recognize an enemy...it's necessary. So, believe me it *was* Johnson."

Doc put one of his arms around my waist and with it proceeded to drag me along with him on his excursion back and forth in front of the hearth as if this action would help to convince me he was right.

"This time, though, Johnson wasn't the brash, arrogant, rich dandy from the city with a beautiful wife on his arm. And it was obvious to me that he wasn't staying at the Wilson House either. He was hunched over, dirty, unshaven and quite shabbily dressed. The only thing he had on his arm this time was a bloke in much the same condition. But, somehow this fellow didn't seem to fit. Maybe it was his bearing. He wasn't hunched like Johnson. He sat ramrod straight the whole time. And although Johnson did the talking, this guy was clearly the boss. It was like Johnson was whining to him and the second man was quite disgusted. This bloke looked like he was wearing a costume. In fact, I think that's what initially drew my attention."

When Doc finally hesitated I took his hands in mine and faced him, escaping his grapple and concluding our sprint.

"Alright, Doc, alright."

When I pressed my advantage by retaking my seat I found it existed only in my mind. Undeterred, Doc used the interval to re-stoke his burners.

"Anyhow, I was so shocked that the fool could be so dumb... or maybe desperate...that he'd come to the village. I just had to share. So I took the opportunity to join Jeremiah and his friends at their table. Do you know who Jer's friends are? Course you don't, course you don't, stupid of me."

Doc stopped pacing, turned to face Ma and me and announced,

"Latham Winslow, Hugh Bradford and Jonas Hollister."

When Ma and I looked at each other and shrugged, Doc raised both hands above his head and shook them in an attempt to break the spell of ignorance which so obviously gripped us both. Exasperated, he plowed on,

"Winslow...Bradford... Hollister? Come on, folks. These chaps are progenies of three of the oldest and richest families in all of Massachusetts. Their forebears came over on the Mayflower, for heaven's sake."

This time it was Ma who cut in and tried to redirect our ever ebullient friend,

"Alright, Doctor Briggs, alright. Jeremiah's friends come from powerful families. But, d'ya' think ya' might get back ta' the Johnson story?"

"Oh, right...right. Well it's the fact that these gents are who they are that make the whole thing possible. Even if it goes wrong their families will never allow..."

Ma and I both screamed as one,

"WHAT THING???"

"The scheme we've hatched...the plot...don't you see? Of course you don't."

Any hopes Ma and I had that Doc would get to the point were quickly dashed as he plowed on:

"We spent the first few minutes speculating as to why Johnson'd take such a chance to show up in town. We decided my speculation that Johnson was on the run was indeed true. Further, if I remember your description of the second man in your vision correctly, the other gent must be his handler from Worcester. Evidently he received much the same treatment as Johnson from the Western Railroad power brokers because he was in the same shape."

"Anyhow, we decided that eliminating the only evidence connecting them to the three murders was the only way to save their asses. If they didn't there'd be nowhere to hide. In their minds either the law would get them or the Worcester bunch would."

"The irony is that if Johnson had simply allowed superstitions of the community to fester after having Ringo Kelley killed... Well, might've taken a week, maybe two but fear would've become so entrenched that there'd have been little the Captain or CJ could do about it and tunnel work would've ceased."

"But the desperate fool didn't. He spent the money and the *Transcript* convinced him the three big mouthed villagers were told *he'd* supplied it. Unfortunately for them, the *Transcript* gave Johnson *their* names too."

Doc paused just long enough to take a quick swig of his now tepid coffee and grimaced,

"Maeve, got any of that elixir of the gods hiding anywhere?"

While Ma went to the walnut display cupboard and poured Doc a splasheen of Da's precious Irish he continued,

"Hope those three guys aren't as stupid as they seemed or they just might have a problem."

'Doc smacked his lips in anticipation, turned Ma's offering bottoms up and held it out for a refill as he resumed,

"We decided that leaving a message at the Constabulary for the Captain might temporarily secure the safety of the three fools; but it wouldn't solve the problem. Evidence connecting the murders to Johnson and his scuzzy friend didn't *really* exist. When they were simply run out of town and not arrested, *they'd* know it too. Even so, while such a close call might convince Johnson to give up, the other guy looked the type who wouldn't. He's a cold bastard, folks. He'd find a way."

"Thank you, Maeve. Telling this story is thirsty work."

"So, a few more drinks and a lot more scheming, Jer, his boys and I thought we'd found a way to kill two birds with one stone: protecting the town criers from the fate their stupidity and greed had wrought and getting Johnson and the second bastard to convict *themselves*."

"And that's where things get interesting. You see, to pull it off we may need to bend a few laws."

At that point Doc paused succumbing to the call of the amber liquid that had been sloshing back and forth in the crystal tumbler he'd been waving and gave it another quick bottoms up.

"Slainte. Straight as an arrow, I am. Another, Maeve, please?"

Ma glanced at me quizzically. I could see she was beginning a slow burn for our guest. I, however, was quite interested by Doc's tale. And so, I returned a shrug, got up and poured another three fingers of Irish into Doc's empty tumbler.

"And we had a perfect group to pull it off. It's no secret Jeremiah and I love to stir the mustard. Wislow, Bradford and Hollister came here for adventure and contact with the netherworld. But our game requires one more member... you, Miss Virginia."

At first taken aback I quickly found myself intrigued.

"Me?"

"Johnson's terrified of you. In case you've forgotten, you scared the shite out of him at the Colgrove's New Year's Eve party."

I guess Ma had heard enough because she sprang from her chair, grabbed Doc's drink from his hand and began shooing him toward the door. If Ma hadn't been so genuinely enraged it would have been comical to see this short slip of a woman attempt to push this only slightly taller cannonball across the great room floor. Logic told me it couldn't happen. My eyes told me it did.

"That'll be just about enough, Doctor Samuel Briggs. It's quietly I've been listenin' ta' your story. I'll be listenin' no longer. I kept askin' myself why you were tellin' *us*. Now I know. Well, it's across the line ya've gone, ya' bloody gobshite. Those are two desperate murderers you're goin' after. Ya've said it yourself that they're ready ta' kill again; three more men if you're right. And ya' call this a game? Ya' want *my* daughter ta' play? Out wit' ya'...OUT."

Now at the door, Ma threw Docs outer garments at him. He caught his coat, but his hat and gloves escaped the bunch and fell to the floor. As Doc bent to gather them up he bellowed,

"But, Maeve, dear, dear woman..."

"OUT...."

"STOP!"

And then I softly said,

"Ma, please stop, please."

I hustled over and rescued Doc from eviction by putting just one hand lightly on her shoulder. She immediately turned to face me, fire still in her eyes. I was so close that she needed to crane her head back as far as it would go to look me in the eye.

What she beheld was a woman, not a girl. One corner of my mouth was turned up a smidge and my expression full of supplication.

"Ma, this home and everyone in it has been tested in a most grievous way this past year. The passion for justice that flows in our Irish blood has tormented every single one of us, and that includes CJ. There has been a pall over this house and this family that I fear will never leave until these murderers atone for their sins."

"They must pay, Ma, and you know it. If there's any way I can contribute to that outcome, I want...no I *need* to hear about it. Please, Ma, Let Doc finish... Please?"

Ma silently turned back to Doc and reached for his outerwear. As she hung up his coat Ma said with more than a touch of pride in her voice,

"Tis the image of Seanmháthair Saorla y'are, Virginia Maureen....in every way. I'll listen."

I led Doc back into the great room and handed him his tumbler of Jameson's. Ma and I sat together on the sofa. Resigned but still full of apprehension Ma said,

"Let's hear the rest."

Doc, who never let a little thing like being tossed out on his ear bother him, never missed a beat. He did, however, judiciously omit any further mention of my role and jumped forward. I guess he figured the more background he offered first the better.

"You'd be surprised what two bits'll buy in this village. To pull off our little game...sorry, Maeve...in order to set Johnson and the second man up to put the noose around their own necks, we'd need help from a few people with, shall we say, a specialized skill set. So we took a little walk over to see Dutchy Gregory...."

*Oh-oh...*

# Chapter 22

## Snagged, Bagged and Gagged

It was just 11:30 when I dismounted Hessey at the mouth of the bloody pit. The night air may have hinted of spring, but the chill breezes that swept down from the still snow-capped Mt. Greylock just to my southwest created perfect conditions which both invaded my clothing and seemed to push me from behind into the maw of the beast. Deep inside, the outflow of winds up the west shaft moaned and whined making the tunnel seem alive...and in pain.

The full moon winked as it peeked through fast moving clouds only momentarily illuminating my surroundings. It was the period of total blackness, however, that made me reluctant to tether Hessie any distance from me. She was my only means of escape and although a native of these hills, the setting was enough to give me goose flesh. I couldn't have felt more vulnerable...almost naked. But Doc's instructions had been quite clear. All I could do was wait...and think.

His plan depended heavily on Dutchy Gregory and his men, not exactly an encouraging prospect. Would they make their delivery...and on time?   I couldn't imagine Dutchy remaining sober long enough to pull it off.

It seemed to me just as likely that Dutch was passed out right now in the back room of his fix-it shop from too much Florida mountain white lightning.  Big Bill Flaherty may have torn apart the Old Black Tavern bar again and was locked up for the safety of both the village and the four constables it usually took to restrain him. Ribs Baker and his partner Smiler Racicot were probably in the middle of fleecing the last pence out of some poor pigeon stupid enough to not notice their teamwork across the poker table from him. And Jordy McSheen had probably wheedled his way for the night into the bed of some equally needy widow.

Part one of the plan, at least, seemed to be on track. Da's messenger knocked on our door at four o'clock.  The note he handed Ma apologized for the late notice and said Da and CJ would be tied up until very late at the constabulary. I don't know how Doc did it; either Da had bought Doc's lie...or he chose to.  More likely it was the latter. If I knew Da, he saw right through Doc but was intrigued by what he might be up to.  Either way, my confidence was much higher when it came to Da and CJ.

It was the crunching of gravel under the massive weight of the draught horses and the squeaking lorry they pulled that shook me from my ponderings. I could see neither the people driving nor the lorry until I was nearly run over. A quick flash of moonlight revealed Dutchy Gregory at the reigns and a cigar smoking Doctor Sam next to him high up on the driver's bench. The alacrity with which each of them descended the three steps needed to reach the ground told me that both, indeed, were sober. As they approached, their faces lit up with smiles communicating that they were having the time of their lives.

"Did you ever doubt us, Miss Ginger?"

When I crossed my arms, turned my head askance and glared down my nose at the gruesome twosome, Doc continued:

"Come on, have look see."

As Doc and Dutchy led me toward the rear, the sides of the storage bed were too high for even me to see over. It wasn't until the rear tailgate was lowered that Big Bill, Smiler, Ribs and Jordy were revealed sitting on a heavy canvas tarp. It appeared that Big Bill was attempting to flatten the lumps under the tarp with an axe handle. Even as I watched, he continued to hit the lumps with a "whomp, whomp" sound.  Each whomp was quickly followed by a muffled scream.

Big Bill's expression told me that he was also quite enjoying his part. Smiler and Ribs...not so much.  They might do just about anything for a stake in their next poker game, but their wincing each time Big Bill brought a descending blow upon the tarp told me they didn't particularly like it. Jordy was a lover not a fighter and couldn't even bring himself to watch.

*What a bunch.*

The quartet jumped down from the lorry allowing Dutchy to pull the tarp off the "lumps." What had been hidden underneath were two wriggling bodies; trussed hands, knees and feet. Their heads were covered with flower sacks and cinched securely with a rope around their necks. The inarticulate unwords they were evoking told me they'd been gagged as well.

Big Bill rapped them both on the soles of their boots and yelled,

"Shut y'er traps, friggin' dilberries."

When one of our guests let out a whining cry, Bill rapped him on the shins.

"Want another? I really like doin' this y' know."

At that the writing stopped and the protests stopped as well.

My incredulous look must have carried through the dimness because Dutchy said,

"Dija' think we was goin' a put 'em in a Brougham complete with footmen?"

Doc put an admonishing finger to pursed lips and waved Dutchy and me to follow him back toward the mouth of the tunnel. When we were far enough away, he was the first to speak,

"They don't know you're here and I don't want them to...yet."

"How in heaven did you ever do this without getting arrested? The Old Black Tavern is right in the middle of the village."

"Ah, but don't forget it's sometimes easier to hide a mugging in the middle of where other muggings are happening. The Tavern may face Main and State on two sides, but the other two are on dark, narrow alleys. There are fights, rollings and various kinds of illicit sexual activities going on there all night. There aren't enough constables in North Adams to keep up with it all. Truth be known, *they* won't even go in there.  So it was a perfect place to hustle the bastards onto the lorry without being seen."

Then Doc paused and gazed off to nowhere with that vacant stare of his, a dead giveaway he was reliving some special moment. He then chortled and resumed:

"Was actually quite easy. I'd already gotten their room number last night so I walked right to the front desk big as life. Told the clerk I'd been called to attend a man who'd taken ill...thought I was cooked when I realized I'd forgotten my bag. Anyways, he wasn't in the least curious about me...who was ill...or even what the man's problem might be. He simply pointed to the stairs, so off I went."

"When I got to Johnson's floor...haven't gone up so many stairs so quickly in years, I can tell you...wasn't even out of breath...Dutchy's crew had already come up the alley stairs and were waiting on the landing outside the locked fire door. When I opened it I could see the blokes were fully equipped for the task at hand, so I pointed out Johnson's room and went down to wait with Dutchy on the lorry."

Still a bit confused I asked,

"But that still doesn't explain how you got through town."

Obviously enjoying his plan of subterfuge, a very pleased Doc continued,

"Who in that alley is going to notice or care about a couple of bagged guys being tossed into the back of a lorry when they themselves are either banging some drunk on the head or invading the knickers of some whore?"

"Oh, gosh, Miss Ginger, I *am* sorry. Just got carried away for a moment."

I seriously doubted the sincerity of Doc's apology because he continued without waiting so much as a breath for my response. Actually, I was thoroughly amused by Doc's story and not at all surprised of his personal familiarity with the goings on in the seediest parts of our village.

"Anyway, from there it was just a short jaunt down State to the railroad yard...deserted on a Sunday night, I can tell you...and a left onto this rutted cow path they plan on naming Chestnut Street...bounced our guests around so hard the boys in the back nearly wet themselves with laughing."

"Once we made the right onto upper Church Street it was clear sailing. Johnson and his buddy could've screamed bloody murder. Nonetheless, Big Bill decided to keep them quiet as possible, if you know what I mean."

I just stood there mouth agape at first, but quickly regained my composure.

Clearly, Doc had been intentionally vague when he laid out his plan...and I hadn't bothered to ask. It had taken a scant few seconds to reassess the moral analysis I had with myself earlier in the day, but it seemed like minutes. The reality before me had filled in details my earlier musings had not...or would not. And I was surprised by them.

I guess I was as stupid as Cullen and his friends in the sense that I'd never really thought this whole thing through. But of this I was sure, Dutchy was right. Johnson and his coconspirator would not have simply accepted a ride here in a Brougham...even with attending footmen.

The vision of those two exiting such a grand carriage holding glasses of wine while footmen assisted was so absurd I grinned from ear to ear as I looked at Doc and said,

"I'm ready. Let's do it.

# Chapter 23

## And So It Came to Pass

Dutchy wasted no time signaling his men with a piercing whistle. Soon after, Big Bill and Jordy approached us, each carrying a passenger slung over his shoulder like a large sack of grain. The shifting and wriggling of Jordy's package nearly caused his knees to buckle, while Big Bill's passively accepted his ride. Observing Jordy's plight, Bill tapped Jordy's guy on the noggin with the axe handle he was still carrying in his other hand. Then he whispered something I couldn't hear to the man.

Let's just say Jordy now had an easier time of it.

I simply shook my head and struggled to conceal my giggles.

*This is starting to be fun.*

By the time the rest of us entered the mouth of the tunnel, Dutchy had already lit a brakeman's lamp illuminating our immediate surroundings. Walking into such drastic change from the near darkness outside was disorienting, almost painful. Crunching and squeaking sounds behind informed us that Smiler and Ribs had already turned around the lorry and were leaving.

Jordy and Big Bill unceremoniously flopped their burdens across the bed of the hand treadle car used by shift supervisors and hopped on. Doc sat sideways next to the treadle mechanism, feet dangling with inches to spare. My perch on the other side, however, was not so convenient. I needed to pull my feet underneath me and ride sidesaddle. Dutchy sat on what little room there was on front and lit the way.

Once everyone was situated Doc raised his free arm and silently pointed down the track. Big Bill and Jordy turned to face each other, grabbed the handles on the horizontal beam of the treadle and with considerable effort commenced the seesaw motion needed to engage the mechanism.

As the overburdened little railcar grumbled into motion so did one of our guests. The other let out a yelp but stopped when Big Bill kneaded him with the toe of his boot. My heart suddenly quickened, my breathing deepened and I began to tingle all over because the next part of our plan depended solely on me.

The efforts of Jordy's men were soon rewarded as the little rail car picked up pace. It seemed only a few minutes before Doc again raised his free arm, this time straight in the air, a sure sign we had arrived. The wheels screeched as the men applied the hand brake slowing us to a stop.

For the first few seconds the silence was deafening; we did nothing. But, as we became accommodated to our surroundings the moaning of the tunnel breezes again chilled both our bones and our being. My eyes were drawn to the ragged tunnel canopy of granite which glistened with the rivulets of water streaming down them.

Yes, I'd been here alright. This was the place of pain, suffering and death.

The last time I was here, however, this was the end of progress. But now there was no wall, no blast bench, no wooden tower on wheels; only the abject blackness ahead signifying a far greater depth.

Doc and Dutchy were first to disembark and took their places behind the car. I went to the front so that Dutchy's lamp illuminated me against the midnight backdrop. Once positioned, I nodded.

*Saints Patrick and Colmcille be with me. What do I do now?*

Jordy and Big Bill proceeded to unwrap their packages and stood them up. Jordy had Johnson by the scruff of the neck while the other man, finding himself completely untethered, quickly turned only to see his huge tormentor smiling down at him while menacingly holding the axe handle with one hand and tapping it into his other.

"Welcome to the Hoosac Tunnel, mate."

Both men had been absorbed with their abductors until Bill spoke. Only then did they swivel their heads around and truly comprehend their plight. What they beheld was darkness leading "there" in both directions and a "here" chiseled from Hell itself.

When I inevitably came into view, each saw a different woman. Johnson's companion laughed and said,

"What the hell is this?"

Johnson, on the other hand fell to his knees, began to sob and screeched,

"She's the devil's handmaiden... She's a witch."

"It's not the divil, I'm servin', you dodgy scoundrel. But it's ta' the divil you'll be goin' when I've had done with ya."

I stretched to my full height and took the few steps necessary to approach my detractor. He'd soon know just, "who the hell *this* was." But the closer I got, the more an inky dark shade wafted from his being and reached out to me.

*Not this night...I'll not be dictated to by the likes o'*
*you.*

I backed off to safety and glowered down at him. The foundation of his arrogance had begun to crack. He'd felt the contact too...and he'd been shaken by it. He knew that I knew. In some way unfathomable to him... he'd told me.

*Yes, I've seen your soul.*

"Y're at the root of it all, you evil man. Your shade is the blackest I've seen. There's a deeper hole than this in hell waitin' for you. And I'm here ta' show ya' the way."

No sooner had I finished than I was shocked to hear voices from behind me blend with the tunnel breeze,

"Why did you have me killed?"

Then a second,

"You didn't need to murder me... I didn't need to die."

And a third,

"I'm in hell because you trapped me to murder...and for what?"

Then the three together,

"You must pay."

I'd felt no presence. Those weren't the voices of Brinkman, Nash and Kelley.

*Jeremiah.*

I looked at Doc with a questioning glance and had returned to me a shrug that said it all. Doc had enlisted Jeremiah and his friends. This was their part.

*Aaaaaggggghhhhhhhh!*

When I looked to Johnson, he was cowering on the tunnel floor in the fetal position whimpering. But, for the dark man the spell had been broken.

"So what is this...some fuckin' party trick? Is that all you've got?"

He turned to stalk out of the tunnel but had forgotten Big Bill who promptly jammed the end of his axe handle into the dark man's gut knocking the wind out of him. The dark man immediately dropped to join Johnson on the tunnel floor... unbowed, but nonetheless in some distress.

As he gasped on the ground I became filled with conflicting feelings. My initial anger with Jeremiah was supplanted with love; love for my dear friend who, for all of his good intentions, would never really understand...And what to do next.

*Seanmáhthair... Saorla....*

Just then the palm of my left hand warmed and I remembered the divination stick I'd carried with me. I wasn't sure why I'd felt drawn to bring it. Did I really think I was going to point it at Johnson and shout some incantation? These two certainly didn't know what it was. For them my riding crop would have had the same effect.

Thoughts of such naiveté both relaxed me and caused my smiling face to flush.

The stick intensified its call to me. Its warmth was alarming but at the same time compelling. After all, the last time I had experienced the divination stick's potential, only some feeling... no, it was more than that...some guide...had helped me avoid a disastrous choice.

But this time was different. I felt the warmth of the divination stick spreading from my hand throughout my entire being. I now knew what I needed to do. I knew where I needed to go.

I approached the two disgusting creatures while holding my stick in front of me. Neither was paying any attention, but it didn't matter. When I came into contact with the outer reaches of their shades I didn't recoil, I allowed them to engulf me. But this time the evil within them was absorbed by the warmth within me. This time I was in control.

The granite tunnel walls became fluid and the light of Dutchy's lamp dimmed only to be replaced by an eerie twilight. The tunnel walls were solid again but loose rocks were strewn about and my head nearly touched the ceiling; the tunnel's end a scant few feet away.

We had arrived.

Johnson and the dark man had accompanied me on this journey and were standing nearby, unscathed but completely disoriented. It was only when they heard a voice call out to them...a voice they both knew... a voice from the grave itself, that they realized the direness of their predicament.

"Ned... Billy...I'm sorry. I really am. But those bastards from the Western Railroad...they own me. It's either you or me. Forgive me."

Terror gripped both men as the flash of the black powder fuse "psssst" by them racing toward its goal of destruction. They tried to run toward the source of the voice, but their boots proved useless, slipping in the loose stones. Johnson fell and when the dark man stepped over him Johnson screamed,

"Cousins, come back. Help, help...You prick, Cousins."

Over his shoulder the dark man yelled back,

"Fuck you, Johnson. This is all your fault."

And then it happened.

A brilliant flash, quickly followed by a thunderous hot wind from hell rolled Johnson along the ground, but tossed Cousins like a rag doll against the tunnel wall. Flying shards of shattered rock filled the air flaying the flesh of the doomed men; their final consciousness the ceiling collapse squeezing one last scream from their lungs and crushing their bones and skulls.

And then we were back.

The blood curdling screams that greeted me reverberated off the tunnel wall. They belonged to the two rolling, writhing beings: one clawing at his face, the other pounding the granite shards of the tunnel floor. The blood they shed, however, was only self-inflicted from their actions.

The faces of the others around me expressed fear, shock... and, in the case of Doc...amusement.

When I addressed the gathering, it was in a calm, surreal tone I hadn't intended, let alone known was possible.

"They will atone. They will pay. There will be justice."

It was as if lightning had struck Johnson and Cousins. Both stopped to look at the source of the statement; then jumped to their feet. The dark man pushed

Jordy so hard that he fell and clambered into the tunnel's deep abyss. Johnson darted by Big Bill slipping and stumbling toward the tunnel's entrance. Their escape had taken everyone by such surprise that no one could intervene. Then I exclaimed,

"Let them go. They'll no longer be able to run from who they are...or what they are. Let them go."

And they did.

# Chapter 24

## How Could We Know?

Our group may have lost two members as Johnson fled in one direction and the dark man the other, but it gained four as Jeremiah and his three friends emerged from the darkness to join us. Jeremiah was grinning ear to ear. He'd seen it before. But this time he had expected it and obviously enjoyed the show. His friends, on the other hand, had clearly gotten a little more than they bargained for. All three hung back and acted as little children hiding behind their mother's skirt.

Although still feeling the effects of my ordeal, their reaction struck me as most amusing and I laughed,

"Jeremiah, what a diabolical man you are."

Quite relieved at my greeting, Jeremiah stepped toward me and we embraced, albeit tentatively. When I whispered into his ear,

"Ego sum remux, meus frater. Pacis vobis,"

Jeremiah released our embrace, looked me squarely in the eye and responded,

"Pacis vobis quoque."

Without another word, we both knew...

"Ahem."

When I turned to the source of the interruption I saw a more than slightly antsy Doctor Sam standing next to the side of the hand car. Big Bill and Jordy had already gotten on, had the treadle bar in hand and were ready to go.

"Do you two think you could finish this a bit later? I, for one would surely like to be outside for the next act. How about you two? Anyways, Miss Virginia, your services may be required to apply the coup de grace. Let's go."

So, on we jumped...all nine of us.

The folly of this enterprise quickly became obvious. No matter how hard Jordy and Big Bill labored, they could not get the cart to budge. Everyone quickly looked first to the person beside them, next to the person across. Then Jeremiah gently touched my shoulder and said,

"C'mon guys, off."

The next thing I knew the little rail car rocked and Jeremiah Colgrove, Latham Winslow, Hugh Bradford and Jonas Hollister were behind propelling the little rail car toward its destination. The start more than enough, Big Bill and Jordy took over increasing our speed. As Jeremiah and his friends receded into the darkness our lamp left behind I saw the four waving to me.

*Now wasn't* that *the most expensive push in the history o' this railroad?*

When we arrived I both was and wasn't surprised to see Da and CJ just outside the tunnel's mouth waiting for us. Other constables were milling around as well and the Constabulary's Black Maria had replaced the lorry.

As I jumped off the cart I brushed off my dress, shrugged and offered a wry grin to Da.

*Ya' didn't buy Doc's story for even one minute, did ya', my most wonderful father?*

All six feet and fourteen stone of that wonderful father simply nodded, hands on hips...and chilled me with "that stare." Clearly, if Doc's play in four parts had backfired, the whole lot of us would have been shown the *inside* of the Black Maria...me included.

But it had, I mean it must have. If it hadn't...well I'd be more than chilled by Da's look right now.
In contrast, CJ was standing next to Da, arms crossed; grinning broadly as he slowly shook his head from side to side. I ran to his embrace. He kissed me on the cheek and said excitedly into my ear,

"We've got him, Ginger...It's all over."

CJ then took my hand and led me to the back of the patrol wagon where Lemuel Johnson, scraped and cut from head to toe, cowered in his torn clothes at the feet of a rather perplexed Father Lynch.

"Father please... forgiveness...please. I did it. I had those men killed. I did it...Just protect me from that witch."

When Father Lynch saw CJ and me he barked over Johnson's constant bray,

"Viginia Maureen O'Leary, what in the name of God have ya' done ta' this man?"

And I answered,

"Why nothin'... nothin' at'all, at'all, your Riverence."

Then I beamed a smile so broad and flushed so brightly that I thought I'd burst,

"Now, didn't he do it ta' himself."

It was now Father Lynch's turn to smile. However, it wasn't until two constables had taken Johnson in charge and locked him away inside the patrol wagon that a now pensive but still skeptical Father Lynch walked over to me and quietly said,

"I'll bet he did, lass, I'll bet he did."

No other words passed among Father Lynch, CJ and me as we walked back to the tunnel where Da was still animatedly raving at Doc.

"D'ya have any idea how foolish and dangerous it'is what y'ave done here? Not ta' mention illegal?"

Da counted off on his fingers for emphasis,

"Let's see: Conspiracy, kidnappin', assault... And worst off, lyin' ta' me... your friend, ya bloody gobshite."

"But what I could strangle ya' for... ya', ya'... I mean throttle your neck like a bloody chicken for... was involving me daughter. If this had blown up in your face I'd a' had ta' 'rest me own daughter. Goddamn ya', Doc."

"Y'are just bloody lucky it worked, I'm sayin'."

As we approached I could hear Da's frustration before I could see it. Once we arrived I completely disarmed Da with two words,

"Ma knew..."

Da pivoted to me,

"What?"

"I'm telling you, Da...Ma knew...and she approved. Doc came to the house this morning and we talked it over."

Of course, I didn't tell Da all of the details Doc *had left out* this morning, but it was just a white lie. After all, I had to save Doc. And from the way things were going, he surely needed saving.

"Virginia Maureen... Virginia Maureen... Virginia..."

Suddenly, I found myself almost smothered by policeman's blue. The bear hug now squeezing the wind from my lungs was far more dangerous than anything I'd encountered this whole night. As Da released me enough to take a breath he said,

"Am I the only one who *didn't* know?"

"Not quite, Da. CJ didn't either. Don't you get it? You couldn't know. And I just heard you count off to Doc the reasons why. What say you *thank him* instead compiling reasons to hang him. It worked, Da. It's over. We got Johnson to confess everything to the whole bunch of you."

Da released me and turned only to see a completely unintimidated Doc Briggs grinning ear to ear.

"How about you give me a hug, Captain?"

And then it happened. A rumbling so deep in the mountain I knew it could only mean one thing.

"Da, where's Jeremiah and his friends?"

As the dust and silt cloud that I knew had to come belched from the mouth of that damned bloody pit, Da answered,

"Who?"

# Chapter 25

## We Simply Must!

"Jeremiah, Da. Jeremiah and three of his friends from Harvard were part of this. They couldn't fit on the rail car so they were left to walk out. Da, how could we know?" I cried.

CJ was already on his way into the tunnel and with him were Big Bill and Jordy.

"We'll get them, Ginger," CJ called out.

"Not without me, you won't."

Da tried to stop me with one of his massive hands on my shoulder, but I looked back and gave Da such a glare that he withdrew it and said grimly,

"Take Doc."

As I caught up with the others I could hear Da behind me barking orders at the few remaining constables,

"Go back ta' the village and sound the alarum. Get Northkutt's ass outa' bed and tell 'im ta' get the tunnel workers out here. There's been a collapse. Go."

I paused for just a second and looked over my shoulder, catching Da's eye and he smiled,

"I'm staying here, Ginger. Someone's gotta' organize this lot...Get Jeremiah, me girl."

The silt storm that had been belching from the tunnel opening had already diminished by the time we entered. However, there was still enough residual air born poison to make everyone gag as Doc unsuccessfully struggled between coughs to light the brakeman's lamp.

But wasn't there intermittent light already ahead of us? It was diffused by the dust and bounced off the ceiling, the ground; this wall, then that. There was neither rhyme nor reason to its motion, only distress.

Was it getting stronger? By the time I could tell, disjointed coughs not our own and sounds of gravel being displaced by several scuffing feet joined us.

They all made it...all four of them. But, nothing was said. The air was still too acrid, their condition too dire. Big Bill was the only one of us strong enough to assist Jeremiah whose lamp smashed on the tunnel floor. Jeremiah's friends were already leaning on each other and shook off further assistance. Doc proceeded to lead the way as was his wont and CJ brought up the rear making sure we all got out.

Once freed from the tunnel's noxious atmosphere we all crashed onto any open space we could find. We had become the tunnel workers of that fateful day when Ned Brinkman and Billy Nash were murdered just over a year ago. We hacked, wretched and struggled to maintain our grip on consciousness for what seemed an eternity, but were in actuality only a few minutes.

One by one we were finally able to stand. One by one we looked back at the tunnel with fear and then at each other with disgust because we all knew that soon someone would have to go back in. There was a man back in there. Granted, he was as evil a person as I had ever encountered; but he was a human being nonetheless. And at least some of us would need to reenter this deathtrap.

*And I knew who.*

I was milling around with the fingers of my hands interlaced behind my neck when I noticed Da double timing up the hill from the engineer's shack with an anxious look on his face. Still yards away he called out,

"Everyone accounted for? Everyone alright?"

CJ was still coughing a bit, but ever the officer, straightened up and reported to his superior,

"Jeremiah and his three friends are all here, Captain. The dust nearly got them, but they're here. Our group is accounted for."

"Is that it, Sergeant? What of Johnson's partner?"

When CJ looked at me with confusion, I answered for him,

"Still in there, Da... He ran away from us and headed farther in...way in."

Da patted me on the shoulder and said,

"Well it's fair play ta' him if he *is* trapped, I say. I'll not lose one man searchin' for the likes o' him."

*But, I know...*

"But, Da..."

He roared,

"Ginger, I'll hear none of it."

Normally I'd run for a hiding place when Da talked to me this way. But on this night I knew...I just knew. It had to be me. It had to be CJ. It had to be Da. *We* had to find the dark man.

Thinking he'd silenced me Da approached slowly and while facing me put one hand on each of my shoulders. He looked me squarely in the eye, smiled and gently said,

"Now listen, Virginia Maureen, we'll get 'im. He's not goin' anywhere. Let's wait until the tunnel clears. By then Northkutt and the tunnel workers'll be here. They'll bring 'im out. There's no reason for any of us ta' risk goin' back in."

*But, there is.*

I reached up and took each of Da's hands in mine; my left hand still holding the divination stick. And when Da looked down to see it all resistance dissolved. I brought both of his hands above my heart and pressed them to my breast. Then I returned Da's manner and almost whispered,

"Now listen to me, my most revered father...please. I've touched this man's soul and he's touched mine. 'Tis true, he's a vile and evil creature. My concern is not for him. It's for CJ. I don't know why, Da, but he must confront this man while he still lives. You and I need to be there. And we need to go now. He doesn't have much time left, Da. We need to go NOW."

Da's resistance melted. Evidently he saw what Ma had seen earlier today when I begged her to trust me. I may not be the reincarnation of Saorla, but I was definitely heir to all she represented.

Without further elaboration Da and I headed toward the mouth of the tunnel. CJ either overheard our exchange or simply had a sense of what he needed to do because by the time we arrived he'd joined us. But, so had Jeremiah and Doc.

Although Jeremiah's nose was still flowing freely and his cherry red eyes full of anxiety, he rasped,

"Let's get the son of a bitch. This whole thing would be over if he'd run out instead of in."

Doc, always quickest on the uptake looked first to Da, then to me and said to the woozy Jeremiah,

"Jeremiah... Jer...you've done enough. Besides, I need help *here* taking care of your friends and filling in Northkutt. The Captain, CJ and Virginia will be just fine, son... just fine."

Although visibly relieved, Jeremiah still looked to us with supplicating eyes.

"We'll be alright, Jeremiah. You're a true friend. We'll find him."

At that the Da, CJ and I turned and entered the tunnel.

I was taken aback that the breezes of earlier evening which served to entice me into the tunnel had now reversed and seemed to be telling us to stay away. But were they? The ambient whistling and moaning of west shaft drafts no longer conflicted with those entering and served to scour the tunnel's gut of all but the tiniest amounts of dust.

Da found the supply of brakeman's lamps neatly arranged on the storage table to our right and quickly passed one to each of us.

"We'll each be needin' our own lamp ta' see inta' every cranny. We wouldn't want ta' be missin' him, now would we?"

*Yeah, and if one ...or even two of us get trapped, the person left will still have light.*

Da and CJ took charge of the treadle bar. I sat on front and positioned the lamps so that they lit our way brightly. Only the three of us aboard, the little rail car's progress was nearly effortless. Nevertheless, machine sounds of the power mechanism and the rumble of steel wheels grinding on iron rails resonated causing my ears to ring.

We soon reached the setting of the so recently concluded act three of Doc's scheme so I raised my hand and waved. The car's brakes screeched as they had such a short time ago and slowed our car to a stop.

"This is the place. This is where we brought them."

"We'll be getting' off and walkin' from here, then. The collapse could be just outa' sight or it could be a couple hundred feet," Da said.

We each took charge of our own lamp and proceeded into the unknown at the same excruciatingly slow pace we used over a year ago on our first adventure into this God forsaken hole.

Sounds of the rail car were replaced by the crunch-crunching of the tunnel floor by six unsynchronized feet. Whistling breezes of the west shaft were again pushed to the fore. We knew we must be getting closer to the collapse because the atmosphere became thicker and more irritating with each step. My eyes picked up grit and my nose began to run. CJ sneezed, surprising everyone and Da's, "Bless you," broke the tension we all felt and we laughed.

"Keep a sharp eye, now. It shouldn't be too much farther," CJ said, but we all agreed.

What he really meant was that we had reached the place of danger...a place where we could easily become victims ourselves.

If our pace had been slow before; now we almost crept. We weren't just looking for evidence of tonight's collapse but also for new weaknesses in the shaft ready to cause another.

So, on we pressed. Step after step. Turn of the lamp...up, down, side to side. My burning eyes couldn't even be certain of what they saw. Nor could I be sure how far we had gone. It all blended...more of the same. What mattered was what we would inevitably find.

*Be alive, ya' gombeen man...Live just a while longer.*

And then, there it was. We all saw it together. Not the end of the tunnel. No blast bench. No wooden gantry on wheels, nothing normal. Just an enormous pile of rocks mixed with gravel. One side of the shaft had simply given way burying the tracks and any access to what lay beyond.

"Porridge stone." Da exclaimed. "Northkutt told me they'd seen the last of it some five hundred feet back."

And then CJ added,

"From the look of it...so many granite boulders mixed in with the mush, a thin layer of granite must have been holding back the mush... and it gave way. There's no way anyone could have known."

At that, all three of us looked behind us and then at each other, leaving unspoken our fear that there may be more of this behind. In any event, there was nothing to be done about it except find the dark man as soon as possible and get the hell out of here. So we continued quickly now to the edge of the collapse.

And there it was.

A hand...that was all, just a hand. Its fingers were flexing and releasing...grabbing handfuls of the tunnel floor in a futile attempt to extricate the body attached to it from its crushing, smothering shroud.

All three of us tore feverously into the debris: Da and CJ lifting boulders and tossing them aside; I digging into the pebble laden muck with my bare hands. We were soon as soaked in sludge as the person we had just unveiled. The difference was this man was cut to shreds and bleeding and his ears oozed a thick orange-gray suspension. When we turned him over, there were grimaces of pain and faltering coughs which puffed breaths of dust. His lungs, now free to expand, attempted a life affirming breath; but instead gasped and coughed out death portending clots of blood.

I tore off a piece of my dress and used it to clean off the man's face. With each swipe more of the man's countenance was revealed. It quickly became evident that this indeed was the dark man...the man Johnson had called...

"Cousins...General Charles A. Cousins."

"I know this man." CJ screamed.

In an instant, my darling Conal's kind and loving face was distorted into an ugly hateful mask.

"You killed my men, you incompetent, heartless son of a bitch. You nearly killed me."

He picked up a boulder and took a step toward Cousins so quickly I could hardly comprehend his intent, let alone intervene.  Da, on the other hand, deftly plucked the boulder from the much smaller CJ and tossed it aside.

CJ dropped to his knees, covered his face with his hands and cried heart wrenching tears of both anguish and anger.

I ran to CJ and dropped to my knees beside him. My attempt at a consoling embrace was met with a violent rebuff.  I had no choice but to kneel back on my haunches and listen to the symphony of death and self-torment filling this devil's temple... this horrible, horrible hole in the ground.

It was then that Da calmly and quietly spoke,

"CJ...Conal, me boy..."

Conal cut off Da and moaned,

"I swore on the souls of my men that if I ever found this man I'd avenge them. He used us, Captain...and when we were blown apart...when we were maimed...he just walked away like we were so much garbage."

"Ah, but 'tis the way of the world, now isn't it, Conal John Mulcahy."

"But could ya' tell me how usin' that rock would accomplish your goal? Think, son. What could ya' do ta' this man that he hasn't already done ta' himself. Surely ya' can see he's dyin' in a most terrible way. In your dreams could ya' have imagined worse?"

"Let it go, Conal... Let it go. "Tis time ta' heal... 'Tis time ta' bury our dead and trust God's justice."

It took a few more minutes, but CJ finally got up, reached out to me with both hands and drew me to join him; our embrace sweeter than any we'd shared. He then approached Cousins whose eyes, although glassy had comprehended the whole scene as it played before him,

"Who are you?" he asked.

And Conal answered proudly,

"Captain Conal J. Mulcahy of the twenty-seventh Massachusetts."

Cousin managed a wry smile and croaked,

"Go to hell....."

And died.

# Chapter 26

## Friday, April 27, 1866

CJ and I had just seen Jeremiah and his friends off from State Street depot. Ironically, the route back to Cambridge would take them to Pittsfield and a link with the southern route along the Western Railroad. Latham Winslow, Hugh Bradford and Jonas Hollister had cajoled Jeremiah into a trip to North Adams in search of adventure and they certainly had found it.

"Well, what do you think, Conal?"

CJ took me by the arm as we turned to leave,

"I think it will take about twenty-four hours for all of Boston to know about you. Those three won't even be off the train and they'll be telling anyone who'll listen about their last few days."

I nodded in agreement and added,

"Well, let's hope Jeremiah can temper the hyperbole. After all, what did they actually see?"

At that, CJ burst out in a belly laugh that filled the air and blurted only one word,

"Right."

"Ginger, you *did* sit next to me last night in the Colgrove's dining room didn't you?"

I poked CJ in the arm with my free fist. He feigned pain and said,

"It took almost an hour before any of those blokes could even look you in the eye... Too bad they don't know you like I do."

CJ released my arm and took two quick steps in front of me before I could poke him again and laughed,

"You'll not strike me again, woman."

His attempt to lighten my mood worked, but only just. Seeing that, CJ took my hand in his and gave it a quick kiss. When his eyes met mine, the love and understanding they showed helped much more than the banter. We rejoined arms and continued our walk,

"You know, Conal, those three are incorrigible. They're convinced I took Johnson and Cousins to the brink of hell and brought them back, when all I did was...um...provide the opportunity for them to go themselves."

At that *I* gave a loud belly laugh.

"But, how they ever came to believe that spirits caused the tunnel wall to collapse killing Cousins is beyond me. Hidden porridge stone did it plain and simple, didn't it?"

CJ smiled and said,

"Sounds like you're the one who needs convincing."

We both laughed and headed up the hill to the Constable station. No sooner had we descended the stairs and opened the door than the despondent wailing of one Lemuel Johnson assaulted us. Doc met us at the door to Da's office and the three of us entered together.

"Well, Captain, it'll take another minute or two, but that should shut him up for a while."

It did and it did.

Johnson's guilt continued to consume him. He believed he had seen hell and was going there. He couldn't stop confessing his guilt to anyone and everyone who came near him or his cell. It was pitiful to see him on his knees, even confessing to the boy who brought his meals from the Old Black Tavern.

The only person who had any effect on him at all was Father Lynch. Although not Catholic, Johnson was adamant that Father was the only one who could grant him salvation. What the good father couldn't get through to Johnson was that he was only God's agent on earth and absolution was solely contingent upon Johnson's sorrow for what he had done, the pain he had caused and the deaths he had ordered.

It was clear Father Lynch wasn't convinced by the man's performance. Every day he'd leave Johnson's cell shaking his head. Father Lynch, like the rest of us, believed that the only thing Johnson was sorry for was he got caught. Ned Brinkman, Billy Nash and Ringo Kelley meant no more to him now than they ever did. And *we* were all sure that if he hadn't been given a taste of what he'd actually done, there'd be three more murders on Johnson's "conscience." So, the actual reason for Johnson's manic contrition was plain and simple. He retained enough of his puritan upbringing to be terrified for his own ultimate fate.

Father's visits calmed Johnson for a while, but inevitably he'd start up again. And so, more for us than for Johnson, Doc administered periodic doses of laudanum to calm him down. Indeed, it was the *only* time those at Constable Station got any peace.

"Thanks, Doc. Johnson's been drivin' us off our nut since early this mornin'. Everyone ready for lunch?"

"Not quite yet, Captain."

Doc plunked his black bag on Da's desk with a dull heavy sounding thud. Opening its jointed mouth revealed a thick stack of folded newspapers had been stuffed into it.

"Take a look at these first and see if you still have an appetite."
Doc pulled out the papers and as he handed copies to Da, CJ and me he said,

"Every single newspaper in Berkshire County has had banner headlines and articles about the capture and confession of Johnson. District Attorney Ainsley had been quite forthcoming of the case against Johnson, implicating the Western Railroad and hinting at powerful political connections in Boston."

"I couldn't help thinking that this was a tremendous mistake, so I telegraphed some friends of mine who live in cities along the southern route and asked them to send me copies of the editorial issues of their daily papers. These came in on the morning train."

"Folks, methinks we have a problem."

Da, CJ and I first read and then passed around copies of the Springfield Daily Republican, Worcester Daily Times, The Westfield News, and The Boston Herald. Every single editorial cited the same tired argument that the

Hoosac Tunnel excavation was a failed enterprise and Johnson was being used as a scapegoat.

The problem was this argument still worked in these cities and except for Westfield any one of them was more populous than the entire Berkshire County. And although small, Westfield was important because it showed how universally the rest of the politically powerful southern region of the state had taken up sides against us.

Da whistled, CJ began pacing and I sat down,

"We've got a problem, alright," Da said.

After thinking it over for a few seconds I got up and addressed everyone,

"What exactly is this problem? Johnson's gone 'round the bend. Every minute of every day is torture for him and will be to the end of his days. Putting a noose around his neck will only transfer his soul to a different one, won't it?"

The smiles on the faces and knowing looks of the other three made me immediately flush...and I wasn't sure why. It was CJ who spoke first,

"Ah, Virginia, what you say is true, so true. But, Mr. Ainsley has turned what should have been a quiet easily won murder trial into a referendum on the Hoosac Tunnel and the northern route versus the southern route.

He has, in fact, resurrected an issue that just about everyone wants to see go away. Why he's chosen to rub their noses in the shite is beyond me."

Then Doc added,

"The tunnel is making excellent progress now and will be finished in the next couple years. The northern route will become a reality, Miss Virginia. When that day arrives every single politician who opposed the project will be doing damage control shouting to the four winds how they were for it all along. In fact, if you read between the lines the political pendulum has started to swing already."

"Not one politician is cited or quoted in any of these articles or editorials. The editors simply rehash the same old tired argument that has been used since 1852. A Johnson trial based upon the charges Mr. Ainsley has alleged could open up a huge Pandora's Box none of them is willing to chance."

Then CJ drove in the final spike,

"The people of North Adams who would have had their futures stolen deserve to see this man pay in a tangible way. Every single tunnel worker who toils in that hellhole every day deserves to see a result. Remember our friend Napoleon Blaise? Mr. Ainsley should have tried Johnson as an ambitious loose cannon operating without restraint. I fear that even though what Mr. Ainsley says is true, his overreach will make any result impossible."

"So what do we do?"

As things turned out, the answer to my question didn't matter because I had no sooner asked the question than two enormous men preceded district attorney Ainsley into Da's office. Their dark blue top coats were open revealing equally dark suits, stark white shirts and black ties. If their mode of dress hadn't screamed "uniform" then the shiny brass shields pinned to the left breast pocket of their suit jackets did. Once inside they parted, flanking the doorway and joined their hands in front of them. There was no greeting in their expressions as they blankly stared at the back wall of Da's office.

A more than slightly rattled Mr. Ainsley skulked to Da's desk. He was holding a large white envelope in his hand and said,

"Captain O'Leary, we need to talk... alone."

Da nodded and made eye contact with each of us. As we left the door was abruptly closed behind us. We gathered around the wood stove located between the captain's and the duty sergeant's offices. I was in the process of filling mugs for each of us from the pot on top of the stove when raised voices rattled the etched glass of Da's office door. And then there was quiet.

The captain's office door then flew open with Da occupying the doorway.

"Sergeant Mulcahy, come in here please."

This was no question. It was an order. CJ looked at me with apprehension on his face and joined Da closing the door behind them.

Always a master of understatement, Doc Briggs exclaimed,

"Well, that can't be good; the Captain has called for his lawyer."

Both of us forgot about our coffee while we strained to hear any snippet of the much quieter conversation now transpiring inside. The time we waited until the door opened again seemed interminable, but the clock on the wall had only ticked off five minutes.

This time it banged off the wall and a scowling Captain O'Leary emerged carrying the cell block keys. The two suited mountains followed and the trio walked briskly to the corridor which housed the cells. I could see CJ leaning arms crossed against the back wall of the office while Ainsley paced fretfully back and forth.

CJ looked at me and said nothing. He didn't need to. The involuntary shaking of his head said it all.

From here I could hear the jingle of the keys, the squeak of the door opening and the clunk of its closing. The clunk which sounded somehow so final proved to be. What next emerged from the cell corridor was a flaccid glassy eyed Lemuel Johnson being supported under each arm. Johnson's legs unsuccessfully attempted to keep up with the stride frequency of the two suits as they swept him out of the station and up the stairs.

I thought Da would tear Ainsley apart when he said,

"Thank you for your cooperation, Captain O'Leary."

Doc shook his head and mirthlessly smirked. I, on the other hand, could only gape.

Lunch was definitely going to wait.

# Chapter 27

## Lunch Is Served

Mr. Ainsley had no sooner left than Da motioned us into his office and closed the door. We all assumed our usual perches: Da sitting in the squeaky chair behind his desk, CJ holding up the outer basement wall by leaning up against it arms crossed, and Doc and I occupying the two visitors chairs in front of Da's desk.

"Well, ain't that a revolting development."

I swear if Da had a gun he would have shot Doc.

Instead Da glowered, "Ya' know, Doc...sometimes...

I thought it best to interrupt Da at this point. Neither CJ nor I wanted to see him get any more wound up than he was...I know Doc didn't.

"So what happened? Who were those guys?"

Da picked up two pieces of paper off his desk. In his right hand he held a letter bearing some official letterhead and in the left what was clearly a court document.

"These are what happened," Da rumbled, "and those two sides o' beef were troopers from the Massachusetts State Police."

When Doc and I returned confused looks, Da shook the letter in his right hand,

"From what I can gather here they're a new agency. Shortly after Appomattox the governor decided that Boston should have a legitimate way ta' exert statewide influence. If those two are typical, I'd say the governor has his own private little army."

Before either Doc or I could react Da leaned forward over his desk and said,

"Save the looks, save comments. This letter is from State's Attorney Fredrikson. He's Attorney General Reed's number one man. It's all in here. What it comes down ta' is Governor Bullock is sick and tired o' the northern route-southern route rivalries."

"Fredrikson says here that... 'The State of Massachusetts is assuming responsibility for disposition of the Lemuel Johnson case'... and... 'you are ordered forthwith to transfer custody of one Lemuel Johnson to the Massachusetts State Police for transport to...' on and on and so forth."

Da then tossed the document in his left hand up into the air and let it flutter, landing on his desk.

"And CJ tells me that piece o' shite gives 'em the authority. It's a warrant from the State Court o' Massachusetts."

At that Doc sarcastically chanted,

"Hip, hip, hurray for Forrest L. Ainsley."

This time Da didn't bristle, he covered his eyes with his hands, leaned back in his chair and laughed out loud,

"Fook it.... We've done all we can... Fook 'em all."

And after only a brief pause he rose from his chair and said one word,

"Lunch."

Clearly, Da had said it all.

*Fook 'em all.*

"It's on me," Doc offered. "Let's go to the Wilson House. Today, steak's on the menu."

I couldn't help retorting,

"For lunch?"

Doc patted his bulbous abdomen and said,

"Just a small one, my dear Virginia, just a snack."

So, we headed down Bank Street and onto Main. Once we crossed to the north side we took a left and headed west. From that point the walk to the Wilson House was short. As we ascended the Wilson House stairs to the second floor a magnificent but completely empty dining room emerged before us. The maître'd was nowhere to be found, but a waitress did approach and inquired,

"Four for lunch or dinner?

It simultaneously hit all of us that we didn't have a clue what time it was. Our expressions must have betrayed our thoughts because the waitress followed with,

"It's two thirty, folks."

We all laughed and Doc said,

"Lunch will be fine, Shirley. Oh... and open the bar, if you please."

The rest of the afternoon flew by as our "lunch" became a round table discussion of the past year or so complete with analyses of the would haves, should haves, or could haves mixed in with a few if onlys. Our interaction was wistful and impersonal, however, not self-deprecating or chiding. It was almost as if we were talking about ancient history. It seemed to be the only safe way we could lick our wounds without being overcome by them.

And it was the creature that helped the process along. We kept time by counting the empty drink glasses in front of us... and even for me there were a few. With each glass the discussion flowed a little better... to a point... and

I had reached it. Fatigue began to grab my eyelids as I noticed the lengthening shadows visible through the dining hall window.  For me at least, it was time to go.

As I stood to leave I said to Da,

"Ma will be waiting for us. Do you want me to tell her what happened and that you'll be a bit late?"

That little woman was probably the only living being who could make Da quake with fear. To be late for one of Ma's dinners without notice... well, I shuddered to think of it.  It was, indeed, time to go.

As we rose to leave an out of breath Western Union delivery boy stormed into the dining hall. He paused for a moment and locating our group he pointed the missive he carried at us and announced,

"Doctor Samuel Briggs... Doctor Briggs... I have a telegram for you, sir. It's marked urgent, sir."

In his haste to complete his task the boy stumbled into a chair as he rushed across the length of the dining hall.

"I was told by Mr. McKay, the telegrapher, to find you post haste and deliver this telegram."

Doc gave the boy a coin and thanked him.  Anxious, he nearly tore it in half as he opened it. After reading its contents, he smiled and called to the waitress,

"Shirley, get me a cheroot... one of those nice stinky ones, dear."

Then he handed the telegram to Da.

I could see Da's eyes scan the paper; then scan it again, then again. It was as if he didn't believe what he had read.

Finally, the suspense was too much for even the usually unflappable CJ.

"Come on, Captain, what in the blue moon does it say?"

Da looked up incredulously from the paper and said,

"Johnson's dead."

Before either CJ or I could react he continued,

"Says here that just outside Westfield he jumped from the train going full speed as it crossed a trestle spanning a river gorge."

Doc inhaled a deep draught of smoke from his disgusting little cigar and through smoke watered eyes chortled,

"Landed on the rocks too. Rotten luck. All that water and he lands smack on the rocks."

I wanted to ask the most obvious question, but Doc's rejoinder shocked me into slack jawed silence.

"Think of the beautiful irony, Miss Ginger. Maybe there won't be a trial, but so what? A trial would've been iffy at best. We all knew that. This way the tunnel boys get some validation and the folks in the village some justice."

"When word starts to get around...as I'm sure it has already, by the way... the people will love it. The forces of evil are confronted by the forces for good and wrecked with despair the evil one takes matters into his own hands. Shakespearean, don't you think?"

Then Doc softened his cynicism and smiled,

"And didn't a little birdie, oh I don't know, about six feet tall I guess, give me a lecture a year ago about Irish justice? I think she said something about true Irish justice not seeking revenge or retribution, but rather a remedy...fairness. We Americans would call it making the best of a bad situation."

"Well, Johnson has gone to the place he deserves to be. The tunnelmen and the good people of this village north of Adams have a just and tangible outcome. And all we did was provide the opportunity. Johnson destroyed himself. Sounds pretty good to me. How about you?"

Suddenly, I couldn't help but tear up. I took two quick steps toward my most unlikely friend and unabashedly embraced him. Our two mismatched bodies resulted in his head nestling... well, Doc *is* very short. And I said,

"Thank you Doc."

Pausing for a moment, but still within my embrace the irascible Samuel Briggs M.D. answered,

"No, thank *you*."

CJ intervened with one word,

"Hey."

Laughing openly, Da finished,

"Come on, everyone, let's go home. Stanley has the evening fire set and Maeve's got supper in the stove."

"That includes you, Doc."

# Afterword

## There is Some Truth to the Tale

Growing up in North Adams, Massachusetts in the 1950's was quintessentially New England. Tales of the spirits of hermits long since dead wandering forests in search of souls to possess or hauntings of homes by those who had life on this plane of existence snatched from them were the stuff of every Boy Scout campfire. To us, the evidence of the truth of these tales was clear. When we went hiking it was not unusual to stumble upon foundations of abandoned buildings deep in the forest or find gatherings of tombstones inexplicably protruding from the forest floor. If there weren't creaks, rattles and whistles in *your* home, there certainly were in the house of someone you knew.

However, tales of the Hoosac Tunnel were the scariest. So many men were killed in its construction. But killed is such an antiseptic term. It hardly describes the grinding, shredding, scorching final moments these men must have experienced. Logic reinforced our blind belief that there simply must be angry souls of at least a few of these unfortunates lurking about. However, experiencing the wrath of their outrage was harder to come by.

While my friends and I might visit the Hoosac Tunnel's western portal located so close to our neighborhood, none of us ever actually wandered into the tunnel. Trains came through too often. At least that's what we told each other. Closer to the truth was our fear of the ghosts we "knew" to be residing there.

As time passed, our visits diminished. Adulthood, fatherhood and career-hood erased these stories from our thoughts and replaced them with the pragmatic rationality of the American treadmill.

But, with retire-hood I was able to take a deep breath and found that there came with it a rebirth of my imagination. I wanted to spin a tale and I wanted it to reflect the excitement of my youth. But what story to tell? Then one cold February day I was at the North Adams Public Library researching the History of North Adams and by chance came across the book HISTORIC HAUNTED AMERICA by Michael Norman and Beth Scott.

Contained within its chapters was a long forgotten campfire story from my youth. It was the story of a tragedy resulting in the deaths of two tunnel workers, Ned Brinkman and Billy Nash, at the hands of their coworker and friend, Ringo Kelly. The question of accident or betrayal is answered when angry spirits of the two men killed within the bowels of the nascent Hoosac Tunnel mete out their retribution nearly one year later when Ringo Kelley is found strangled at the very same spot he murdered his friends.

So, this was it. The story... my inspiration. You jut can't make this up. Even the names were right out of Hollywood central casting! So there is indeed some truth to the tale.